BREAKOUT

Books by Kate Messner

The Brilliant Fall of Gianna Z.
Sugar and Ice
Eye of the Storm
Wake Up Missing
All the Answers
The Seventh Wish
The Exact Location of Home
Breakout

BREAKOUT

KATE MESSNER

BLOOMSBURY
CHILDREN'S BOOKS
NEW YORK   LONDON   OXFORD   NEW DELHI   SYDNEY

BLOOMSBURY CHILDREN'S BOOKS
Bloomsbury Publishing Inc., part of Bloomsbury Publishing Plc
1385 Broadway, New York, NY 10018

BLOOMSBURY, BLOOMSBURY CHILDREN'S BOOKS, and the Diana logo
are trademarks of Bloomsbury Publishing Plc

First published in the United States of America in June 2018
by Bloomsbury Children's Books
Paperback edition published in June 2019

Bloomsbury books may be purchased for business or promotional use. For information on
bulk purchases please contact Macmillan Corporate and Premium Sales Department at
specialmarkets@macmillan.com

"We Real Cool" is from *The Bean Eaters*, published by Harpers, © 1960 by Gwendolyn Brooks.
Reprinted by Consent of Brooks Permissions.

"We Wear the Mask" is from *Lyrics of Lowly Life*, 1896, by Paul Laurence Dunbar.

ISBN 978-1-68119-538-4 (paperback)

The Library of Congress has cataloged the hardcover edition as follows:
Names: Messner, Kate, author.
Title: Breakout / by Kate Messner.
Description: New York : Bloomsbury, 2018.
Summary: From multiple perspectives, tells of a time capsule project and
the middle schoolers who contribute, including future journalist Nora
Tucker and newcomer Elidee Jones, whose brother is in the local prison.
Identifiers: LCCN 2017034344 (print) • LCCN 2017045606 (e-book)
ISBN 978-1-68119-536-0 (hardcover) • ISBN 978-1-68119-537-7 (e-book)
Subjects: | CYAC: Time capsules—Fiction. | Community life—Fiction. |
Journalism—Fiction. | Prisons—Fiction. | Schools—Fiction.
Classification: LCC PZ7.M5615 Bp 2018 (print) | LCC PZ7.M5615 (e-book) | DDC [Fic]—dc23
LC record available at https://lccn.loc.gov/2017034344

Interior design by Kay Petronio
Printed and bound in the U.S.A. by Berryville Graphics Inc., Berryville, Virginia
4 6 8 10 9 7 5 3

All papers used by Bloomsbury Publishing Plc are natural, recyclable products
made from wood grown in well-managed forests. The manufacturing processes
conform to the environmental regulations of the country of origin.

To find out more about our authors and books visit www.bloomsbury.com
and sign up for our newsletters.

For Ella

Dear Library Board,

Enclosed is my contribution to the Wolf Creek Community
Time Capsule Project. This folder includes my letters as well
as public documents and things I've collected from friends and
family members, shared with permission. I labeled everything
with Post-its and added notes so you don't get confused.
When I collected this stuff, I didn't know if I'd submit it all, but
sometimes you need to hear a lot of points of view to get the
whole story. Journalists have to pay attention to things like that.

Altogether, I think these documents tell a true and honest
story of this June, which is what you said you wanted. You have
my permission to include all these things in the time capsule, but
you don't have my permission to pick and choose only some of
them. That's the deal.

When you started this project, you probably thought you'd
end up with a lot of stories about everybody eating Popsicles
and swimming in the creek. But that's not what you're getting.
Because this summer was different.

Sincerely,

Nora Tucker

* | *

Friday, June 7—
Morning announcements
from Mr. Simmons
(He's our middle
school principal.)

Just FYI . . . I don't know if you
future Wolf Creek people still do this,
but our school puts a transcript of
the morning announcements online for
students who are hearing-impaired. I think
that's cool, and also (bonus!!) it means I
can print announcements for the time
capsule without typing them up myself.

Friday, June 7

Good morning, Wolf Pack! Please stand for the pledge to the flag.

(Pledge)

As the school year winds down, Mr. Russell would like to remind everyone that library books are due by the end of the day unless you've made prior arrangements.

Language arts teachers will share a special project with you today—a request from the public library for students to contribute to the community time capsule project. We'd love to have all our middle school voices represented.

The drama club end-of-year party is after school today in the auditorium until 3:30.

The final chess club tournament begins Monday. See Ms. Baker in room F-4 to sign up.

Wolf Creek Middle School field day will be a week from today, on June 14. Like always, we'll have the Wolf Pack cookout, the giant soccer field Slip 'N Slide, and the Mad Mile Race. Despite my lobbying to have a different prize for this year's winners, our water-balloon-the-principal tradition remains in place. To register for the race, see Mrs. Roy in the gym.

Happy birthday to Rory Burke, Patrick Fountain, Jessica Maynard, and Mrs. Howard (in the cafeteria). And let's have a warm Wolf Creek welcome for a new seventh-grade student joining us today, Elidee Jones.

Our quote of the day is from Thomas Edison. "Our greatest weakness lies in giving up. The most certain way to succeed is always to try just one more time."

That concludes our announcements.

Friday, June 7—
Wolf Creek
Community Time
Capsule Project for
Ms. Morin's
English class

SUMMER HOMEWORK: Submit at least five items for the Wolf Creek Community Time Capsule, which will be opened in fifty years. These may be letters you've written to future residents or other pieces you've written that you wish to include. Anything you'd put in your writer's notebook will work, too. Ideas might include:

- ☑ Letters
- ☑ Personal narratives
- ☑ Descriptions
- ☑ Conversations
- ☑ Poems
- ☑ Jokes (must be appropriate)
- ☑ Student-written news articles, editorials, comics
- ☑ Lists
- ☑ Notes to yourself
- ☑ Hopes, dreams, wishes, and fears
- ☑ Master plans and evil plots
- ☑ Other ideas of your own!

SUBMISSION #1: A letter to future Wolf Creek residents about how you see your community and what's on your mind as we finish the school year. This is a quick note typed on the classroom computers, due at the end of class. I'll provide feedback on this one to make sure you're on the right track.

SUBMISSIONS #2–5, due July 30: More letters, or whatever you'd like from the list above, either handwritten or typed. Turn these in to Mrs. Raymond at the public library no later than July 30. She'll keep a list of students who turn in all five entries, and those students will start eighth grade with extra credit.

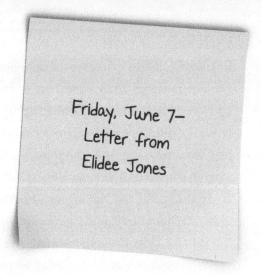

Friday, June 7—
Letter from
Elidee Jones

Dear future Wolf Creek residents,

I'm supposed to write you this letter for an assignment, but I just got here, so I don't have much to say about your town yet. The mountains are pretty.

It seems strange to be starting a new school and finishing the year at the same time, but I guess that's what happens when your mom gets a new job at the beginning of June. It took us six hours to drive here with the U-Haul trailer.

My old school was a lot different. It was in New York City, so it was a lot more diverse than this one. There was more to do there, too. The last day I went to school back home, my after-school drama group got to take a field trip to a Broadway play about Alexander Hamilton, America's first Secretary of the Treasury. That sounds boring, but it wasn't. None of us had been to a Broadway show before because it's super expensive. But I guess some old rich lady liked this show a lot and donated a bunch of money so middle and high school kids could see it, too. So we could appreciate the poetry. And we did. We all loved it. Especially the rap battles the Founding Fathers had in their cabinet meetings. They were dressed in old-fashioned clothes, all up in each other's faces, spitting rhymes like Drake and Jay Z. The truth is, I don't even like rap music much, but the songs in this play were amazing. After the show, my friends Alaya and Rachel started planning a freestyle contest for lunch next week. I was all over that, already making up lyrics in my head on the subway back to school. Only then I remembered I wouldn't be there.

It's nice here, though. It sounds like the end of the school year will be pretty good. Field day seems fun. I'm looking forward to making new friends and being an 8th grader at Wolf Creek Middle School next year. It's not where I was hoping to go to school, but it seems like it will be okay.

I hope things are going well for you, whatever you're doing in the future.

Sincerely,

Elidee Jones

Welcome, Elidee! I'm glad you're in my class. I understand what it feels like to be missing friends. I love Wolf Creek, but I still miss my college friends. It sounds like we have a love of poetry in common, too! One of my favorite poems is "The Red Wheelbarrow" by William Carlos Williams. You should look it up. Sometimes, students like to make up their own versions, and I bet you'd be good at that.

My students all got poetry notebooks when we were celebrating National Poetry Month in April. I know you weren't here then, but there are some extras on the shelf by the door if you'd like to take one to write in over the summer.

—Ms. M.

Dear future Wolf Creek residents,

Ms. Morin said we should tell you how we see our community
and what's on our minds as we wrap up the school year. I'll start
with the first part.

HOW I SEE MY COMMUNITY:

I see my community as a pretty cool place because it's safe and
friendly, and everybody knows everybody. That's my opinion.
If you get a letter from my older brother, Sean, he'll tell you it's
boring and that he can't wait to get to college. But you can make
up your own mind about that, I guess. Sean's biased because
his girlfriend Emily moved to Syracuse to go to SU, where Sean
wants to go the year after next, even though my parents think he
ought to stay put and go to Wolf Creek Community College. Sean
says that is the absolute last school on his list. He liked it better
in Wolf Creek before Emily left. All he does now is work to save
money for Syracuse.

Even though fifty years is a long time, I doubt Wolf Creek will have changed much by the time you open this time capsule. Probably everybody still works at the prison and goes deer hunting in November and lines up on Main Street for the Fourth of July Parade, right?

WHAT'S ON MY MIND:

Field day! I've been waiting forever to be in 7th grade so I can run the Mad Mile. I'm under seven minutes now—I've been practicing so I can throw water balloons at Mr. Simmons. That's the prize. The fastest girl and fastest boy each get to throw three water balloons, and Mr. Simmons isn't allowed to run or duck or anything. He just has to stand there and get water-ballooned. That's been the seventh-grade field day prize forever. My mom got to water-balloon her principal, Mr. Snyder, when she was in seventh grade, and my brother Sean got to water-balloon him, too, right before Mr. Snyder retired. I'm going to be the first Tucker to water-balloon Mr. Simmons.

Sleepover! My friend Lizzie is coming over for a sleepover tonight. We're going to watch movies and eat her grandma's minty chocolate brownies, which are the best. They taste like a York Peppermint Pattie. I'll try to get the recipe to put in the time capsule. You'll love them!

Voldemort! (You know who that is, right? From the Harry Potter books? You must.) He's on my mind because he's on my little brother Owen's mind ALL THE TIME. Dad made the mistake of reading Harry Potter aloud to him, and now Owen won't go to bed until somebody checks the bathroom, the linen cupboard, the hall closet, Owen's bedroom closet, behind his desk, and under his bed. Mom used to do it, but Owen thought she did a crummy job and didn't look carefully enough, so I am the designated Voldemort-checker now. I haven't found He-Who-Must-Not-Be-Named yet, but I'll keep you posted. Owen's birthday is next Saturday, and I got him a wand, which I hope will make him feel braver.

My Alcatraz book that I'm writing! It's like this book we read in English class last year, only different. I loved that book, and not just because it has a prison superintendent's daughter as a character, which you don't see very often. I could relate to her because my dad's always busy with inmates at Wolf Creek Correctional Facility, just like her dad is always busy at Alcatraz with Al Capone and everybody. I've read that book four times. (In fact, I just remembered I still have it signed out and I'm not sure where it is, but I need to look because they just said on the announcements that Mr. Russell wants his books back.)

Anyway . . . back to my own Alcatraz book. The truth is, I haven't worked on it in a while because it got hard right after I started the first chapter. I had all this great research, but when you're trying to figure out something that happened in history, it's like a big, messed-up puzzle. You have to look at all kinds of different documents and reports and interviews, and half the time, people say totally different things about what happened. So you have to piece everything together to figure out the real deal. That's why my book has been so tricky. I might work on it more this summer, but maybe not, because I need time for . . .

THE WOLF CREEK MIDDLE SCHOOL GAZETTE!: I want to be editor next year, when I'm in eighth grade. I'm trying to get

Lizzie to do it with me, but she doesn't like news all that much. She likes math, though, so I'm going to see if she'll make some of those infographics like they have in the big-city newspapers. Maybe she can do some kind of newspaper comedy, too. Lizzie wants to be a comedian someday, if she doesn't end up being a mathematician. I want to be a journalist who covers all the exciting breaking news stories. We don't get many of those in Wolf Creek, unfortunately. Usually, our local paper runs stories about missing cats. But a journalist has to be ready, just in case. I'm planning to write news articles for most of my entries for this project. That way, opening your time capsule will be like reading a newspaper from the past!

The last thing on my mind is lunch. Because English is almost over and I'm so hungry that even school grilled cheese sounds good. Maybe by the time you read this, there will be better school lunches here, but I wouldn't count on it.

Your friend from the past,

Nora Tucker

This is a great letter, Nora! I think future Wolf Creek residents will appreciate your reflections, and I *LOVE* that you're going to include newspaper articles. Have fun reporting!
—Ms. M.

PS I found a copy of that Alcatraz book left outside on a bench by the track this week and took it to the office Lost and Found. Check there!

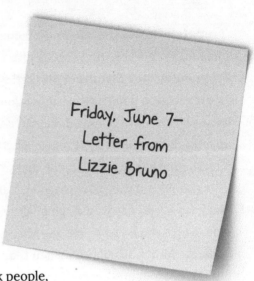

Friday, June 7—
Letter from
Lizzie Bruno

Dear future Wolf Creek people,

I don't know what this town will be like when you're reading this, but right now, it's kind of boring and could stand to lighten up a little, so I present to you . . .

LIZZIE BRUNO'S TOP TEN THINGS TO DO IN WOLF CREEK
(If you think I'm being sarcastic about
some of these, you're right.)

10. **Attending Wolf Creek Middle School**—This is not to say that everything about our school is great. I'm pretty sure they serve better lunches at the prison, and our annual fitness test in gym is a special kind of punishment. (We have to try a pull-up every single year, even when there's no hope whatsoever.) But school still makes the Top Ten List because most of our teachers are okay. Also, once a month, they have a staff workday, so I get to stay home eating chocolate

pretzels, watching Elizabeth Chin comedy videos, and making bar graphs and Venn diagrams.

9. **Shopping at Joe's Mountain Market!**—They really do have an exclamation point on the sign. I don't think they mean for it to be ironic. I guess when you're the only place to pick up milk and bread, you get to use whatever over-the-top punctuation you want. Also, the market is on our walk home from school and they have Swedish Fish, so . . .

8. **Field day**—Field day would rank higher without the Mad Mile, which *should* be called the Miserable Mile. I'll never understand why people run when they're not being chased. But the cookout and soccer field Slip 'N Slide are cool, so field day still makes the list.

7. **Sleepovers at Nora's house**—This would also be ranked higher if it weren't for Nora's mom, who won't let us watch PG-13 movies because Nora's birthday isn't until August and her mom says no, that's not actually close enough.

6. **Walking down our beautiful Main Street**—perfect for those who like a view of the prison while they're out shopping at the exclamation-point market or Bob's Hardware.

5. **The public library**—For real, because Mrs. Raymond lets us do whatever we want with the teen room, so there are beanbag chairs and video games in there.

4. **The Wolf Creek Firefighters' Carnival and Cookout**—This is pretty much my favorite day of the summer. We hang out watching water ball fights and eating fried dough. Fun fact: this used to be called the Firemen's Carnival, but when the old chief retired and Mrs. Labray got the job, she said it was time for that sexist carnival name to retire, too.

3. The Fourth of July Cookout

2. The Founders Day Cookout

(We are really into cookouts here)

1. Recording conversations on my new WhisperFlash Z190 digital audio recorder—Grandma got it for me for my birthday because she heard an NPR interview with a comedian who said she learned all about how people talk and comedic timing by recording regular conversations and listening to them, sometimes even writing them down. I'm bringing the recorder to Nora's this weekend. It can store up to fifty hours of audio, and it's so small that you can have it turned on, recording in your pocket. Maybe I'll include a flash drive of audio recordings for this time capsule project so you can hear our important conversations about what brand of hot dog they should get for the Fourth of July Cookout.

For the record, I'm not joking about this. Hot dogs are on the town council agenda next week. They're meeting to vote, and I know . . . the suspense must be killing you. But it's time for lunch, so I have to go now.

—Lizzie Bruno

What a fun list, Lizzie! I think future Wolf Creek residents will appreciate your sense of humor. I'm afraid that if you want to include recorded conversations in the time capsule, you'll need to type them up. We have no way of knowing if your flash drive will still be readable fifty years from now. Also, when you share recordings, please be sure to add a paragraph with your own reflections, so you're not just writing other people's words. The future wants to hear from _you!_

—Ms. M.

Friday, June 7—
Note posted outside the gym (I took this photo on the day of our practice run, when I still thought this whole time capsule was going to be about field day and Popsicles.)

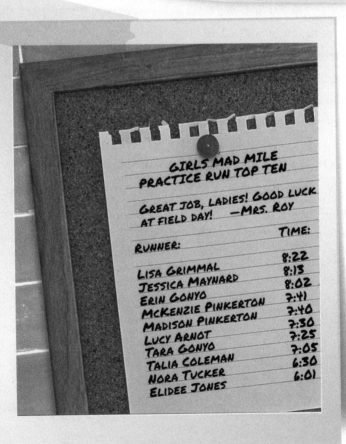

GIRLS MAD MILE
PRACTICE RUN TOP TEN

GREAT JOB, LADIES! GOOD LUCK
AT FIELD DAY!   —MRS. ROY

RUNNER:	TIME:
LISA GRIMMAL	8:22
JESSICA MAYNARD	8:13
ERIN GONYO	8:02
MCKENZIE PINKERTON	7:41
MADISON PINKERTON	7:40
LUCY ARNOT	7:30
TARA GONYO	7:25
TALIA COLEMAN	7:05
NORA TUCKER	6:30
ELIDEE JONES	6:01

Friday, June 7—
Text messages between
Lizzie & Nora

Just FYI . . . . I used
our computer's messaging app
to print out these text messages. In
the olden days, people sent handwritten
letters, and reading those now tells us a
lot about what life was like back then.
Texts are kind of our version of letters,
so I decided to include them, even though
they'll probably seem old-fashioned by
the time you read this. You probably
communicate telepathically or something.
Good luck saving that for your extra-
credit time capsule project.

NORA: Omg who moves to a new school 2 weeks before classes end?

LIZZIE: I saw the list outside the gym and knew you'd freak out

NORA: I beat my best time by like 30 seconds and she was soooooo far ahead

LIZZIE: Tomorrow's newspaper headline.

NEW KID SPEEDS INTO TOWN, DESTROYS TUCKER MAD MILE LEGACY

NORA: I need to train harder

LIZZIE: Hard enough to make up 30 seconds in a week?

NORA: Yup

LIZZIE: WOLF CREEK SEVENTH GRADER DROPS DEAD OF EXHAUSTION, LAST WORDS: "JUST 20 MORE SECONDS TO GO . . ."

NORA: 😊 Seriously
where did she even come from?

LIZZIE: I heard she came bc somebody in her family's in the prison

NORA: Really???

LIZZIE: Yup

NORA: Whoa

LIZZIE: She seems really nice though. Her locker's near mine and she had strawberry Pop-Tarts this morning so we got talking about how the frosting kind is way better. I like her

NORA: So does Mrs Roy. Did you hear her after our run? She was all, "Whoa! Our new student is quite the athlete!" and trying to get Elidee to sign up for cross-country next fall

LIZZIE: That's good isn't it?
So your team can win

NORA: I guess

LIZZIE: Gotta go finish my math

NORA: Bring your notebook tonight ok? I have an idea for the time capsule

LIZZIE: ?

NORA: We should write news articles about what's happening in town so it's like reading a newspaper from our time when they open it

LIZZIE: Can't we save ourselves some time and just stick in a copy of the actual newspaper?

NORA: No! This way it's our perspective and also good practice for the school paper

LIZZIE: I don't remember signing up for that

NORA: It'll be fun! I'll be editor and you can just do the parts you like and we can have math stuff like those graphs you like in USA TODAY! And a comedy page!

LIZZIE: I'll do parody articles like they do in The Rutabaga

NORA: What's that?

LIZZIE: An online newspaper that publishes articles making fun of real news

NORA: It'll have to be a separate section so people don't think we're publishing fake news

LIZZIE: You are such a nerd

NORA: We have journalistic standards!

LIZZIE: I'll bring my notebook tonight

NORA: Can you also bring your grandma's brownie recipe?

LIZZIE: Doubt it because whenever people ask she says it's a secret

NORA: Tell her it's for the time capsule so nobody will know for 50 years

LIZZIE: Idk she'll only be 117 years old then so she might still be baking them

NORA: Ask anyway

LIZZIE: Okie dokie

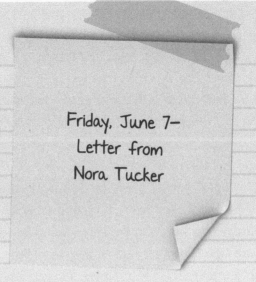

Friday, June 7—
Letter from
Nora Tucker

Dear future Wolf Creek residents,

Sorry this letter is a little messy. I'm writing on the school bus. Do you still have buses or do you hover-craft home from school?

There was actually some news today—we got a new student at school! I don't see why she didn't finish the year at her old school. Her name is Elidee, and she's in seventh grade like us. Her brother is in Dad's prison. (Technically, the prison doesn't belong to my dad. I call it that because he's the superintendent and in charge of everything.) We also call the college where my mom works "Mom's college" even though she's only in charge of the admissions office. But by the time you're reading this, the prison will be somebody else's prison anyway because Dad's going to retire in a few years.

It took us a while to figure out Elidee's deal because Lizzie heard this morning that her dad was in prison. Then Tommy Dunbar said it was Elidee's mom, but Lisa Grimmal said that couldn't be true because Elidee's mom was in the office with her before homeroom.

Tommy asked Lisa how she knew, and Lisa said, "Duh, because it definitely wasn't Paul Washington's mom." (I don't know what Wolf Creek is like in the future, but in order for you to understand what Lisa said, you probably need to know that not too many African American people live here now. Paul Washington is the only one in our school. He was until today, anyway. So that's what Lisa was getting at.) Anyway, Tommy kept arguing that maybe the lady in the office was Elidee's aunt or something, but Lisa was right. (Also, there are no women in the prison here—just men. Tommy should have known that because his dad works there. But I guess that tells you something about Tommy Dunbar, and if you get a letter from him, you should probably keep all this in mind when you read it.)

Anyway, Elidee's brother is the one in prison. I found out after gym because Ava Porter's aunt is Elidee's mom's landlord and says the reason they moved is so they can visit without taking the bus from New York City. Her brother's only nineteen, which seems too young to have done something that bad. Dad's prison is maximum security, so you don't get thrown in there for stuff like stealing candy bars from Joe's Mountain Market. I didn't get to ask Ava what the brother did, because Elidee came into the locker room, so we had to stop talking about her.

I realize that what I just wrote makes us sound gossipy and not very nice, but most people were actually going out of their way to be nice to Elidee. When she had trouble opening her locker, three people swooped in to help. Tara Gonyo said she liked Elidee's sneakers, and then the Pinkerton twins started talking about theater stuff because Elidee was in her school's drama club in New York and McKenzie and Madison are in ours.

I bet the situation with Elidee's brother is hard, though. I can't imagine having to visit my older brother in prison. If he got a life sentence, I'd probably get his room. But Sean would never do anything like that. He works at Joe's Mountain Market and doesn't even take the day-old doughnuts without asking first.

The bus is almost at my house, but I have to tell you one more thing about Elidee. She ran a six-minute mile in gym today. I am really hoping this is not a regular thing.

Your friend from the past,
Nora Tucker

MAMA: You home yet?

ELIDEE: Yes

MAMA: How was your first day?

ELIDEE: Ok
People were pretty friendly

I'm like the only black person here though

MAMA: I thought there were some other families

ELIDEE: One other kid in our grade

Paul something

He nodded at me but I didn't talk to him

MAMA: What did you do in your classes?

ELIDEE: Not much because everything's winding down

Ran a mile in gym

MAMA: How did that go?

ELIDEE: I got the best mile time because nobody's very fast here

MAMA: It's a smaller school. Maybe you can run on a team in the fall

ELIDEE: The gym teacher was all excited and wants me to run cross-country

MAMA: That's great!

ELIDEE: I doubt they're as good as Morgan Academy

MAMA: So run for your new team and show those Morgan Academy people what they missed

ELIDEE: Maybe

MAMA: Got homework?

ELIDEE: Just a thing we're supposed to do over the summer for extra credit in English

MAMA: You should do that tonight because we're going to see Troy tomorrow

ELIDEE: Ok

MAMA: Have a snack & I'll make dinner when I get home from the hospital

ELIDEE: See you later

MAMA: Love you to the moon and back xo

ELIDEE: To Pluto and back

MAMA: That's not even a planet anymore

ELIDEE: Still counts

MAMA: Then I love you to RR245 and back

ELIDEE: ?

MAMA: Dwarf planet out past Pluto

They found it in 2015

ELIDEE: You win

Love you

MAMA: Love you too

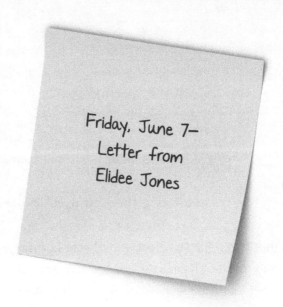

Friday, June 7—
Letter from
Elidee Jones

Dear future Wolf Creek residents,

This is the second of five letters I'm supposed to write to you for extra credit. My new English teacher told me to check out a poet she likes, so I got a William Carlos Williams book from the school library. This was harder than you might think because the librarian here likes to get all his books back before school ends so he can lock them up for the summer. At my old school, Ms. Sanchez sent us home with books to read while school was out. She never seemed worried about what came back and what didn't. I had to promise to bring this poetry book back on Monday.

That works out fine because the poem Ms. Morin likes is really short anyway. It's about how so much depends on a red wheelbarrow. That's it. I haven't seen any wheelbarrows in Wolf Creek, but maybe that's a thing here? Anyway, I wrote my own version of the poem on the bus ride home:

So much depends
On a thick concrete wall
Smudged with bird ~~poop~~ droppings
Beside Joe's Mountain Market!*

*That's Joe's exclamation point—not mine.

It's not as pretty as the other poem, but neither is your Main Street. Also, I'm definitely no William Carlos Williams. I looked him up online at school, and he was a grumpy-looking old white guy. Maybe I'll get a different poetry book at the public library if they let people borrow books over the summer there.

Sincerely,
Elidee Jones

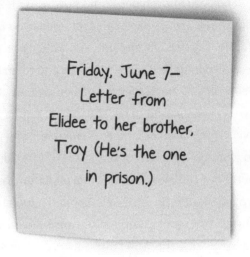

Friday, June 7—
Letter from
Elidee to her brother,
Troy (He's the one
in prison.)

Dear Troy,

It's messed up, living here now. Our school bus drove by your big old wall this morning and again this afternoon, and I thought about where you might be and what you were doing in there. You get up early, right? So by the time we drove by at 7:30, you were probably eating toast at a long table full of men in green pants and shirts. When we drove by this afternoon, I wondered if you might be in the yard. Mama says you get to go outside an hour a day. Maybe you were out there throwing a basketball around with a bunch of other guys who hung out with the wrong people. Or maybe you were back in your cell already. Maybe you were reading or writing up stuff for your appeal. Mama prays for that every night, you know. Even though Aunt Maya told her every single inmate in there's working on the same thing and none of them are going anywhere.

But you know what? You know who Alexander Hamilton was, right? You always liked social studies class best, so I bet you do. He was one of America's Founding Fathers who fought for freedom for other white guys. He ended up being America's first Secretary of the Treasury and some other stuff, too. He used to live on some island in the Caribbean until a hurricane destroyed everything, and then he wrote about it and got sent to America to go to college. He wrote his way off his island. Wrote his way out. They talked about that in a play I saw on a field trip before we left New York, and I kept thinking about your appeal. You've always been pretty good with words, so maybe you can write your way out, too. You never know. And let's face it—you don't have a whole lot else to do in there, so I think you should keep working on it.

We're coming to see you tomorrow, so I'm not mailing this letter; I'll bring it then. Mama bought some nuts and beef jerky and Starbursts for you at the market. She's going to try and bring them. The rules on the website for prison families say you have to have everything a certain way, just so, and only some kinds of packages are allowed. We're trying to be careful to get it just right so you can have your stuff. Mama says you've been complaining the food's ten times worse than a school cafeteria's in there. I'm not so sure. You've never gone to school in this town, and I doubt those prison cooks could come up with much worse than the school's grilled cheese. It's like eating salted snot pressed between a couple pieces of bread that got left out on the counter too long.

I hope that made you laugh.

I bet not much is funny in there, but I miss hearing you laugh.

I miss a lot of other things, too, now that we live here. I miss walking home from school with Alaya and Gina and Rachel instead of riding a smelly bus. I miss stopping at the bodega for chips. I miss hearing languages that aren't English and seeing faces that aren't white. I miss petting Mrs. Cruz's dog Onyx when they're out walking in Mullaly Park. I miss the park, too—the playground and the old men reading newspapers on benches and the sound of the 4 train rumbling over the track by the basketball courts. Our apartment here has a yard, which Mama said would be better than a park, but it's empty and weedy and way too quiet. At least Mrs. G. lives in the apartment upstairs. Even though I don't see her much, it's nice knowing she's up there when Mama's at work, which is a lot. I miss having her around more.

Also, I miss the planetarium. Remember when we used to go to the Friday night shows? Mama and I still play that love-you-past-the-moon game. It started with that book where the bunny tells his mama he loves her to the moon. And then the mama says, "Oh yeah? Well, I love you to the moon and back!" I don't know if you remember this, but when I was little and learning about the solar system, Mama started saying that with other planets at bedtime. I'd tell her I loved her to the moon, and she'd be like, "Well, I love you to Mars!" or Saturn or Neptune. It's funny—we still do that when we text now, only we try to find things that are farther away. It was easier to get ideas when we lived near the planetarium. We live so far from everything now.

I really miss Grandmama. I miss her suppers and her hand on my shoulder and the way she French braids my hair, with one fat braid on each side. When we left, she gave me a bag full of hair oil because she said stores here might not even sell it. Mama's braiding my hair for me now, but she only does one braid and never gets it as tight. Grandmama braided it so tight I'd have a headache.

I bet pretty soon I'll even miss the headache.

You probably miss a lot of things, too. I hope Aunt Maya's wrong and your appeal works out and you get out and we can all go home.

Love you,
Elidee

PS You might meet my English teacher, Ms. Morin. She told our class that she teaches at the prison sometimes, and you guys are going to do the same project we're doing in class, where you get to tell your stories as part of a time-capsule project for the library. You should do that if you get the chance. They say they want to include everyone's voices, and your stories are probably more interesting than most people's. Plus then we can both be in there. The time capsule, I mean. Not the prison.

LIZZIE: Hi!

NORA: Hi! Did you bring your notebook?

LIZZIE: Yes and I also brought this! It's recording right now.

OWEN: Is that spy gear? It looks like a pen that shoots poison darts that I read about in a book once.

LIZZIE: Nope. It's a digital audio recorder.

NORA: Oh cool! We can use it when we do interviews for the time capsule project!

LIZZIE: I'm actually using it to record everyday conversations to get a better sense for language and timing. Grandma says she heard on NPR that it's important for comedians.

NORA: Can't we also use it for interviews for the articles?

LIZZIE: Sure.

OWEN: I'll help!

NORA: But you don't like to write.

OWEN: I like to draw. I'll be the comics guy.

MRS. TUCKER: Nora!

NORA: What?

MRS. TUCKER: Come get your clothes out of the dryer so I can finish this wash!

NORA: Coming!

LIZZIE: I was hoping things would be more interesting and hilarious over here, but this sounds just like my house.

NORA: It's a mom thing. Let me get my clothes, and I'll meet you in my room so we can start writing!

LIZZIE: Cool. Can I use your computer?

NORA: Sure. How come?

LIZZIE: Ms. Morin says I have to type up any conversations I want to put in the time capsule project. I want to transcribe what we just recorded while you're folding so I can figure out how long that's going to take.

LIZZIE'S REFLECTIONS: This tiny two-minute conversation where absolutely nothing happened just took me 19 minutes to type, and there is no way I'm going to keep doing this. Nora's brother Sean says there might be some app that will transcribe audio for you, but unless I can get that, this is going to be my only recorded conversation in the time capsule. Sorry, future Wolf Creek residents. But I hope this little sample makes you feel better. As you can see, you're not missing much.

Friday, June 7—
Staff Writer Bios
for the *Wolf Creek
Community Time
Capsule Times*

Nora made me write this cheesy
biography as if we're award-winning
journalists who work at the New
York Times or something, so I'm
making her add this Post-it. Let it be
noted, future Wolf Creek residents,
that I understand how silly this is
and am only doing it for Nora. I also
love that Owen drew pictures to go
with our bios. —Lizzie

THE WOLF CREEK COMMUNITY
★★★ TIME CAPSULE TIMES ★★★

Owen drew this picture
of me. My hair isn't quite
this big in real life.

MEET THE STAFF WRITERS
NORA TUCKER is a rising eighth grader and future
editor in chief of the *Wolf Creek Middle School
Gazette*. A lifelong resident of Wolf Creek, she lives
with her parents and two brothers, Sean (who's 17)
and Owen (who's 8). When Nora is older, she wants

to be a journalist or a novelist or both. Probably both. In addition to writing, her interests include running, reading, Alcatraz history, and fighting imaginary villains in defense of her younger brother.

Owen also drew my picture,
and my braces really are this enormous.

LIZZIE BRUNO is an almost-finished 7th grader and reluctant journalist. She's an only child who lives with her mom in Wolf Creek except for when her dad makes her spend a week with his family in Massachusetts every summer so he can prove what a great dad he is. I'm guessing there's only about a 20 percent chance you're still reading this, but just in case you're one of the one in five, Lizzie's favorite things are math, comedy, Nora, potato chips, and her grandma. Not necessarily in that order.

THE WOLF CREEK COMMUNITY
★ ★ ★ TIME CAPSULE TIMES ★ ★ ★

MIDDLE SCHOOL PREPARES FOR ANNUAL FIELD DAY

by Nora Tucker

Students and staff of Wolf Creek Middle School are preparing for the annual field day competition next week. The event is a local tradition, dating back more than forty years.

"We looked forward to it all year," said Lisa Tucker, who took first place in the girls' Mad Mile Race in 1980. "There used to be a dodgeball tournament, too, but they got rid of that because parents complained. Those red balls really do hurt when you get hit with one."

In place of dodgeball, the school now offers a Slip 'N Slide on the soccer field, which has been a big hit.

"It's pretty fun," said seventh grader Lizzie Bruno. "My favorite part is when the teachers decide to try it. Last year, Mr. Russell got going so fast he slid right off the end of the plastic and kept rolling down the hill."

This year's field day will be Friday, June 14, rain or shine, in back of the school.

*"Parody" means this isn't actually real news; it's Lizzie's comedy piece making fun of the news here. Also, the quotes aren't real. Lizzie made them up.

FRANKFURTER FACE-OFF:

TOWN COUNCIL SIZZLES WITH RED-HOT CONTROVERSY AS WHINERS ARGUE OVER WIENERS

by Lizzie Bruno

Wolf Creek's town council is set to debate what may be its most crucial issue of the century next week: What brand of frankfurters should be served at the Fourth of July Cookout?

This hot-dog hullaballoo began when Mr. Ledbetter got a raging case of poison ivy last summer.

"It was all over his face and up and down his arms, and I don't even want to know where else," said Ledbetter's hiking buddy Stuart Eldridge.

Ledbetter had to step back from his traditional role as Independence Day Grill Master. Local resident Bill Tucker (that's Nora's dad!) offered to help out, which everyone thought was nice of him at the time.

However, on the morning of the cookout, Mr. Tucker went out and bought some kind of hot dog he found on sale instead of Blazing Bob's Red Hots, which is the tradition. It turns out most people liked the on-sale hot dogs better (see pie chart below).

But now, Mr. Ledbetter is back at the grill and wants only Blazing Bob's again. The town council has been flooded with letters from emotional residents who are weeping for their fabulous foot-longs and don't know how they'll be able to go on if the substandard sausages prevail instead. "If it ain't a Blazing Bob's Red Hot," said longtime resident Doug Toole, "then it ain't worth the mustard."

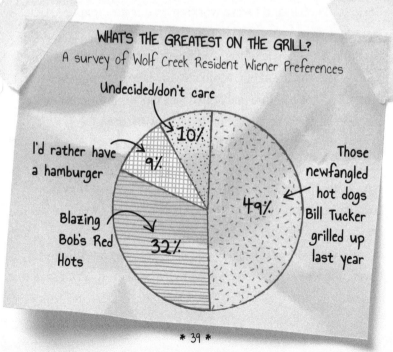

WHAT'S THE GREATEST ON THE GRILL?
A survey of Wolf Creek Resident Wiener Preferences

Undecided/don't care 10%

I'd rather have a hamburger 9%

Blazing Bob's Red Hots 32%

Those newfangled hot dogs Bill Tucker grilled up last year 49%

Saturday, June 8—
Letter from Nora Tucker
(Whatever you do, don't
skip this one, because
we actually have something
to report now!!)

Dear future Wolf Creek residents,

BREAKING NEWS: **TWO INMATES BROKE OUT OF DAD'S PRISON OVERNIGHT!!!**

Seriously! Lizzie and I were working on our newspaper articles last night, and we went to bed at around ten. Then at eight this morning, the doorbell rang, and it was a state trooper who told Mom about the breakout. Mom already knew, though, because I guess Dad got a phone call at five this morning, when they were discovered missing, so he had to go to work then.

(By the way, you know those alarms on the prison towers that are supposed to go off to warn everybody if inmates break out? Yeah, they totally didn't go off. I don't know if they'll be fixed by the time you're reading this or not, but I wouldn't count on them if I were you.)

Anyway, Mom told Lizzie and me not to say anything to Owen because she doesn't want him to be scared. Mom says this isn't going to last very long because it's June in the mountains, so even if the police don't find those guys right away, it won't be long before the blackflies do, and then they'll be begging to go back to their cells. (Do you still get blackflies in the woods every June? Maybe by the time you read this, you'll have found a way to get rid of them, and if that's the case, you're lucky because they're mean little things. Dad says they're vampires with wings.)

Mom also told us she got an early-morning call from Lizzie's mom, who's at the hospital with Lizzie's grandma. Her grandma was supposed to go to work this morning—she's a civilian worker at the prison—but I guess she woke up with chest pains, so they went to the emergency room to have her checked out. She's fine—it wasn't a heart attack or anything—but they're still at the hospital, so Lizzie's mom can't pick her up until later.

And that reminds me—I got that recipe for you from Lizzie's grandma:

Priscilla's Magical Minty Brownies

1. Mix up two packages of any brand fudge brownie mix according to the directions.

2. Pour a little less than half the mix into a 10 x 15 inch baking dish.

3. Put a layer of York Peppermint Patties on top of that.

4. Pour the rest of the mix over it and bake at 350 degrees for about 45 minutes or until they seem done.

I was expecting something fancier, but I guess that was the secret of her secret recipe. Sometimes things aren't quite how they seem.

Anyway, back to the prison break. Lizzie and I wanted to go out reporting, but Mom said no because of the manhunt happening now. I told her I think that's pretty unfair, since Sean was allowed to go to the market for work, but she didn't care. I kind of wish college was still in session so Mom would have less time to worry and make new rules. Unfortunately, she gets to work from home a lot of the time until it gets busy again in August.

So now Lizzie and I are going to collect background information instead. Our school paper adviser says that's important to have in news stories so readers can see how what's happening now fits into the bigger picture. So Lizzie's making some charts about the prison, showing the population and stuff, and I'm collecting all my notes about Alcatraz history from my book research so we can compare the two escapes. There are some pretty cool stories from Alcatraz. One team of guys who tried to escape made dummies and left them in their beds so it would look like they were sleeping instead of running around free. Pretty smart, right? More to come . . .

Your friend from the past,

Nora Tucker

Saturday, June 8—
Text messages between
Lizzie & her mom,
8:45 a.m.

MOM: You up yet?

LIZZIE: Yes how's grandma?

MOM: Ok docs say it's not heart related. Just anxiety

LIZZIE: That's good

MOM: They want to run more tests so are you ok staying with Nora again if they keep her overnight tonight?

LIZZIE: Sure

Hey did you hear about the prison break?

MOM: Yes but doctor is here so I have to go. I'll keep you posted Love you!

LIZZIE: Love u too

NORA: What are you doing? I thought you were gonna work on charts and stuff.

LIZZIE: I will. I'm recording a conversation first.

NORA: ~~Yahoo~~ You ought to save the batteries, so we can use it when we go out later.

LIZZIE: Your mom's ~~now leading a sow~~ not letting us out until those guys are caught.

NORA: She might ~~lead her~~ later if we're with Sean. Come on. Save space so we can record stuff at the market.

LIZZIE: I will. I just want to test that app Sean told us about.

NORA: ~~Doesn't~~ Does it listen and turn the audio file into words?

LIZZIE: That's the idea. But the reviews ~~also~~ all say you might need to

correct stuff later.

NORA: Okay. But do you have enough now? Because you

should work on the charts, and I'm gonna stop talking

so I can find my Alcatraz stuff.

LIZZIE: Yeah, this should be good. This is Lizzie and Nora, ~~over a noun.~~

over and out!

LIZZIE'S REFLECTIONS: The app worked! Mostly, anyway. I had to type in who's saying what, because obviously the app doesn't know us. Also, after I printed this out, I noticed that it made some mistakes. It had Nora's mom "leading a sow" (Ha!) but I corrected those in pen. Sorry about that. I'll fix them on the computer before I print next time. The app reviews all say that it works better once it gets used to your voice, so hopefully there won't be much to correct anyway. My reflection is that I'm really glad this works now and I hope our next recorded conversation is more exciting. I have to go now because Nora says we have to use this time to get all the "background information" for the story.

Saturday, June 8—
Lizzie's chart and
timelines about prison
history and population
and stuff, for
background

WOLF CREEK CORRECTIONAL FACILITY TIMELINE

(These notes are from the Department of Corrections website,
Nora's History Day report from last year, and Wikipedia, which I
know is not a 100 percent reliable source, but we're not allowed
to go to the library because we're locked in the house, so that's
as good as it gets tonight.)

1850	Opens as a mining prison—inmates work in mines nearby
1892	Prison expands to hold maximum security inmates
1899	5 inmates try to escape—it doesn't work out for them
1908	Construction begins on concrete wall all around prison property
1910	Construction complete (it's a REALLY big wall)
1910-this week	Wall keeps inmates inside prison
June 7	BREAKOUT! 2 inmates escape overnight, discovered missing at 5 a.m. the next day
June 8	Police still looking for guys who broke out TO BE CONTINUED

WOLF CREEK CORRECTIONAL STATISTICS

(Source: NY Department of Corrections & Census Bureau)

Population of Wolf Creek, NY: 3,261

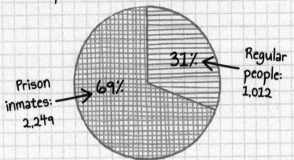

31% ← Regular people: 1,012

Prison inmates: 2,249 → 69%

Wolf Creek Correctional Inmate Demographics
(this means people's backgrounds & stuff)

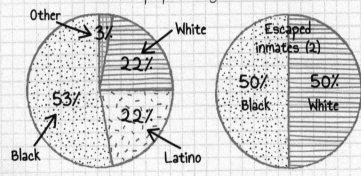

Other → 3%

White 22%

53% Black

22% Latino

Escaped inmates (2)

50% Black   50% White

Wolf Creek Correctional Facility Officers

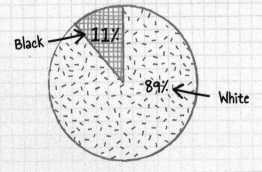

Black → 11%

89% ← White

LIZZIE'S REFLECTIONS: I've always known Wolf Creek is a small town with a big prison, but I've never realized that most of our town is made up of inmates. There are more than twice as many people living in that prison as there are out here. That's weird. But it goes to show how cool pie charts are. They help you see things.

Another thing these charts made me see is that more than half the prison population is black but almost none of the corrections officers are. I'm wondering if that's right or if it's a typo on the website, so I'm going to ask Grandma about this when she gets out of the hospital. Hopefully, that'll be first thing tomorrow. Mom says whatever it was, she's much better and just getting some rest now before she comes home.

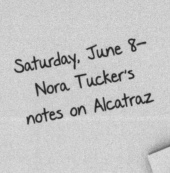

Saturday, June 8—
Nora Tucker's
notes on Alcatraz

Most famous Alcatraz escape attempt—Frank Morris,
John Anglin & Clarence Anglin in 1962

   ★ Sharpened tools & used them to dig out of their cells
   ★ Went down to water
   ★ Made inflatable raft out of raincoats (???HOW???)
   ★ Launched homemade raft into bay
   ★ Probably drowned (but nobody knows for sure . . .)

Other guys who tried to escape from Alcatraz:

        Joe Bowers   1936
        Theodore Cole & Ralph Roe   1937
        Thomas Limerick   1938

TO BE CONTINUED LATER BECAUSE MOM JUST
CAME IN & SAID WE CAN GO TO THE MARKET AS
LONG AS WE'RE HOME BY DINNERTIME!

Saturday, June 8—
Letter from
Elidee Jones

Dear future Wolf Creek residents,

This is the third of five letters I have to write to you for extra credit. (Yes, I did mean to say "have to." I know extra credit is supposed to mean something's optional, but if you think that's how it works around here, you've never met my mom. Even though I didn't get into that fancy school I applied to, she says I can go to any college I want as long as I don't slack off and start making bad choices like skipping extra-credit assignments.) Anyhow, this will probably be my most interesting letter because two inmates broke out of the prison overnight. A state trooper came to our door this morning and asked Mama if we'd seen or heard anything. We didn't.

Mama asked the trooper who the inmates were but he wouldn't say. He told us to lock the doors, and Mama said okay, as if we didn't do that anyway. Do you Wolf Creek people not lock doors unless the police make a special point to say so? That's not too smart. The trooper asked if he could look in the garage we share with the other renters, and Mama said sure, so he did that and then left.

I turned on the TV news and found out that the two men who escaped were both older guys who are in prison for life. I hope they catch them soon and nobody gets hurt.

Sincerely,
Elidee Jones

Saturday, June 8—
Letter from Elidee to
her brother, Troy

Dear Troy,

We were supposed to come see you today, but we can't because
two guys broke out of your prison. Have you heard about that
yet? You must have. It's not like people break out of that place
every day. When I first heard, I was so scared it might be you and
you'd get hurt or killed. We were on our way to the prison when
we found out visiting day got canceled.

Mama had your big bag of Starbursts and stuff all packed.
We were going to get there right when visiting hours started, but
we didn't even make it to the end of the street. The cops were
stopping every last car. When Mama pulled up, they looked in
the back seat and asked where we were headed. She told them,
and one guy laughed. The other guy said there wouldn't be
visiting hours for a good long time. So we went home. Mama just
left for work. She says I can eat your Starbursts. She'll get new
ones whenever it turns out we can see you.

Do you know those guys who broke out? You probably can't answer that. Probably shouldn't, even if you can. Probably, I won't even send this letter. Mama says you won't be able to get mail for a while either. I guess I'm just writing so it feels like I have somebody to talk to. Everybody at home is busy with end-of-school stuff, and there's nobody here. I don't know any of the kids, and Mama's busy with her new job and church stuff. You know that's part of the reason we had to come here, right? Mama's church friend Mrs. Gonzalez moved here last fall so she could visit her husband more, and she said Mama and I should come, too.

That wasn't supposed to happen, though. We were supposed to stay in the Bronx. I was supposed to go to Morgan Academy, this fancy school you have to apply to get into, and everything was going to be great. Mama was going to be ten kinds of proud. Only, then I didn't get in. I worked so hard on that application and wrote it all fancy. I wrote about reaching for the stars and working hard and being grateful for opportunities—exactly what I figured they'd want at a school like that. But then a letter came in the mail saying I didn't get in. I still don't get it. My grades and test scores and everything were fine. I guess they didn't like my essays or something.

Mama decided that letter was God's will, telling her we ought to move up here to be closer to you and Mrs. G. after all. So here we are. And now she can't see you anyway because those guys got out.

I hope you don't know those two. I hope it happened far away from you because it sounds like the kind of thing that could get everybody in trouble, and you definitely don't need more trouble than you have already. None of us do.

Did I tell you I started school here this week? It's okay. I talked with this one girl whose locker is near mine. She seemed pretty nice.

I won't ask you how it is in there. I know it's awful, even though Mama says it's not so bad and you'll be okay getting through your fifteen years.

I hope having us closer helps you remember there's a life waiting for you. Mama says you're just as smart as I am, except when it comes to choosing friends. She says you'll be able to take college classes when your time's up. Sooner if you win your appeal. I used to think Aunt Maya was right about that being some silly dream, but I keep thinking about that Hamilton guy I told you about.

You would have liked that play. Even though it's about dead white guys, the actors and actresses looked like us. It was your kind of music, too—rap and hip-hop. It was so good even I liked it, and you know I don't usually like that stuff. In one of the songs, Hamilton said he never thought he'd live past twenty. I'm pretty sure he ripped that line off from Kanye, but it made me forget that the story happened so long ago, you know? Like it could be happening in our old neighborhood right now. Like maybe you really could write your way out of that prison, just like Hamilton wrote his way off his island.

So keep working on your appeal, okay? I'll wait awhile to eat your Starbursts in case we get to see you soon.

Love you,
Elidee

Saturday, June 8—
Signs on the door of
Joe's Mountain Market!

(I took these photos on my phone Saturday, June 8, but some of the signs have been there a lot longer than that.)

WELCOME,
LAW ENFORCEMENT
& MEDIA!

BEST SUBS IN TOWN
Half $2.50
Whole $4
Extra meat $1

JOE'S MOUNTAIN MARKET!

OPEN 6 A.M.–MIDNIGHT, 7 DAYS A WEEK

WELCOME TO THE ADIRONDACKS!

PLEASE LEAVE BACKPACKS & LARGE BAGS AT THE COUNTER

Lawn Mowing, Garden Weeding, Odd Jobs
CALL JASON AT
555-0132

ADIRONDACK ADVENTURES WITH JESUS
✝
Vacation Bible School: June 24–28

Wolf Creek Community

Join Us for B...
Outdoor A...
Crafts, ar...

$50 REWARD
Orange Tabby named Nebula
Lost June 3
near corner of
Trudeau Rd. & Old Edwards Quarry Rd.
Please call
Judy Heggleson

Sorry if this offends anybody in the future. I told Lizzie she might not want to make fun of Jesus in her parody, but she says no subjects are off limits when it comes to comedy. Also, she says she's not really making fun of Jesus anyway—just VBS and Mrs. Mizzleman, a little.   —Nora

ANNUAL VACATION BIBLE SCHOOL FEATURES EXCITING SPECIAL GUEST!

by Lizzie Bruno

Joe's Mountain Market! was abuzz with chatter this week after a sign on the market door announced that Jesus Himself will be this year's special guest at Vacation Bible School.

"Last year, we had Father James stop by during our craft time most days, but the kids got bored with him, so we went for the big guy this summer," said VBS coordinator Marge Mizzleman. "We're hoping it boosts attendance."

"I hope He comes by the market for lunch," said Joe's manager, Martha McKnight. "I'll give Him a discount on whatever sub He'd like. Though personally, I don't think I'd recommend the tuna. Our Italian mix is much better."

McKnight ordered five hundred loaves of bread in the hopes that this year's VBS special guest could multiply them into five thousand loaves, thus ensuring a record profit year for the market. However, just after placing the order, she learned that the claim was actually a VBS publicity stunt and that Jesus would not actually appear in person. "Well, that's a shame," McKnight said.

"But we do promise that He'll be there in spirit," Mizzleman added after she admitted to the exaggerated claim. "Also, we will have really great snacks."

Dear future Wolf Creek residents,

Now that Lizzie and I have been hanging out at the market a little while, we've agreed that we need to take a break from writing fun stuff and be serious. We're going to focus on real investigative reports because it's been more than six hours since those guys broke out, so things are getting intense. Lizzie and I are going to split the reporting work—I'm making observations about what's happening and taking notes, and Lizzie is collecting conversations and taping interviews on her fancy new digital recorder thing. (It probably won't seem fancy or new by the time you read this, but it's pretty cool right now.)

Probably by tomorrow they will have caught those guys, but for now, we promise to be your number one source for professional, investigative news on the Wolf Creek prison break! More to come soon . . .

Your friend from the past,

Nora Tucker

PS Lizzie wants me to add that comedy can be an important way to make statements on current events, so she might still do some parody stuff. But mostly it'll be serious investigative reporting.

Saturday, June 8—
Notes from Joe's
Mountain Market!
by Nora Tucker,
investigative journalist

* Market is WAY crowded: 17 people in deli line, mostly state troopers w/ puffy chests (bulletproof vests?)
* Martha running around yelling at people & moving cartons of bottled water
* Sean & other workers are slicing tons of lettuce & tomato
* Betty the cashier has police scanner on behind counter

PEOPLE AT TABLES:

* Mrs. Hemingway (local newspaper reporter w/ *Wolf Creek Free Press*)
* Mrs. Hemingway's son Josh w/ camera
* Paul Washington's dad & 2 other corrections officers eating subs
* 3 state troopers—one w/ huge mustache, one bald, one really tall & skinny

* Skinny stranger-guy w/ funky glasses & notebook talking on phone
* Guy with TV news camera (CNN) taking video of market & people
* Blond woman in dress & heels taking notes

OMG! THAT'S ELIZABETH CARTER WOOD FROM CNN!!!!

OUTSIDE:
* Main St. blocked off to traffic except for COs & cops
* 1 p.m.: 8 X 9 TV trucks with satellite dishes on top outside prison
* 5 p.m. ↗

Saturday, June 8—
Notes from Elizabeth
Carter Wood's notebook
(She left it open on the
table when she went to
use the bathroom)

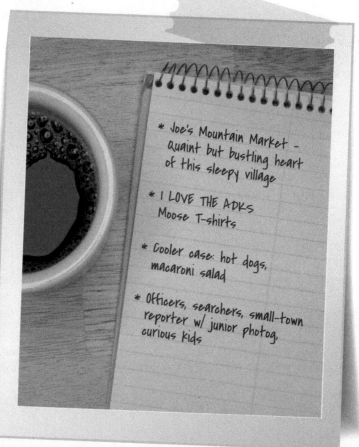

* Joe's Mountain Market –
  Quaint but bustling heart
  of this sleepy village

* I LOVE THE ADKS
  Moose T-shirts

* Cooler case: hot dogs,
  macaroni salad

* Officers, searchers, small-town
  reporter w/ junior photog,
  curious kids

State troopers' lunch conversation (I don't know where they're from, but they're not from here)

MUSTACHE GUY: My wife's gonna kill me if this search goes more than a few days. Our twentieth anniversary's next weekend.

BALDIE: Better not miss that one.

SKINNY: Hope those two aren't as sharp as the guys who escaped from downstate in '96. We were out two months on that one.

MUSTACHE: If we're gone that long, I'm gonna need to sleep on one of your couches when I get back. You gonna finish that sub?

* * *

Elizabeth Carter Wood from CNN interviewing Martha (Joe's manager)

ECW: Must be busier than usual today, huh?

MARTHA: Oh yes, cheese some!* We're almost out of coffee. Bottled water, too. Good thing I got the Pepsi guy coming today.

ECW: Thirsty searchers?

MARTHA: Yep. They've been out since 5:30 this morning with dogs and helicopters and the whole deal. My cousin over on Trudeau Road thought he saw somebody in his yard late last night. Hollered at him to get outta there, and the guy said sorry, he took a wrong turn. We figure it must have been one of the escapees. Makes me shiver to think about it.

ECW: Wow. I can imagine. Hey, any idea where I can get better cell service? I only have one bar.

MARTHA: Nope. Sorry. Welcome to the Adirondacks.

Just FYI, I corrected most of the app's mistakes on the computer before I printed this, but I left "Cheese Some" because it's awesome. Martha really said "Geezum" (that's an expression people use here, but the app obviously doesn't speak North Country). I like "Cheese Some" better anyway.

Nora interviewing Paul Washington's dad

NORA: Must be busier than usual for you guys today, huh?

PAUL'S DAD: Yep.

NORA: Any idea where those two inmates might be?

PAUL'S DAD: Nope.

NORA: Wow. So you're going to keep searching?

PAUL'S DAD: Yep.

*   *   *

NBC NY camera guy at deli

NBC GUY: You don't have sushi, do you?

MARTHA: Ha! No.

NBC GUY: That's okay. I told him you wouldn't. In that case, we need four ham subs, three roast beef, and one mixed Italian. Also one turkey.

MARTHA: Lettuce and tomato?

NBC GUY: Do you have arugula or spinach?

MARTHA: We have lettuce and tomato.

NBC GUY: Any hummus?

MARTHA: What do you think?

NBC: Got it. No hummus. No arugula. No cell service. But the subs are only four bucks. It's like 1987 here.

MARTHA: Welcome to the Adirondacks.

LIZZIE'S REFLECTIONS: The recorder did pretty well today, but it didn't pick up the scanner they had running in the market. The police kept getting calls about inmates being seen in all kinds of places where they turned out not to really be. Here are some of the most interesting places people thought they saw them:

✡ At Nancy McNichols's garage sale on Trudeau Road, buying curtains
✡ West Lake Road boat launch, near the beach, with a bright green Jet Ski
✡ In a red Honda Accord on the interstate
✡ In a blue Corvette at the stoplight on Tom Goddeau Road
✡ Eating frozen yogurt with sprinkles at Sweet Treats
✡ Getting breakfast at McDonald's
✡ Ordering onion rings at Moby's Red Hots

The inmates were not actually at any of those places, eating any of those things or buying curtains. All we really know is this:

The inmates are named John Smith and James Young, which are super boring names for two guys who did something so exciting. Their pictures are all over the news now. James Young is a tall, skinny African American guy with short hair. John Smith is a short, muscular white guy with shaggy blond hair and a tattoo of a dragon on his neck.

They're both in prison for killing people a long time ago in NYC. They were discovered missing at the 5 a.m. bed check.
There are 220 officers out searching now & more are on the way.
City newspeople get really bummed out when there's no arugula.

Finally, here are the headlines I would have used for my parody articles today if I hadn't promised Nora I'd try to be serious for a while . . .

BREAKOUTS AND BARGAINS: ESCAPEES SCOUR LOCAL YARD SALES FOR WINDOW TREATMENTS

ARUGULA OUTRAGE: BIG-CITY REPORTERS THREATEN TO BOYCOTT MARKET OVER PATHETIC PRODUCE OPTIONS

RAINBOW SPRINKLES ON THE RUN: INMATES STEAL TIME FOR TREATS AS THEY FLEE POLICE

My Moby's onion ring and McDonald's breakfast stories would have been pretty great, too.

Saturday, June 8–
Text messages
between Nora & her
mom, 5:10 p.m.

MOM: Have you left the market yet?

NORA: Nope still here

MOM: Head home please

NORA: We're going to watch the tv newspeople do their live reports on main st at 6 and then come home ok?

MOM: You can watch them on tv. Head home now

NORA: But we really really want to see the live reports

Please???

MOM: NOW

Saturday, June 8—
Text messages between
Elidee & her mom

MAMA: Hey there

ELIDEE: Hi

MAMA: I'm not going to make it home for dinner. Sorry

ELIDEE: That's ok I can make mac & cheese

MAMA: Have some salad too

ELIDEE: Ok

MAMA: What have you been doing all afternoon?

ELIDEE: Listening to music

MAMA: You should work on that extra-credit assignment

ELIDEE: Done for today

I'll write another letter tomorrow

MAMA: Door locked?

ELIDEE: Yes

MAMA: Did you check?

ELIDEE: We've been here 2 days and you think I've already turned into some country person who leaves the door unlocked?

MAMA: Don't sass

ELIDEE: Sorry

I checked and it's locked

MAMA: Good girl. See you around 11

Just call Mrs. G upstairs if you need anything

ELIDEE: Ok

Love you to RR245 and back

MAMA: Love you too copycat

ELIDEE: You're not going to show me up with something farther away??

MAMA: Too busy here. I'll have to make up for it next time xo

Saturday, June 8—
CNN report, 6 p.m.

NOTE FROM NORA: I watched CNN and then printed out this report from the website because people who aren't allowed to stay out to do their own reporting sometimes have to rely on other reporters whose parents don't stomp all over the First Amendment by making them come home and restricting their freedom-of-the-press rights.

The search continues for two killers who escaped from a maximum security prison in upstate New York. Police are pouring into the sleepy town of Wolf Creek, hoping to track down the two men, who authorities say are extremely dangerous.

Corrections officials say John Smith and James Young escaped by cutting holes in the walls of their cells and making their way through electrical passageways and heating pipes—all the way to freedom.

Police say the pair emerged from a manhole near the prison early Saturday morning. It is not known at this time if they had a vehicle or other help from the outside, but police are following several leads.

Despite the prison wall that looms over Main Street, Wolf Creek is a quaint, small town where safety is usually taken for granted. But not anymore. At the local market, where conversation is usually about moose sightings and macaroni salad, everyone—from prison employees to curious youngsters—is talking about the escape.

HELEN JABLONSKI, WOLF CREEK RESIDENT: "I hope they get 'em, that's for sure. We never lock our doors around here, but you better believe I'm locking 'em now. And Tony's keeping his shotgun loaded by the bed just in case."

Police have been checking unoccupied buildings and hunting camps, but so far, there's been no sign of the prisoners.

STATE POLICE SERGEANT TED PHELPS: "We're asking anyone who might have information to call our tip line. We are fully committed to tracking down these two individuals."

But if the inmates have managed to make their way into the mountains, that may be easier said than done. The terrain around here is some of the most rugged in the state.

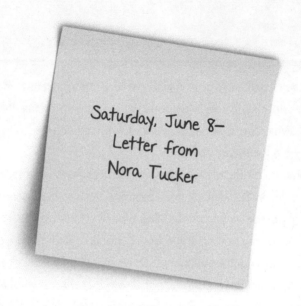

Saturday, June 8—
Letter from
Nora Tucker

Dear future Wolf Creek residents,

I'm back to writing letters because our super serious investigative reporting is not going all that well. I can't believe Mom made us come home so early, but I had to write to tell you the good news that you couldn't tell from the CNN website printout—Lizzie and I were on TV tonight!!

We were at the market earlier when Elizabeth Carter Wood was there with her cameraman, and I kind of noticed that he was pointing the video camera our way, but I tried to just look busy, and then THERE WE WERE ON TV AND IT WAS SO COOL!

The not-cool thing is that she called us "curious youngsters," which makes us sound like little kids when really, we were taking just as many notes as she was.

After Lizzie and I got ordered home, we walked to my house (actually, we ran—Mom was being intense). When we got close, we could see her standing at the front window like she'd been waiting for us all day. After we got inside, she locked the door and turned the bolt thing, which I don't think we've ever used.

So now Dad's at work. Mom says he might stop home for a late dinner. Sean's stuck at the market, too, because the deli line is so long. For now, it's just Lizzie, Owen, and me, hanging out in our never-locked, double-locked house.

Owen found out about the inmates when he heard Mom on the phone today, and she was right—he did freak out. Mom says I have to distract him now. I almost gave him his birthday wand early, but I really want to save that, so instead, I told him about the time capsule project and said he could write stuff, too. I showed him my assignment page from Ms. Morin, and he loved the idea of making master plans and evil plots, so Mom found Owen a notebook and you'll probably be getting stuff from him, too. Please understand that most of us who live in Wolf Creek are not as weird as my brother.

Your friend from the past,

Nora Tucker

Saturday, June 8–
This is a picture of
Owen's new notebook

PLACES THE
INMATES MIGHT
BE HIDING

Saturday, June 8—
From Owen's Master
Plans & Evil Plots
notebook

Searching for
themselves in the
woods (dressed in
police uniforms*)

Garages   Closets   Trees behind
                              school playground

Old fire tower on
Blueberry Ridge
Mountain

Shop-Mart
(disguysed as
clerks or shoppers)

Tree
forts

Trees
behind our
house

Hospital
(disguysed as
doctors)

Inside rusty
school bus
behind Mason
Tallmudge's
house

Basements

Under beds

Shed next
to library

*This really happened with bad guys in one of my Green Flash superhero comics once.

Saturday, June 8—
Dinner at Nora's house,
recorded on Lizzie's
WhisperFlash Z190

NOTE FROM LIZZIE: We missed a few things because the recorder was muffled from being in my pocket the whole time. We didn't take it out because Nora's mom is still all stressed out and we're pretty sure she would have said no to having the WhisperFlash at dinner, so we had to be stealthy.

This is totally legit, by the way. In New York State, it's legal to record a conversation as long as one person in the conversation knows and is okay with it. That might not sound fair, but it's the law. Nora looked it up. And since Nora and I are people in this conversation, we're good. Just don't tell Nora's mom, okay? She might not care about the law.

MRS. TUCKER: Nora, can you grab the salad dressing, please?

SEAN: I'm starving. Didn't get a break today. We were
slammed with cops.

MRS. TUCKER: It'll probably be busy tomorrow, too.

SEAN: Yeah, Martha already asked if I could come in early.
She's kinda hoping this goes on for a while. It's been
great for business.

MR. TUCKER: With all due respect to Martha, the rest of us
hope otherwise.

NORA: I can't believe they're still out. We were on CNN!

MRS. TUCKER: Nora, please. Dad could probably use a break
from this.

MR. TUCKER: It's not going to be a long break. I need to get
back.

NORA: Okay, but can I ask something about Lizzie's chart?

MR. TUCKER: What chart is that?

LIZZIE: For Nora's news story. I made a chart showing Wolf
Creek's population and the prison population and stuff.
The numbers I found said only 22% of the inmates are
white—the rest are black or Latino or other—but almost
all the corrections officers are white. Is that true?

MR. TUCKER: Sounds about right.

MRS. TUCKER: It makes sense that the CO numbers would
be similar to Wolf Creek's population, girls.
It's not as diverse here as it is in bigger cities
downstate.

NORA: Yeah, but what about the inmates?

SEAN: That's not just Wolf Creek. Prisons all over the
country are like that because of bias in our criminal
justice system.

MR. TUCKER: Our corrections officers don't see black and white, Sean. Only blue and green.

OWEN: You have blue and green inmates in there?

NORA: He's talking about what they wear, Owen. Corrections officers have blue uniforms and the inmates wear green.

SEAN: Ms. Madora says it's incredibly problematic to say that you don't see color. She says that's refusing to acknowledge our country's history of racial injustice.

MR. TUCKER: So I'm incredibly problematic now? Who's Ms. Madora?

SEAN: Our English teacher.

MRS. TUCKER: We met her at parent-teacher conferences—the one with all the earrings.

SEAN: She's our adviser for Mock Trial, too. And she does a lot of current events stuff in class. We read an article last week about how changes to drug laws in the 1970s led to America imprisoning more people than any other country. Like, way more if you base it on population. And even though white people were using drugs, too, more black and Latino people got arrested based on those laws.

MR. TUCKER: It's not that simple. And you know what? People who have never worked in a prison like to point fingers, but when you're dealing with the population we're dealing with—

SEAN: I know. And poverty plays into crime rates, too. But that's also tied to systemic racism. Emily took a sociology class this year that talked about that, and it blew her away. Ms. Madora says this really ought to be the civil rights movement of our time. And she'd tell you Lizzie's chart is proof we need criminal justice reform.

MR. TUCKER: Ms. Madora should stick to teaching Shakespeare.

OWEN: Can somebody pass me the bread, please?

SEAN: Dad, it's not personal. And it's not just Wolf Creek. It's the whole—

MRS. TUCKER: Sean, not tonight.

NORA: But you always say we should bring up interesting topics for dinner conversation.

MRS. TUCKER: That's enough interesting conversation for one day. Right now, we all just need to make a circle of support around Dad.

OWEN: I'll be in your circle, Dad.

MR. TUCKER: Thanks, buddy.

SEAN: You can support Dad and still want the criminal justice system to change.

MRS. TUCKER: Sean, please. Let's talk about something else.

MR. TUCKER: I actually need to head out. I told Chuck I'd be back before eight.

MRS. TUCKER: Will you be home to sleep later or don't you know?

MR. TUCKER: Depends on what happens.

MRS. TUCKER: Good luck. We'll keep our fingers crossed.

NORA: Night, Dad. Love you.

SEAN: See ya, Dad.

OWEN: Love you!

MR. TUCKER: Love you, too.

LIZZIE'S REFLECTIONS: Looks like my chart was right after all. I had no idea it was like that. And if Sean is right and it's because of racist policies and stuff, that's pretty messed up. Nora says we should try to find out more about those drug law changes, but her parents got all stressed out talking about it, so I'm pretty sure that won't be happening at the Tucker dinner table for a while. At least not until those guys get caught.

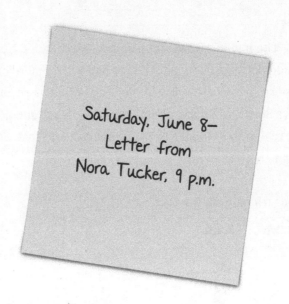

Saturday, June 8—
Letter from
Nora Tucker, 9 p.m.

Dear future Wolf Creek residents,

We just finished cleaning up from dinner. It's been a long day here, and they still haven't caught the inmates. The police are looking everywhere. Mom and I are also looking everywhere because Owen keeps making us search the house. Inmates are the new Voldemort, apparently. Here are all the places we checked before Owen would go to bed:

Our garage
Our basement
Owen's tree fort
Attic
Linen closet in upstairs hallway
Owen's closet
Under Owen's bed

The inmates were not in any of those places. Neither was Voldemort. I'm going to bed now and will do more investigative reporting tomorrow. I'd also like to ask Dad more about those laws Sean was talking about, but Lizzie says I should wait until we're done with our "circle of support" to do that. She's probably right.

Your friend from the past,

Nora Tucker

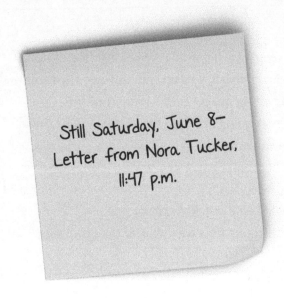

Dear future Wolf Creek residents,

I know I said I'd write tomorrow, and it's not tomorrow yet, but
the helicopters are keeping me awake. Maybe by the time you
read this, there will be quiet helicopters or some other way to
search that doesn't keep people up all night, but ours are all
loud and choppy. Uncle Tommy, who's a state trooper, came
by on patrol earlier. He told Mom the helicopters have a fancy
night-vision, heat-sensing thing to look down into the woods.
I hope it works.

    It's weird thinking those inmates are out there somewhere.

    Maybe far away by now.

    But maybe not.

    Lizzie's staying over again. She started snoring halfway
through our movie, so I turned it off and tried to sleep, too. Even
though it's really hot, we had to close and lock all the downstairs
windows because of the inmates. My bedroom is upstairs,

though, so I got to keep my window cracked to hear the crickets. At least until the helicopters showed up and drowned them out.

The whirring is getting quieter now. Maybe they saw something, so they're sending men into the woods. Maybe Uncle Tommy's out there searching.

I can't hear the helicopter anymore.

I guess I'll try to sleep again.

I wish Mom would come check my closet, too.

Somehow, now the quiet feels even scarier than the noise.

Your friend from the past,

Nora Tucker

PS You might read this and think that I'm overreacting, but if you've never looked out your window knowing there might be two murderers in the woods, you can't really understand.

Dear future Wolf Creek residents,

This is the fourth of my five letters. Mama's at work, so I'm
locked up and can't go anywhere until she gets back. Back home,
she worked in a really nice nursing home, taking care of old
people who can't remember things anymore. She thought she'd
be able to get another job like that, since there are plenty of
senior centers here. She sent out applications but didn't get a
single interview, so now she's working at a hospital that's half an
hour away.

Mama says if that's God's will, it's fine with her, and she'll end
up where she ought to be. Aunt Maya says God has nothing to do
with it. She's pretty sure it's because people here aren't used to
seeing names like Latanya on job applications. Everybody else's
mom here is called Donna or Kathleen or something. Is it still
like that in Wolf Creek in the future? Probably. Seems like this
might be the kind of place where nothing ever really changes.
Anyway, I figured I'd get this letter done now because there's
nothing else to do. We don't have Wi-Fi hooked up yet, and I

can't go to the library until Mama gets home. I need to look up some new faraway planets for this game we play. I also want to get poetry books. Until Mama gets home, all I have is that one by the wheelbarrow guy. He writes poems like this:

So much depends
On a blue milk crate
Full of shorts and running shoes
That are no good because I'm not allowed outside

So much depends
On a police helicopter
Circling like a hungry vulture
Casting shadows on the mountains

So much depends
On Mama getting home on time
Because the public library's only open
Until five

No offense to the wheelbarrow guy, but the lyrics in the *Hamilton* musical were way better poetry than this.

Sincerely,
Elidee Jones

NAME
POEMS

Mama

Make a good impression.
Always do your best.
Make me proud.
Always.

Troy

Trouble and guts
wRong place at the wRong time
One choice. One mistake. One day.
Your sentence: 15 years.

Elidee

Everybody says
Love your mama, she's been through enough so
I try to be perfect.
Doubt I'll ever come close enough.
Every once in a while, it would be nice if
Even one thing could be about me.

**Wolf Creek
Public
Library**

*Sunday, June 9—
Elidee's library checkout
receipt*

RECEIPT

Patron: Elidee Jones
Date: June 9

TITLES CHECKED OUT:

The Hubble Space Telescope: A Universe of New Discovery by the
Associated Press
Due date: June 23

Brown Girl Dreaming by Jacqueline Woodson
Due date: June 23

The 100 Best African American Poems edited by Nikki Giovanni
Due date: June 23

One Last Word: Wisdom from the Harlem Renaissance by Nikki Grimes
Due date: June 23

Alexander Hamilton by Ron Chernow
Due date: June 23

TITLES REQUESTED VIA INTERLIBRARY LOAN:

Hamilton: The Revolution by Lin-Manuel Miranda and Jeremy
McCarter

(In Transit: Expected Monday, June 10)

THANKS FOR USING YOUR LIBRARY!

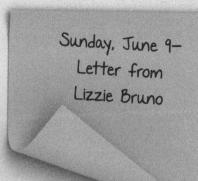

Sunday, June 9—
Letter from
Lizzie Bruno

Dear future Wolf Creek people,

This is Lizzie Bruno, reporting LIVE on day two of the GREAT WOLF CREEK MANHUNT!

Actually, it's not great at all because we're not allowed to do anything fun. At least I'm getting this extra credit done early. For this entry, I'm sharing a conversation I recorded in the car when we went to my house to pick up more clothes and my school stuff for Monday. My grandma's fine, but they're keeping her another day for a few more tests, so I'm staying with Nora again and using her computer to get this done. Here's what happened when the police stopped our car . . .

OWEN: Why are we stopping?

MRS. TUCKER: Just a roadblock . . . Morning, officer.

TROOPER: I need you to roll down the rest of your windows, ma'am, and open the trunk, please.

OWEN: What's in the trunk?

NORA: Nothing, Owen. They're checking everybody's. Remember how Mom said there are lots and lots of helpers? The troopers are keeping us safe.

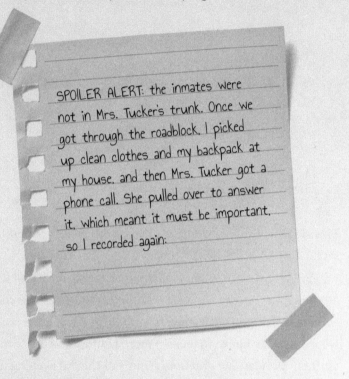

SPOILER ALERT: the inmates were not in Mrs. Tucker's trunk. Once we got through the roadblock, I picked up clean clothes and my backpack at my house, and then Mrs. Tucker got a phone call. She pulled over to answer it, which meant it must be important, so I recorded again:

MRS. TUCKER: Hey there, how's it going today? . . . Still nothing, huh? . . . Will you get a break later? . . . Oh really?! Wow . . .

NORA: Wow what?

MRS. TUCKER: Shhh . . . Well, that's a good sign, I guess . . . okay . . . I will . . . I know . . . I hope so . . . Okay, love you. Bye.

NORA: What's going on? Why'd you say wow?

MRS. TUCKER: The governor's coming to town for a news conference this afternoon.

LIZZIE: Whoa!

NORA: What time?

MRS. TUCKER: Noon

NORA: That's in half an hour. Where is it? At the prison? Lizzie, we should go!

MRS. TUCKER: You can't just waltz into a press conference without credentials.

LIZZIE: We have our Wolf Creek Middle School Gazette press passes somewhere. But I spilled orange juice on mine, so the marker is kind of smudged.

NORA: I bet Dad could get us in!

MRS. TUCKER: Dad has enough to worry about without—

NORA: Can we go to the market and watch from there?

OWEN: What if the bad guys are there?

MRS. TUCKER: The bad guys are not going to be at the news conference, honey.

OWEN: I meant at the market.

MRS. TUCKER: They're not going to be at the market either.

NORA: Then can we go? Please?

LIZZIE: I'm only going if I can write something funny about it.

NORA: Fine. Mom, can we?

MRS. TUCKER: I suppose. I'll drop you off. Come straight home when it's over.

Sunday, June 9—
We found our
press passes!

PRESS PASS 🐾
Wolf Creek Middle School Gazette
Reporter: *Elizabeth Bruno*
Adviser signature: *Melissa Mohin*
NOTE TO FACULTY: Please accept this as equal to a hall pass.

PRESS PASS 🐾
Wolf Creek Middle School Gazette
Reporter: *Nora Tucker*
Adviser signature: *Melissa Mohin*
hall pass.

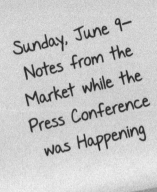

Sunday, June 9—
Notes from the
Market while the
Press Conference
was Happening

11:55 a.m. at Joe's Mountain Market!
Market's very, very quiet—only Sean and Martha here
HUGE crowd down at press conference by prison
TV reporters & camera people w/ satellite trucks
Many police officers
Looks very safe over there
Would be dumbest place ever for inmates to show up

11:57 a.m.
Old lady came into market
She bought toilet paper

11:59 a.m.
Another CNN satellite truck parked in front of market
Totally blocking view of prison, so we can't tell if they're
   starting the press conference yet or what

Sunday, June 9—
Letter and notes
from the actual
press conference

Dear future Wolf Creek residents,

If you're thinking "Hey, you were supposed to stay at the
market!" you are correct about this. But we couldn't see anything
from the market. It looked very safe over at the prison, so we
had to make a judgment call. Dad talks about that sometimes
when he has to think on his feet and make a quick decision at the
prison. He uses his best judgment. That's what we did, too.

   Also, Mom was wrong about us not being able to waltz
into the press conference. Nobody checked for press passes or
anything. So we waltzed in and my notes are pasted below:

12:05 p.m. Big white tent with wooden podium set up
   outside prison
Bunch of microphones rubber-banded together up on
   podium—kind of looks like a bouquet of flowers
Easel set up w/ big posters of inmates' faces
NBC News reporter leaning against birch tree, peeling

off bark (lucky Mom isn't here or she'd tell him to knock it off because that's bad for trees)

WNBC reporter—wearing nice dress w/ mud boots

Camera people & sound people with big furry microphones on sticks

Dad & two other prison officer guys holding phones, clipboards

Dad keeps tugging at his tie—probably nervous because he has to explain to all these reporters how his inmates got away.

12:15 p.m. Black car with tinted windows—governor?
Camera guys all pick up cameras
Reporters poking at phones
Lizzie just got so excited she dropped her recorder
OMG ELIZABETH CARTER WOOD FROM CNN PICKED IT UP
& TALKED TO US

12:20 p.m. Press Conference starts—Speakers:
Dad
State Police Captain Bradley Mason
Governor Sonia Ramos

(Lizzie's recording what everybody says & she'll print that all out later)

12:32 p.m. Press conference ends & everybody leaves

I wish I'd gotten to ask a question. I tried to ask one about prison history because everybody else was asking really hard questions, and some of them sounded kind of mean. I thought Dad would have an easier time answering my question, but nobody heard me.

Your friend from the past,

Nora Tucker

Sunday, June 9—
Recorded on Lizzie's
WhisperFlash Z190 at
the press conference

NOTE FROM LIZZIE: I put my recorder up on the podium with all the microphones, and it picked up two reporters talking before the press conference started, so I'm including that conversation, too.

REPORTER GUY: When did you guys get in?

REPORTER LADY: Last night. We got pulled off the Wall Street protest to come up here.

REPORTER GUY: Bummer. This isn't exactly Manhattan.

REPORTER LADY: No kidding. At least the fresh air's nice. Where you staying?

REPORTER GUY: Some bed-and-breakfast two towns over. I woke up this morning with a sheep looking in my window. Nice room, though.

REPORTER LADY: Consider yourself lucky. They have us at Max's Motor Lodge off Exit 30.

REPORTER GUY: Let's hope this ends soon.

MR. TUCKER: Good afternoon. I'm Bill Tucker, superintendent of Wolf Creek Correctional Facility. This is State Police Captain Bradley Mason, and we're also joined by New York Governor Sonia Ramos. As you know, early yesterday, two inmates were discovered missing, and it was determined that they used stolen tools to cut through their cell walls. From there, we believe the men crawled through pipes to a manhole cover several blocks from the prison and escaped. Both are serving life sentences for murder and should be considered extremely dangerous. A massive search is under way and Captain Mason will share more on that.

CAPTAIN MASON: State Police and Corrections Department search teams are performing a grid search of the area surrounding the prison. We will continue to man roadblocks and request the public's support and patience. We've set up a hotline and ask anyone with information to call immediately. We have already received more than five hundred tips and are investigating those. We're grateful for the support we've received from Albany, and now I'd like to introduce Governor Ramos.

GOVERNOR RAMOS: Good afternoon. First, I'd like to thank the officers involved in the search. They've been out all night, and as you know, the territory surrounding this prison is mountainous and rugged, so hunting down the escapees is no small task. But our officers will search behind every tree, under every rock, and inside every structure. And I'll promise you right now that we will find these men and bring them to justice. Thank you.

MR. TUCKER: One at a time, please!

NBC LADY: How many officers are out searching?

CAPTAIN MASON: Approximately five hundred. We have more arriving from downstate tonight.

NBC LADY: Have they found any clues?

CAPTAIN MASON: There were some articles of clothing and canned goods found in bushes not far from the prison, and we're looking into that.

ELIZABETH CARTER WOOD: There's been talk of an accomplice. Do you know if the inmates had help?

MR. TUCKER: That investigation is continuing. We're interviewing a number of people who had contact with the inmates to determine if anyone provided assistance.

ELIZABETH CARTER WOOD: So prison employees might have been involved?

MR. TUCKER: We're investigating that possibility. Next question?

REPORTER GUY: This is an unprecedented escape. As superintendent of the prison, can you explain to the public how prison safety policies could have failed so badly?

MR. TUCKER: That's all part of our investigation. To the best of our knowledge, the 11 p.m. bed check was done as scheduled. However, the inmates had made dummies out of rolled-up clothing to make it appear that they were in their beds asleep. We continue to investigate and are taking this very seriously.

NORA: Can you tell us about the history of the prison?

REPORTER GUY: Superintendent Tucker, this is a prison with a history of questionable reviews, based on state inspections. Did inadequate training of your officers play a role in this escape?

MR. TUCKER: I'm not going to speculate when our staff members have been working more than thirty hours straight. All I can tell you is we're cooperating fully with state investigators.

GOVERNOR RAMOS: And I can promise the public that there will be a full and independent investigation. But right now, our top priority is finding these two inmates, and our officers need to get back to work. Thanks for coming.

(Everybody shouted more questions here, but Nora's dad and the state police captain and the governor pretended they couldn't hear them anymore. The rest of this is a conversation we had with Elizabeth Carter Wood when we went back up to the podium to get the recorder.)

ELIZABETH CARTER WOOD: Get some good quotes?

NORA: I like the one about looking behind every tree and under every rock.

ELIZABETH CARTER WOOD: That'll take a while around here. You have more trees and rocks than we do in New York City.

NORA: Isn't CNN in Atlanta?

ELIZABETH CARTER WOOD: We're based there, but we have reporters all over. Maybe you two will join us someday!

NORA: That would be awesome!

ELIZABETH CARTER WOOD: Do you live in Wolf Creek?

NORA: Yep. My dad's the prison superintendent, so we live right in town.

ELIZABETH CARTER WOOD: Your dad is . . . Bill Tucker? Wow, I bet he's been busy.

NORA: We've hardly seen him since this started.

ELIZABETH CARTER WOOD: I bet it's been a tough couple of days.

NORA: Mostly for my little brother. He doesn't even want to sleep in his room now. He's afraid the inmates might be in his closet.

ELIZABETH CARTER WOOD: Aww . . .

(PHONE RINGS)

NORA: Oh! That's my mom. I better go.

ELIZABETH CARTER WOOD: Wait—take one of my business cards, okay? You can call me if you'd like to chat more. Maybe we can compare notes on the big story and you can sort of be an assistant reporter for CNN this week. How does that sound?

NORA: Great!

ELIZABETH CARTER WOOD: Super! See you later.

LIZZIE'S REFLECTIONS ON ALL THESE CONVERSATIONS:

1. News conferences don't have much news sometimes. This one was three people saying the same stuff we already knew.

2. Reporters all try to talk at the same time.

3. And what's their problem with Max's Motor Lodge? We stayed there when my cousin got married last summer. There was a pool and everything.

Sunday, June 9—
An investigative
report by Nora
Tucker

PRISON OFFICIALS AND POLICE VOW TO CATCH ESCAPED INMATES

by Nora Tucker, Investigative Reporter

Officials held a press conference at Wolf Creek Correctional Facility today, promising to find two inmates who escaped from the prison. John Smith and James Young were both serving life sentences for murder and are considered very dangerous. Police are looking for help to track them down.

"We've set up a hotline and ask anyone with information to call immediately," said State Police Captain Bradley Mason.

Prison superintendent Bill Tucker has been working around the clock since the escape. So have searchers from the state police and Corrections Department. Governor Sonia Ramos, who came to Wolf Creek today, promises that the state will support those efforts one hundred percent.

Prison officials are still trying to figure out how this happened.

"That's all part of our investigation," said superintendent Bill Tucker. "We're taking this very seriously."

Police say even more searchers will arrive soon to help.

Sunday, June 9—
A not-so-investigative
report by Lizzie Bruno
(This is another one of
Lizzie's made-up
parody articles)

MANHUNT CONTINUES:

POLICE COMPLAIN OF TOO MANY TREES AND ROCKS AROUND HERE

by Lizzie Bruno

Police are still searching the woods around Wolf Creek Correctional Facility for two inmates who busted out of the prison. The governor even came to town today, promising that searchers would check "behind every tree, under every rock, and inside every structure."

However, some searchers are taking issue with that order.

"Every tree? Really?" said Trooper Ima B. Tired. "There must be thousands of them. Millions if you count shrubs. Do we have to search behind the skinny trees, too? Because both of those inmates are pretty big guys, and only the bigger trees would hide 'em."

"It's not realistic," added Officer Ben Tover. "I've flipped over every pebble and stone between the prison and the river. So far, all I found is a lot of ants and one really fast beetle."

Police supervisors say regardless of these hardships, the search must continue. "It's hard work, but we'll be back at it first thing tomorrow morning," said Sergeant Brighton Early. "I'm sure we'll find them eventually."

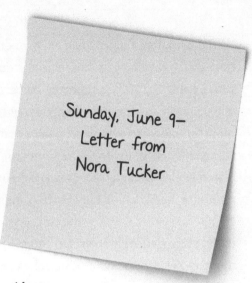

Dear future Wolf Creek residents,

I liked my news story on the press conference, so I was in a great mood until we turned on CNN just now. Read this part of Elizabeth Carter Wood's report, and then I have some advice for you.

The man in charge of Wolf Creek's prison refused to talk about who's to blame for this unprecedented lapse in security.

Prison superintendent Bill Tucker: "I'm not going to speculate when our staff members have been working more than thirty hours straight. All I can tell you is we're cooperating fully with state investigators."

It's obviously a stressful time for prison officials. And fear is running high in this community, even in the prison superintendent's own home. Tucker's young daughter told CNN that she's hardly seen her father since the escape. She says her little brother is afraid to sleep in his own bed, for fear the inmates might be hiding in his closet. Everyone is hoping this comes to an end very soon.

I don't know if journalism will work the same way by the time you're reading this, but in case it does, here's my advice. If you're going to talk to a reporter, be careful what you say, even if it seems like you are just hanging out being investigative-reporter buddies. Otherwise, you'll get in trouble for accidentally doing an interview with CNN. Mom gave me a big lecture about responsibility to family. She says Dad's under enough stress right now, and keeping our "circle of support" does not include giving interviews with the national press. I think I was about to get grounded, only then Dad called and Mom went in her room and closed the door. When she came out, she forgot about yelling at me because she was too busy double- and triple- and quadruple-checking the locks on all the doors and windows. She even locked the window Sean crawls through when he forgets his house key.

Owen watched Mom do all that locking and checking, and then he went around the house testing the locks himself. Then he was worried the inmates might break his window and climb in. Mom reminded him his room is on the second floor and the inmates aren't that tall. Owen said, what if they had a ladder? Mom said they didn't. Owen thought they could probably find one. What if they stole one from Bob's Hardware?

There's really no reasoning with Owen once he starts what-iffing, so Mom dragged his mattress into her room and said he could stay up until she was ready to come upstairs, too. So now Owen's in the living room, writing in his Master Plans and Evil Plots notebook.

Lizzie and I brushed our teeth and changed into our pajamas, but neither of us can sleep, so now Lizzie's making a Venn diagram to compare our prison break to the one at Alcatraz. (I know this sounds geeky, but in our time period, lots of newspapers use graphics like this. Have you ever seen USA TODAY?)

This just reminded me that I haven't returned that Alcatraz book to the school library. You should look for it if they still have it when you read this. It's really good. I've read it four times, so it's not like I don't know what happens, but that makes it perfect reading for tonight. I'm not up for any more surprises right now.

Your friend from the past,

Nora Tucker

Sunday, June 9—
Lizzie's Venn diagram

NOTE FROM LIZZIE: You'll probably notice there are some arrows & stuff here. In a regular Venn diagram, there are two circles and you write the differences between the two things in the circles and put the similarities in that space where the circles overlap. But once we started working on this, we figured out that even our similarities have differences. Like both groups of escaped inmates made dummies to put in their beds, but the dummies were made of different stuff. Also, Nora and I think the Alcatraz guys did a better job. So that's what all the arrows are about.

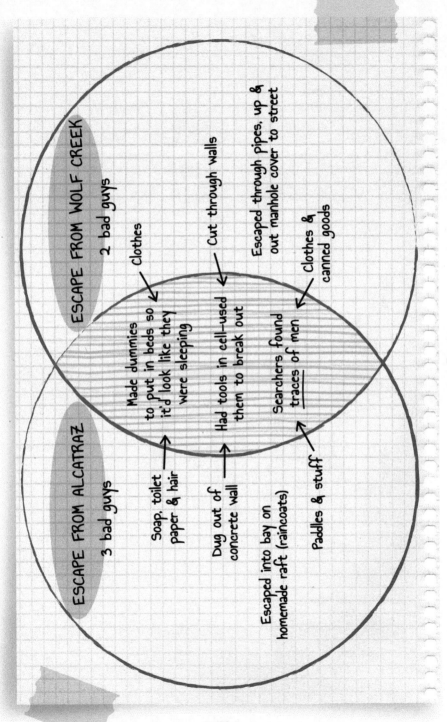

ESCAPE FROM WOLF CREEK
2 bad guys

Clothes

Cut through walls

Escaped through pipes, up & out manhole cover to street

Clothes & canned goods

Made dummies to put in beds so it'd look like they were sleeping

Had tools in cell—used them to break out

Searchers found traces of men

ESCAPE FROM ALCATRAZ
3 bad guys

Soap, toilet paper & hair

Dug out of concrete wall

Escaped into bay on homemade raft (raincoats)

Paddles & stuff

Sunday, June 9—
From Owen's Master
Plans & Evil Plots
notebook

SUPER SECRET PLAN
FOR DEFEATING BAD
GUYS WITH LADDERS

OUR HOUSE AT BEDTIME

INMATES' EVIL PLAN

Good guy tools

me

SECRET HIDING SPOT FOR DEFEATING
BAD GUYS WITH LADDERS

* III *

ACTION TIME!

GOOD GUYS WIN!

"Thank you, Owen Tucker, for your brave work capturing these bad guys!"

Monday, June 10 — Wolf Creek Middle School morning announcements

Monday, June 10

Good morning, Wolf Pack! Please stand for the pledge to the flag.

(Pledge)

You probably noticed as you entered the building that we have some visiting law enforcement. That's related to the escape of two inmates from the prison over the weekend. There is nothing to suggest the escapees are anywhere near our school, but the police are committed to keeping everyone safe. They'll be on hand as long as this situation continues, to make sure there are no disruptions to our learning. You'll see them in the traffic circle during drop-off and dismissal, and we'll have a police presence both inside and outside the building during our school day as well.

Some other announcements . . .

Gym classes will be held inside today.

The eighth-grade science water-monitoring field trip out to Calder Creek has been postponed.

Another reminder from Mr. Russell that library books were due last week. If you still have some, please turn them in today or tomorrow.

The chess club tournament starts after school today in room F-4.

Wolf Creek Middle School field day is this Friday! I hope you've all been practicing for the Mad Mile. If you signed up to bring plates or napkins for the cookout, those can be dropped off at the office any day this week. Baked goods, veggie plates, and other perishable items should be brought on Friday.

Happy birthday this morning to Alyssa Beals and Jake Irving!

Our quote of the day is from children's rights activist Marian Wright Edelman, who said, "Education is for improving the lives of others and for leaving your community and world better than you found it."

That concludes our morning announcements.

Dear future Wolf Creek residents,

Our principal says the police are at school so learning doesn't get interrupted, but nobody's getting anything done today. I get that the officers are supposed to make us feel safe, but seeing them in the halls with their guns kind of makes it feel like the world is coming to an end.

Lizzie and I are in study hall now, doing nothing, just like we've done in all our classes so far. I thought math would be different because of Mrs. James. She's been around forever and will probably still be hanging in there when you read this letter, so here's a tip: do NOT forget to bring a pencil to her class. Mrs. James is the kind of teacher who answers any complaint with a story about how back in her day, they walked to school barefoot in the snow, and they never would have slacked off on algebra just because two killers were wandering around the woods.

When Mrs. James asked for today's assignment, Walker Tremont said he didn't have it because his math book was in his dad's car when his dad got called out to man a roadblock. I thought Mrs. James would give her usual lecture about responsibility, but she just nodded and told Walker to bring it tomorrow. Then it *really* felt like the world was coming to an end.

She at least tried to do her regular math lesson, but when she had to take a phone call, everybody started talking about the breakout. Josh Randall says his mom works at the prison and is convinced the inmates had help, probably from a corrections officer who gave them the tools they used. Cole Bordeau's dad works there, too, and Cole says there's no way a CO would have helped, because guards know what those guys are like better than anyone, so Josh and his mom don't know what they're talking about.

Then Mrs. James hung up the phone and tried to review probability for our final exam. That didn't work because when she asked for an example, Josh raised his hand and said there's an 80 percent chance some guard gave those inmates the tools. Cole didn't bother raising his hand before he said there's a 99 percent chance Josh was going to get punched if he didn't shut up. I think there's a 100 percent chance that Mrs. James was glad when the bell rang.

I heard about a million rumors at my locker today.

Somebody gave the inmates a cell phone.

Somebody picked them up in a getaway car.

The inmates are in Vermont.

They're in Mexico.

They're in Canada.

It feels like they're everywhere and nowhere, all at the same time.

The only person not blabbing on and on about it is the new girl, Elidee. Walker and Cole were kind of bugging her at the end of math class, asking about her brother. Elidee ignored them, but I kind of wish she hadn't. I'm curious about her brother, too. I told Lizzie maybe we could interview Elidee later, but Lizzie said it would be crummy to even ask because people at school are already treating Elidee more like a news story than a person.

Lizzie's probably right. It seemed like people were being really nice to Elidee when she first got here, last week, but everybody's in a gossipy mood now with the inmates out.

Asking Elidee for an interview about her brother probably wouldn't be cool. It reminds me of how Elizabeth Carter Wood got me in trouble by putting our friendly conversation on the news. Sometimes, there's a fine line between being a journalist and being a jerk. I'd still really like to know about her brother, though.

Your friend from the past,

Nora Tucker

Monday, June 10—
Recorded on Lizzie's
WhisperFlash Z190 at
lunch

In the Lunch Line:

WALKER: Hey, new girl! Talk to us . . . Come on . . . Your brother know those guys who escaped?

ELIDEE: No.

WALKER: What's he say about being in there?

COLE: I bet he's seen some wild stuff go down.

ELIDEE: Excuse me . . . I need to get my lunch.

COLE: Too good to talk to us? I don't think so.

MRS. KAPPELLI: Is there a problem, boys?

WALKER: Nope. Just wanted to introduce ourselves to the new girl.

MRS. KAPPELLI: That's nice that you're making her feel welcome. But you'd better sit down and start eating. You only have twenty minutes.

At Our Table:

ELIDEE: Is it okay if I sit here?

NORA: Sure.

(Then it was quiet for a long time because Elidee sat down and ate her sandwich and Nora and I didn't really know what to say because we had been talking about the prison break. But that would have been weird because of Elidee's brother, so we all just sat and chewed for a while.)

NORA: How'd you like Mrs. James's math class?

ELIDEE: It was okay.

NORA: Is Wolf Creek different from your old school?

ELIDEE: Yeah. A lot.

NORA: What was your old neighborhood like? It was in the Bronx, right?

ELIDEE: Yeah. Highbridge.

NORA: So did you move here for any particular reason?

LIZZIE: Geez, Nora! Let her eat her lunch.

NORA: I was just asking. Sorry. Go ahead and eat.

LIZZIE: Have you heard what we're doing in gym today?

NORA: Practicing for field day, but we can't go outside. It's so dumb.

ELIDEE: I don't see why we can't be out on the track.

LIZZIE: I know, right? What's the likelihood of the inmates showing up to crash gym class? What if they don't catch them by field day?

NORA: They won't cancel that. There's no way.

ELIDEE: What's so special about field day?

NORA: Everything. We should throw out our trash because the bell's going to ring.

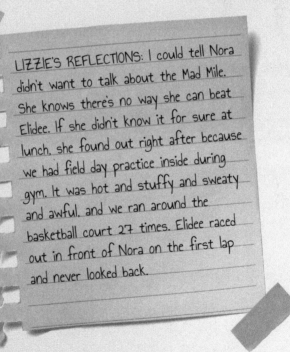

LIZZIE'S REFLECTIONS: I could tell Nora didn't want to talk about the Mad Mile. She knows there's no way she can beat Elidee. If she didn't know it for sure at lunch, she found out right after because we had field day practice inside during gym. It was hot and stuffy and sweaty and awful, and we ran around the basketball court 27 times. Elidee raced out in front of Nora on the first lap and never looked back.

Monday, June 10—
Text messages between
Elidee & her mom

MAMA: You home yet?

ELIDEE: Just got off the bus

MAMA: What are you doing?

ELIDEE: Writing some stuff

MAMA: There's fruit cut up in the fridge if you're hungry

How was school?

ELIDEE: Ok

A couple of the boys were bugging me about Troy

MAMA: How do they even know?

ELIDEE: Idk

Seems like everybody knows everything about everybody here

MAMA: You want me to talk with somebody in the office?

* 122 *

ELIDEE: Nah it wasn't a big deal

Just annoying

MAMA: You keep your head high

ELIDEE: I know. I am

MAMA: Got homework?

ELIDEE: That extra credit thing again

MAMA: Get it done and I'll see you for dinner

ELIDEE: Ok

MAMA: Love you to the moon & back

ELIDEE: I love you to Epsilon Eridani b and back

That's a planet outside our solar system

MAMA: I love you to Epsilon Eridani c and back

That's a planet just beyond Epsilon Eridani b

ELIDEE: Seriously??

MAMA: You left your library book in the living room so I was reading it after you went to bed

ELIDEE: This was easier when I could get away with loving you to Pluto every time

MAMA: xo

NORA

Nosy
Opinionated
Really super fast (not)
Attitude

WOLF CREEK

Welcome to Wolf Creek, where we
Open our hearts and
Love our neighb-
Find the inmates!

Call the police if you see anything!
Report anybody different!
Everyone lock your doors!
Eventually we'll catch them or
Kill them.

NIKKI

Nikki Giovanni and Nikki Grimes—
Imaginative. Inspiring.
Kissing the page with poems.
Kinda makes me want to write my own.
I want my words to shine, too.

Dear future Wolf Creek residents,

This is the last of those five letters I have to write to you for
extra credit.

I bet you're tired of hearing about the prison break. I know I
am. You'd think everybody in the whole prison got out, the way
people here are reacting. I know those guys are dangerous, but
there are only two of them. How is it that five hundred cops can't
find them?

My impressions of Wolf Creek haven't changed much. Your
mountains are still pretty. I like your library, even though it's
small. I found some good books, including one about distant
planets and stuff for this game I play with Mama. (Long story
that I don't have time to explain here.) I also got *Brown Girl
Dreaming*, which Ms. Sanchez, my librarian at home, said was
good, and two other poetry books—one by Nikki Giovanni and
one by Nikki Grimes. (I should probably change my name to
Nikki if I decide I want to be a poet.) I also got a book about
Alexander Hamilton and a book with all the lyrics to the musical.
I had to request that one through interlibrary loan, but it got

here really quick. So that's one good thing about Wolf Creek. Your library is quick.

People here don't run all that fast, though. Everybody's whispering about my six-minute mile, which is no big deal back home. They whisper about a lot of other things, too. Other than that, school is mostly okay. I wish people would mind their own business, though.

It's kind of lonely here, too. There are plenty of people, but it still feels that way. If you've never been the only brown face in a classroom, you wouldn't understand.

That's fine. This is the last time you'll hear from me anyway. The English teacher said we could write extra letters if we wanted to share more. But I didn't especially want to share even this much with you, so I'm going to write some poems for myself now. Have a good life.

Sincerely,
Elidee Jones

LEARNING FROM
NIKKI (Giovanni)
(Inspired by "Knoxville,
Tennessee" and also
some haikus I read)

Haikus for a Wolf Creek Summer Day

Pretty mountain town
Buzzes with birdsong, crickets,
And whispered rumors.

Running tight circles
Under the basketball net
Round and round the gym.

Prison on Main Street
Towers like castle turrets
Here the guards are kings.

Haikus for a Bronx Summer Day

Honking city streets
Cousins run through sprinkler spray
Puddle-splashing day.

Corner bodega
Gray cat in a patch of sun.
Door jingles open

A hot grill sizzles
Peppers, onions, ground beef, grease—
One chopped cheese to go.

Sidewalk lemonade
Ice cubes and puckered-up laughs
Sour-sweet taste of home.

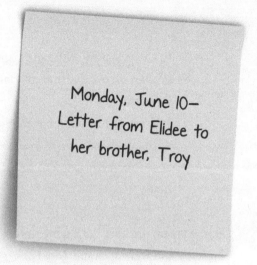

Monday, June 10—
Letter from Elidee to
her brother, Troy

Dear Troy,

I had some of your Starbursts while I was reading my new library book tonight. We'll get you new ones whenever we can come again, but there are no visiting hours or packages allowed until this manhunt ends, so these would probably be stale by then anyway. Just like the news in this letter I probably won't even send because it won't get to you anytime soon. But I'd rather talk to you than to the future residents of Wolf Creek. I had to write five entries for that time-capsule thing they're doing. And hey—I just remembered you were supposed to do that, too, but now you can't because they're not even letting the teachers in for their classes. That's what Ms. Morin said. So she won't get to do that writing with you guys. So much for their time capsule including everyone who calls Wolf Creek home.

Unless you get transferred again, you'll be here thirteen more years, but I bet you'll never call this place home. I know I don't.

There's nothin' like summer in the mountains
Someone coasting on a bike or splashin' in a fountain
Till a newcomer shows up and tensions start mountin'

With these skinny white girls and their skinny white thighs
Best I can surmise is that my dark brown skin took 'em all
    by surprise
They stare at me just for walking down their street. Talking
    with heat
That ain't some hoedown, run-down, small-town country
    beat.

Go easy on me here . . . It's my first try. I've been reading some poetry and writing some, too. I also got the lyrics from that *Hamilton* musical and decided to try some verses of my own. I figured maybe you miss rapping with J. P. and those guys, so I thought I'd write you a few lines.

A few lines, a few rhymes (because I know you got the time)
I know it's not the best—you might even say it's a hot mess
But I sought the rhyme, and I brought the rhyme
Except it's harder than I thought this time
So now I better wrap up this rap extravaganza
'Cause what rhymes with that? Amanda the panda?
I was trying to write mad responsibly, keepin' it loose
But I'm more like some sad wannabe Dr. Seuss than Lin-
    Manuel Miranda.

Ha! Man, it's good you'll never get this letter or you'd be laughing at me for the rest of our lives for that one. You'd think that growing up in the birthplace of hip-hop would help my rhymes, but I guess not. I'll have to keep practicing.

    One of the other books I'm reading right now is a memoir—a

true story about this writer Jacqueline Woodson's life. It's a lot like mine in some ways, even though she's older. She had to move around a bunch, and her uncle got sent to a prison that sounds like yours. She wrote her memoir all in poems, and you know what? It looks like she learned poetry by trying out other people's styles, like I've been doing. Jacqueline Woodson wrote like Langston Hughes in her book. He had a poem about how he loved his friend, so she wrote one about loving her friend, too, and called that page "Learning from Langston." Earlier today, I was reading this poem about summer by Nikki Giovanni, so I tried some of my own summer poetry in the notebook my English teacher gave me. I think I'll go back and change my title for the page to "Learning from Nikki." I'm going to try some other poems, too, but don't worry, I won't start sending you all of them—only the cool ones.

I miss you.

Love,
Elidee

PS Mrs. G. just knocked on the door all of a sudden and scared me half to death. She only came to drop off cookies and went back upstairs, and now I feel dumb for getting rattled. But the littlest sounds make me jumpy now. Maybe I just feel that way because those inmates are still out there somewhere, but I'm not sure. At home, there were always people around making noise. In Wolf Creek, it's so quiet you hear every little sound. Every person walking by on the sidewalk. Every faraway shout. Every creak. And every sound that you can't quite place. Then it gets quiet again, so you have lots of time to wonder what it was.

LEARNING FROM GWENDOLYN

We Real Cool
by Gwendolyn Brooks

THE POOL PLAYERS.
SEVEN AT THE
GOLDEN SHOVEL.

We real cool. We
Left school. We

Lurk late. We
Strike straight. We

Sing sin. We
Thin gin. We

Jazz June. We
Die soon.

We Break Rules
by Elidee Jones

THE INMATES.
TWO OUT IN THE
WOODS SOMEWHERE.

We break rules. We
Sneak tools. We

Bust bars. We
See stars. We

Hide well. We
Won't tell. We

Run fast. We
Won't last.

We Real Brash
by Elidee Jones

THE STUDENTS.
400 AT WOLF CREEK
MIDDLE SCHOOL.

We real brash. We
Talk trash. We

Run slow. We
Low blow. We

Stand guard. We
Stare hard. We

Tight crew. We
Hate you.

We Wear the Mask
by Paul Laurence Dunbar

We wear the mask that grins and lies,
It hides our cheeks and shades our eyes,—
This debt we pay to human guile;
With torn and bleeding hearts we smile,
And mouth with myriad subtleties.

Why should the world be over-wise,
In counting all our tears and sighs?
Nay, let them only see us, while
　　We wear the mask.

　　We smile, but, O great Christ, our cries
　　To thee from tortured souls arise.
　　We sing, but oh the clay is vile
　　Beneath our feet, and long the mile;
　　But let the world dream otherwise,
　　We wear the mask!

I Wear the Mask
by Elidee Jones

I wear the mask with downturned eyes,
Quiet words and nods and sighs.
I run the fastest gym-class mile
But never gloat—I only smile.
A humble grin is my disguise.

When you're new, it's never wise
To let them hear your angry cries.
They wonder what's inside me while
    I wear the mask.

    So in this place that I despise
    I wear my perfect-girl disguise.
    Another day, another trial
    And no real way to reconcile
    The me that's real with all these lies,
    So I wear the mask.

Golden Shovel poem: Take a "striking line" from a poem you love and make a new poem out of that by writing the words of the line down the right side of your paper & using them as the last words in each line of your new poem.

Home
by Elidee Jones

LEARNING FROM NIKKI (Grimes)

(Inspired by "Emergency Measures"
in **One Last Word** by Nikki Grimes)

Striking line: "How can I stay strong in a world where fear and hate wait outside my door?"

We've unpacked the boxes but I still don't know **how**
This place is ever gonna feel like home. How **can**
It when there's no stairway up to the sixth floor? No one **I**
Love living upstairs. No Grandmama or Aunt Maya to **stay**
With after school, no crowded homework table, no **strong**
Cousins tossing me into the park swimming pool, no chickens **in**
The community garden, pecking at bugs and scratching at weeds. It's **a**
Different New York up here. Another planet. A **world**
Where all the men in town wear uniforms in gray or blue, **where**
The twilight air buzzes with mosquitoes and **fear,**
Where everybody knows everybody except for me **and**
Whispers poke my sides every time I walk the halls. I **hate**
The feel of so many eyes on the back of my head. Can't **wait**
For school to end every day. But then what? Can't go **outside**
Until Mama gets home. Home? No. Not yet. Maybe not ever. **My**
definition of home involves more than four walls and a locked front **door.**

Another Story
by Elidee Jones

(Inspired by "Through the Eyes of Artists" in *One Last Word* by Nikki Grimes. Her poem was already a Golden Shovel poem, based on a line from "To a Dark Girl" by Gwendolyn Bennett. So I guess mine is a Double Golden Shovel poem.)

Striking line: "Your life's story is a tale worth telling."

Mama used to tell Troy and me, "Follow **your** Dreams and you can be anything. Anything at all." But **life's** Not fair sometimes. Sometimes your **story** Changes. Your plot twists and whirls and the wind **is** Blowing you in five different directions. That dream gets lost and it's **a** Wonder you're even still here to tell the **tale**. But you are. So you find a new dream **worth** Following. Another hope. Another story worth **telling**.

August 24, 2004
by Elidee Jones

LEARNING FROM JACQUELINE

(Inspired by "February 12, 1963" in *Brown Girl Dreaming*
by Jacqueline Woodson)

I am born on a Tuesday at Bronx-Lebanon Hospital
New York,
USA—

While the rest of the country was still gushing over
Michael Phelps and all his gold medals,
Mama was in labor,
Watching the TV over her round belly and
Cheering on the Kenyans in the steeplechase
(They swept all three medals, oh yeah).
Then I showed up
And there was even more to celebrate.
Six pounds, fifteen ounces,

Daughter of Latanya and Joe,
They're leaning into one another in a blurry photo
With me all wrinkle-faced and hungry in the middle,
Troy squeezed into the corner by the nightstand,
Daddy's arm around him.
One
Happy
Family.

Daddy's cancer is there, too—
Growing quietly in his belly.
Couldn't see it in the picture
But it was already bigger than all of us.
Took him eleven months later,
Right after I learned to walk.

I was too little to understand,
Too new to have a hole left in my heart.
I didn't remember the hospice bed in our apartment
Or the weeks of saying good-bye,
But Troy did.
Mama always says that messed him up.
When you've lived seven years with a
Big strong hand on your shoulder,
You sure must miss it when it's gone.

Monday, June 10—
Letter from
Nora Tucker

Dear future Wolf Creek residents,

Today, everybody was talking about what they'd do if they were the inmates—where they'd hide or not hide, how they'd survive in the woods. Walker said if he were the inmates, he'd hide someplace the police already searched, and then Cole asked how he'd know that, and Walker said he'd watch the news, and Josh said, "Dude, you think they have TV in whatever cave they're hiding in?" Then Walker told Josh to shut up because he's an idiot.

I think Walker had a pretty good idea. If I were the inmates, I'd try to steal a smartphone so I could follow the news. I'd google where they think I am and then hide someplace else.

But I'm not the inmates, so I'm going outside while I can, to jump on my trampoline.

Your friend from the past,
Nora Tucker

NORA: U there?

LIZZIE: Yeah

NORA: Omg I just got sent inside because someone saw one of the bad guys on our block!

LIZZIE: No way!

NORA: The police r searching now

LIZZIE: Whoa!

NORA: I was practicing handsprings and Mom was on the porch and then a state police car came screeching up the street and stopped and the guy jumped out and shouted get her inside!!

LIZZIE: Are they searching the woods behind your house or what?

NORA: Hold on I'll look

2 cops are pointing guns up toward Owen's fort

LIZZIE: !!!!!

NORA: One's climbing up a little

LIZZIE: Omg what if they're up there?

NORA: I'm freaking out

LIZZIE: Me too and I'm not even there

NORA: Hold on

Ok he must not have seen anything because he came down

LIZZIE: Good

NORA: 4 more police cars just pulled up

LIZZIE: Whoa

NORA: The police just got out and are all running toward the woods

LIZZIE: How many?

NORA: Like ten I think

Too fast to count

They're in the trees behind the fort now

LIZZIE: Can you imagine if the inmates are in there?!

NORA: No

Actually yes

I kind of imagine them everywhere

LIZZIE: Can u see anything now?

NORA: No

My heart is still beating so fast

LIZZIE: Me too

Anything yet?

NORA: No but those woods don't go back very far so

Wait

2 guys just came back out

They're all out now

They're leaving

LIZZIE: Wow

Another false alarm you think?

NORA: I guess

I wish they'd find them

LIZZIE: Me too

NORA: Hey how's your grandma? She's home right?

LIZZIE: Yeah she's better but I haven't seen her much because she's been in her room all afternoon

NORA: I don't blame her

LIZZIE: Gotta go

Mom's making me go with her and grandma to the store

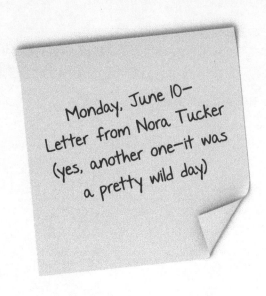

Monday, June 10—
Letter from Nora Tucker
(yes, another one—it was
a pretty wild day)

Dear future Wolf Creek residents,

Earlier today, I got kicked off my trampoline and locked in the house because somebody thought they saw an inmate running from a garage, so the police had to search all over. They didn't find anything.

I wonder where the inmates are.

I'll be looking out the window on the way to school, staring into the woods and thinking maybe they're in there. In those trees. In that barn. Behind that trash bin. Maybe they're down by the riverbank or hiding in that old shed.

Owen's worried the inmates will show up at his school. Mom keeps telling him that's not likely because one sure way to get caught if you're an escapee is to show up somewhere with lots of people. She told Owen the inmates are probably hiding far away by now.

Those Alcatraz inmates who got away made inflatable rafts out of raincoats once they got to the bay. What if our guys made rafts, too, or stole a boat and escaped down the river?

Lots of people think the Alcatraz guys drowned. The FBI found a homemade paddle and some of their stuff but no bodies, so nobody knows for sure. Probably they drowned. But it's not a hundred percent.

It's hard to break out of prison and not get caught. Our guys will probably get caught soon.

Your friend from the past,

Nora Tucker

BAD THINGS THAT THE INMATES COULD DO (WITH SOLUTIONS BY GOOD GUYS)

BAD GUYS: HIDE IN TREE FORT TO AMBUSH TUCKER FAMILY

GOOD GUYS: SURROUND TREE FORT WITH SUPER SOAKERS & SPRAY THE BAD GUYS DOWN

BAD GUYS: CRASH WOLF CREEK
YOUTH SOCCER GAME

GOOD GUYS: LET BAD GUYS PLAY UNTIL
THEY ARE NEAR GOAL. THEN TIP OVER GOAL
AND TRAP THEM UNTIL POLICE ARRIVE.

BAD GUYS: TAKE SCHOOL BUS HOSTAGE*

GOOD GUYS: THROW TUNA SANDWICHES
UNTIL INMATES ARE BURIED. THEN ESCAPE
FROM BUS & LOCK THEM IN.

*Noah says this could really happen. Mom says Noah is a dimwit
sometimes. She also says I have to stop drawing the inmates
before bed and think about something fun like birthday plans.

BIRTHDAY PARTY PLANS

hot dogs
buns
ketchup
marshmallows
graham crackers
chocolate
cheese puffs
cookies
Mountain Dew
NO SALAD

AWESOME BONFIRE

THINGS TO DO
Tell scary stories
Joke contest
Eat cookies
Play Monopoly
keep an eye out
for inmates, just
in case

AWESOME TREE FORT SLEEPOVER

LEARNING FROM JACQUELINE #2

Highbridge Lullaby
by Elidee Jones

(Inspired by "Lullaby" from *Brown Girl Dreaming*
by Jacqueline Woodson)

The 4 train rumbles me to sleep at night.
Sometimes when the Yankees hit home runs
The stadium crowd joins the chorus, a happy roar
That soars out of the park, over the streets,
Right up to Mrs. Diaz on her fire escape.
I can hear her laughing into the phone.
She calls her mother every night at ten
While her son Robert plucks guitar inside by the
     window and
Below skateboarders roll over every seam in the
     sidewalk
Ka-thunk, ka-thunk, ka-thunk,
And bass-heavy songs pour out car windows

Booming their way up six stories, into mine.
J. P.'s basketball thumps on the floor above me
Until Mama knocks the ceiling with a broom handle,
And his mama makes him stop.
I can tell time by the night songs.
Eleven o'clock comes with the click of a lock and
The bodega's metal door rolling down.
Mr. Bello rings in midnight.
When his shift at the fire station ends,
I count his slow boot steps up up up the stairs
Until his apartment door squeaks open and closed.
A city serenade—horn, siren, horn, brakes
Shouting in the street and underneath it all
The hum of air conditioners
Water leaking from the one above onto ours.
Drip . . .
Drip . . .
Drip . . . .
Splat.

Wolf Creek Lullaby

Crickets chirp.
Owl hoots from a tree.
Who-who-who-whoo-oooo!
(Seriously, that's the sound,
Like he's trying out to be the owl in a book for
    little kids.)
Then quiet.
Crickets.
Little bit of a breeze.
Somebody's lonely dog barks twice.
One car. Far away.
Maybe it wasn't even a car.
Crickets . . .
Crickets . . .
Crickets . . .

In New York City, they sell night-sound machines
to drown out city noise
with gentle waves and rain.
Maybe here, they sell a different one—
City traffic, neighbors laughing,
stadium crowds heading home.
If they did, I'd buy one
To drown out all this quiet.

◎ WCRK-TV

Good morning, North Country. It's day four in the search for two killers who escaped from Wolf Creek Correctional Facility. Police believe they may be closing in on the inmates, and that's prompting new safety concerns. Local schools are asking students to wait inside until buses arrive this morning. This may cause delays, but officials say keeping kids safe is their top priority.

Local corrections officials are speaking out against a piece in this morning's *New York Times*. The report claims at least two inmates have suffered beatings at the hands of guards since this weekend's escape. An inmate told the *Times* he saw another prisoner being dragged down a hallway after refusing to answer officers' questions about the escape. Corrections officials deny that report.

Bill Tucker, prison superintendent: "Obviously, we've asked inmates to share any information they have, but guards are gathering information in their usual professional way. Frankly, it's irresponsible of the *Times* to report such a rumor when our officers are putting their lives on the line to ensure public safety."

Meanwhile, searchers are preparing for wet weather. The

forecast calls for pounding rain right into this evening. That could be a problem for police dogs brought in to track the inmates. Handlers say light rain is actually helpful because moisture can enhance a scent. However, today's downpour is likely to wash everything away, and the wind can scatter scents as well.

Sergeant Jennifer Oates, New York State Police K-9 Unit: "We'll probably give the dogs a break today. But this rain is going to stop late tonight, and then cool, wet conditions will make tomorrow much better for searching. With eight hundred officers in the woods now, the inmates don't have the luxury of staying in one place. They may find shelter for a few hours or a night, but they have to stay on the move, and as soon as they're running, they're vulnerable again. We're going to find them."

Rain or shine, community members are rallying around law enforcement. Blue ribbons are popping up all over town as a show of support. Tomorrow evening, the Wolf Creek Community Church will host a ham supper for searchers. Church leaders say they have enough food donations, but volunteers are still needed to serve and clear dishes. The supper gets under way at 5 p.m.

Tuesday, June 11—
Recorded on Lizzie's
WhisperFlash Z190 on the
way to school (Our bus was
stopped at a roadblock, and a
soaking-wet trooper got on, so this
was not an ordinary slice-of-life
sort of morning.)

TROOPER: Good morning.

EVERYBODY ELSE: . . .

NOTE FROM LIZZIE: We probably
should have said good morning or
hi or something, but we were too
busy staring at the trooper's gun.
It wasn't the usual kind that police
have on their belts. It was a great
big rifle thing over his shoulder.

TROOPER: Anybody see anything unusual last night? Any
strangers in the woods?

EVERYBODY ELSE: . . .

TROOPER: No? Okay. Please remind your folks to keep doors
and windows locked. And call if anyone in your
family notices anything unusual. We'll be patrolling
again tonight to keep everybody safe.

SOMEBODY IN THE BACK OF THE BUS: Thank you!

TROOPER: You're welcome. I really appreciate that.

Good morning, Wolf Pack! Please stand for the pledge to the flag.

(Pledge)

Gym classes will be held inside again today.

Mr. Russell would like to remind everyone to return those library books. Having materials out this late makes it difficult to finish end-of-the-year work.

Congratulations to students who advanced to round two in the chess club's June tournament. Match play continues after school in Room F-4.

We have a special announcement now from student council vice president Lucy Arnot . . .

Hi, everybody! I'm Lucy, and most of you know that my dad is a corrections officer. The COs and state police have been putting in really long hours searching for the inmates and keeping everybody safe, so the student council thought it would be nice if our school did something to show support. We'll be passing out blue ribbons all day. You can tie one around your wrist or in your hair as a way to say thank you. We're also making signs in English classes, except for Mrs. Light's eighth-grade honors class because she says they're behind in reading *Fahrenheit 451*, and she's going to finish before school ends if it's the last thing she does. Thanks for your support of our brave officers.

Thank you, Lucy. A few more announcements . . .

Wolf Creek Middle School's field day and Mad Mile race are still tentatively planned for this Friday, provided things are safe. If you signed up to bring plates or napkins and haven't already dropped them off, please do so before the big day.

We're wishing a happy birthday this morning to Isabella Watts and to State Police Trooper Lara Elliott. She's the officer who's been greeting you at the seventh-grade entrance this week.

Our quote of the day is from one of America's Founding Fathers, Alexander Hamilton. He said, "Those who stand for nothing fall for anything."

That concludes our morning announcements.

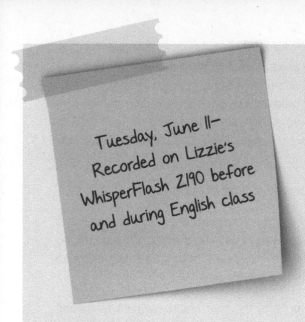

Tuesday, June 11—
Recorded on Lizzie's
WhisperFlash Z190 before
and during English class

BEFORE CLASS:

LUCY: Did everybody get a blue ribbon in homeroom?

NORA: I didn't. They ran out.

LUCY: Here. My mom gave me fifty-five yards but we could use even more, and my mom's super busy getting ready for the ham supper, so could you maybe pick some up for us before tomorrow?

NORA: Uh, maybe. I'll try. I think my mom's going shopping tonight.

LUCY: Great! Hey, what's that new girl's name?

NORA: Elidee?

LUCY: Elidee! Do you want a blue ribbon?

ELIDEE: No, thanks.

LUCY: Why not?

ELIDEE: I just don't want one.

LUCY: You should take one. They're to say thank you to all the officers. Here . . .

ELIDEE: Thanks.

BELL RINGS TO START CLASS:

MS. MORIN: You probably heard we're doing something different in class today. The student council made these big signs for law enforcement. Each one says Thanks for Keeping Us Safe. You can color in the letters and add your own little notes if you'd like, too. We'll all sign ours and put it up in the seventh-grade hallway, okay?

LUCY: Can I tell them about the bags?

MS. MORIN: Sure.

LUCY: We also need to decorate these brown paper bags I brought in because my mom and some of the other moms arranged for Joe's Mountain Market to donate subs for dinner for the officers working roadblocks. And the moms thought it would be nice if the bags had personalized artwork from students, so you should decorate one whenever you finish with the sign.

MS. MORIN: All right then, we've got a sign to decorate and bags to personalize. Your choice of activities today. Whenever you finish what you'd like to do, you can work on letters for the time capsule or read your books.

Dear future Wolf Creek residents,

I'm in English class and we're finishing our thank-you sign for the police, but I already colored in my letter (I got the H) and decorated a brown bag for some officer's sub. Lucy brought in a huge stack of those bags, and if they all get used, that is going to be a TON of subs. Sean's going to be at work until midnight shredding lettuce and slicing tomatoes.

Everybody helped with the sign except Elidee. She didn't want a ribbon either, but she took one because Lucy was bugging her. She didn't put it on, though. I wonder why. Maybe because of her brother being in prison? But he's not one of the guys who broke out or anything, so wouldn't she still want to support the police who are searching? The troopers guarding our school are keeping Elidee just as safe as everybody else, so I think it's crummy not to say thank you. Elidee just sat and read her book most of the period. She doesn't seem all that nice.

(Just so you know, I'm not a gossipy person. I'm only saying this because by the time you read it, we'll be grown up and probably living somewhere else, anyway, so it's not really like I'm talking behind Elidee's back.)

★ ★ ★

I'm writing in study hall now. At the end of English class, one of the state troopers walked in to make sure our classroom windows were locked (they were). While she was talking to Ms. Morin, Walker and Cole went up to Elidee's desk and asked why she wasn't helping with the sign. She ignored them, but they didn't go away. Lizzie was in the bathroom when this happened, so we didn't record it, but Walker said something like "Seriously? You're not even gonna say thank you?" Cole said his dad and the other officers in his unit were out all night so the least Elidee could do is color in a dumb letter on a sign.

To be honest, I was thinking the same thing, but then Walker and Cole started being really mean and talking about Elidee's brother. Cole said Elidee was probably just like him and she ought to go back to Brooklyn or wherever she came from. And that seemed unfair because it's not Elidee's fault her brother did whatever he did to get in prison.

Anyway, that's when the trooper came over and asked if there was a problem. Cole said yeah and asked the trooper if *she* thought everybody should support the police and help with the sign. He looked all kinds of smug, but then the trooper totally burned him and said no, what *she* thought was that everybody had a right to make their own decisions, and if *somebody* can't respect a person's right to do that, then *he's* the one who's out of line.

That made Cole and Walker shut up. It also made me think maybe I was being kind of mean, too. Just not out loud. I guess I was being a quieter jerk.

Elidee didn't say anything about any of that. But after the trooper left, she went and got a bag and decorated it with these cool trees that looked magical and real at the same time. When she finished, she took it up front and said something to Ms. Morin, who said, "I'll make sure." I took a quick picture of the bag with my phone on the way out.

Your friend from the past,

Nora Tucker

Tuesday, June 11—
This is a picture of
the sub bag Elidee
decorated.

Tuesday, June 11—
Recorded on Lizzie's
WhisperFlash Z190
during gym class

MRS. ROY: Okay, everybody! We're practicing for Mad Mile again. That's twenty-seven laps around the gym!

NOTE FROM LIZZIE: I didn't record while we were running because it would have been all huffing and puffing, aside from Mrs. Roy shouting "Come on! Push it, ladies!" every few seconds. All you need to know about our run is that the gym was stuffy and horrible, I almost barfed up my tuna sandwich, and Elidee beat Nora by five whole laps. Then I started recording again.

ELIDEE: Nice run.

NORA: Thanks. You, too.

WALKER: Nice run? You got burned, Tucker!

COLE: She wasted you! Ha!

NORA: What are you laughing at? She beat you, too.

WALKER: Yeah, but black people are always fast.

COLE: So they can outrun the cops.

NOTE FROM LIZZIE: Elidee said something really quiet here. I'm pretty sure I heard what it was, but I think kids are going to be reading this time-capsule thing, and it isn't appropriate for them, so I'm going to leave it at that.

NORA: You guys, stop. That's awful.

WALKER: Oohhhh . . . watch out, Cole. You made her mad.

NORA: Don't be a jerk. Just because she's better than you.

WALKER: Hey, don't look at me. They're fast. I just stated a fact.

NORA: You can't just say that . . . that all black people are a certain way.

WALKER: Come on, Nora. You know we're just messing around. It's not like we're racist. Paul Washington's one of our best friends.

COLE: And he's fast, too!

NORA: That's still—

NOTE FROM LIZZIE: That was Mrs. Roy blowing her whistle because the last two people finally finished, and we all went to the locker rooms to get changed. I kept recording because Nora and Elidee were talking even though Cole and Walker were gone.

NORA: Those guys are jerks.

ELIDEE: Yeah.

NORA: I tried to get them to shut up.

ELIDEE: I can take care of myself.

NORA: I was trying to help.

ELIDEE: I don't need help.

NORA: Look . . . I'm sure it's hard to be new, but if you were a little nicer to people, they'd probably be nicer to you, too.

ELIDEE: Nicer?

NORA: Like with Lucy's ribbons and the sign. I mean . . . nobody can force you to wear a ribbon, but the student council worked hard on that project. Almost everybody's dad here is a cop or a CO, and it's a really stressful time. But people in Wolf Creek are friendly if you give them a chance.

ELIDEE: People like your two buddies out there? Really? If that's your idea of friendly, girl, then—

MRS. ROY: Ladies, is there a problem?

ELIDEE: No, ma'am.

NORA: We were just talking.

MRS. ROY: Elidee, I don't know what your old school was like, but at Wolf Creek Middle School, we use language respectfully and responsibly. I do not want to hear you using that tone with your classmates again.

ELIDEE: Yes, ma'am.

MRS. ROY: If I need to arrange a conference with your mother to talk about that, I'd be happy to do so.

ELIDEE: You don't need to do that. I'm sorry I raised my voice.

NORA: Mrs. Roy, that wasn't actually Elidee's fault. I said something that—

MRS. ROY: That's kind of you to say, Nora. But we just don't put up with that kind of attitude here.

Tuesday, June 11—
I saw this note on the
counter in the office
& took a picture with
my phone.

Dear Mr. Simmons,

The quote you shared in the
announcements wasn't from Founding
Father Alexander Hamilton, like you
said. I've been reading about Hamilton,
and he never said that. Your quote came
from some British radio guy named Alex
Hamilton two hundred years later.
Other people might have said it before
that (nobody's really sure about this
quote) but the British Alex Hamilton
guy is the reason the quote gets
misattributed to Alexander Hamilton,
the Founding Father. If you want
students here to be responsible with
language, you should probably be more
careful about it yourself.

Sincerely,
A concerned morning announcement
listener

Tuesday, June 11—
Pages from Elidee's
notebook

wolf creek
by Elidee Jones

(Inspired by "new york city" in *Brown Girl
Dreaming* by Jacqueline Woodson)

Maybe it's another Wolf Creek
Mrs. G. was talking about. Maybe that's where
The summer breeze blows soft and cool and sweet,
Where the mountains really are purple
Just like in the song.
Where you can knock on any door—
Any one at all—
If you need to borrow an egg and
People are so friendly you don't miss home
Even a little.

Here the prison wall feels taller than New York
    skyscrapers,
Casting dirty shadows on a shabby Main Street
And one sad little Chinese restaurant
With a white guy behind the counter.

Ever since those inmates busted out,
This place is all locked doors and side-eye,
All pull-over-to-the-side, let-me-check-your-trunk, and
watch-that-tone-we-don't-need-your-attitude-here.
I haven't tried to borrow any eggs
But I doubt that would go very well either.

Dear future Wolf Creek residents,

I'm on the bus and I have a stomachache because I started a fight with Cole and Walker today. It was dumb because it was about Elidee, and she's not even my friend or anything.

Actually, I'm not sure I want this in the time capsule. I've gotten used to writing to you, though, so I'm going to write and decide later if I want you to read it. That way, I can write without worrying about what you'll think of me.

Anyway, Cole and Walker said something about black people. I'm not going to repeat it because it was racist, even though people here aren't usually like that. It was dumb, and I should have ignored them, but instead, I kept thinking about Mr. Langdon's "leadership moments" lecture in social studies. He said when discrimination was happening a long time ago, most white people just kept their mouths shut. A few engaged in civil disobedience— when you break the law to stand up for what you believe in. But tons of other people knew discrimination was wrong and went along with it because they didn't want to make trouble.

I didn't want to be like that. So I said something. Walker and Cole got mad at me, which stinks because I have to see them every day, and my dad works with their dads.

And Elidee didn't even say thank you. I was obviously trying to be nice, but she got all snippy and told me she could take care of herself. Then I got mad at Elidee because if she hadn't come here and refused to help color the stupid sign, none of this would have happened in the first place. So I told her that. Not that exactly, but pretty much.

Then Mrs. Roy heard us arguing, and she yelled at Elidee but not me, which totally caught me off guard. Mrs. Roy was practically Elidee's best friend last week after Elidee ran that six-minute mile, so I don't know what changed, but she sure didn't like her much today.

Actually, I do know what changed. Those inmates broke out, and it feels like everybody's acting different now. Is this what a circle of support looks like? Elidee hasn't lived here forever like everybody else, so I guess she's outside the circle.

Anyway, after Mrs. Roy yelled at her, Elidee took a deep breath. She held it so long I thought she might explode. Then she apologized, all calm and quiet. Like she'd practiced it a thousand times. She didn't say it wasn't fair, even though we both knew it wasn't. I started to say something, but Mrs. Roy cut me off, and then I just shut up.

Now I feel all prickly. Like maybe I shouldn't have said anything to anybody. Actually, no. It's that I didn't say enough. I don't know. I wish they'd catch those inmates so everybody wouldn't be so touchy.

Your friend from the past,

Nora Tucker

Tuesday, June 11—
Letter from Elidee to
her brother, Troy

Dear Troy,

I messed up today. Not like you. It wasn't like that. But I'm mad at myself for not keeping quiet.

I was so stupid. Two white boys in my class were talking trash, and I was doing all right. I was staying calm just like Mama always taught you to do if the police stop you, like she taught us to do when teachers try to push our buttons.

And I was doing fine. I was pretending those boys weren't even there until this Nora girl butted in and told me if I'd be nicer and color their dumb sign and tie a blue ribbon on my wrist, I'd have fewer problems. And I was like, "Seriously???" Barely had ten words out of my mouth before the gym teacher told me to watch my tone or she'd haul Mama in. Like Mama needs that.

The sign I didn't help with was a thing they made in English class, saying thanks to the police working on the inmate search. I didn't sign it because I don't know the police here. But if they're anything like that cop who beat on Rachel's brother James last fall, I'm not interested in sending any kind of thank-you note. Helping with the sign wasn't supposed to be mandatory anyway. Ms. Morin said we could read if we wanted, and that's what I was doing when people started getting all up in my business. And then it happened again in gym.

You probably would have punched those boys. Punched all of them.

But I don't get to do that. I'm Mama's saving grace and her hope for the future and blah blah blah. You know what it's like hearing her prayers come into my room every night? They land on top of my blankets like bricks until I can barely breathe.

"Thank you, Lord, for my perfect child, and continue to show her the way . . ."

She prays for you, too. That you'll be safe and all. But she prays for me to stay perfect. That's my job. Ever since you broke her heart, I have to keep holding all the pieces together for her. And I've been doing that, you know? I smiled and nodded when she told me we were moving up here to the middle of nowhere.

I'll be fine starting a new school two weeks before summer, Mama. Of course. I'm your girl. We'll make it work.

But I forgot to make it work today. I forgot and let my voice get a little too loud. Sometimes I think you have it easier in there. Nobody expects you to be good.

You know that those guys who escaped are still out, right? I heard Mrs. G. talking to Mama last night. She said the cops are trying to find out from other inmates what happened. Mrs. G. heard two officers beat up one guy because they thought he knew something and wasn't talking. Have they been asking you about all that stuff? I hope not. I hope you're all right. I hope you don't know anything, and I hope the guards believe you when you say so.

Someday when you can get mail again, I'll write you a real

letter. One you can actually read, instead of just talking to myself. I'd never be able to send you this letter, even though it's all true. You've got enough to worry about.

Love,
Elidee

Tuesday, June 11—
Recorded on Lizzie's
WhisperFlash Z190 on
our way shopping

MRS. TUCKER: I hope the store's open past five.

OWEN: I need that poster board tonight.

MRS. TUCKER: I know. How was everybody's day?

NORA: Boring. We had gym inside again.

OWEN: Recess got canceled. There were police with guns on the playground.

LIZZIE: I heard they were checking a hunting camp in the woods near school.

MRS. TUCKER: See? Nothing to worry about, Owen. Oh . . . roadblock.

TROOPER: Evening. Can you open your trunk, please?

NORA: It's going to stink if we have police cars hanging around field day on Friday.

MRS. TUCKER: I can't imagine they'll hold field day if the inmates aren't caught by then.

TROOPER: All set, ma'am—thanks for your patience.

MRS. TUCKER: Thank you for your service. Have a good night.

NORA: They can't cancel field day. That'd be like canceling Christmas!

OWEN: Or canceling my birthday!

MRS. TUCKER: Well, that's not going to happen. But we should probably make a plan B, Owen, just in case you guys can't sleep out in the tree fort Saturday. Maybe an indoor campout.

OWEN: That's not camping.

MRS. TUCKER: Sure it is! We'll make the living room into a superhero's lair, like Batman's cave. We can have pizza and—

OWEN: You said we could roast hot dogs and s'mores over the bonfire.

MRS. TUCKER: We may need to do that over the fireplace instead.

OWEN: Why can't we have a bonfire?

MRS. TUCKER: Well, the police have been watching for smoke, in case the inmates try to build a fire, so they're asking the rest of us not to have campfires for now.

OWEN: Even birthday campfires?

MRS. TUCKER: Even those, buddy. But hopefully, we're making backup plans for nothing. With any luck, the manhunt will be over by then and we'll be able to have your tree fort sleepover. Let's get that poster board now . . .

Tuesday, June 11—
Letter from Nora Tucker

Dear future Wolf Creek residents,

I'll be glad when these inmates get caught. Mom's not letting me out of her sight. This manhunt is making everybody scared and grouchy and weird. Lizzie called me last night, all upset because she could hear her grandma crying, but when Lizzie tried to go see her, her mom sent her away. She said Lizzie's grandma was just shaken up, knowing the inmates were out there. Lizzie could tell her mom was scared, too. All the parents are. It's messed up when the people in charge of telling you everything's going to be okay are as afraid as you are.

We just got back from getting Owen's poster board. Lizzie and I also got the craft store's last two rolls of blue ribbon. We aren't on student council, but Lucy Arnot gives jobs to anybody who's standing too close, so now we're cutting it into strips to give away tomorrow. When we finish, we have to peel potatoes. Mom's making scalloped potatoes for the ham supper and wants everything ready so she can pop them in the oven after work tomorrow.

Lizzie's sleeping over tonight. Her mom asked if she could stay with us again because her grandma could use some peace and quiet. I'm glad she's here, and not just because I want help with the potatoes. It's been too quiet with Dad at work. He's still trying to figure out how this happened because if he doesn't, that means it could happen again, and that's pretty awful to think about. Sean's been staying late at work every night, making subs for the searchers. Owen's here. He's supposed to be folding napkins for the supper, but he's writing in his evil plots notebook, so Lizzie and I will probably have to do napkins, too.

Are ham suppers still a thing in your time? I can't imagine they would be, since they already sound old-fashioned. Maybe in the future you'll have sushi and hummus and arugula suppers instead. Then those city reporters would be happier about coming to Wolf Creek.

Your friend from the past,

Nora Tucker

BIRTHDAY
BACKUP PLAN

SECRET PLAN FOR CATCHING BAD GUYS TO SAVE BIRTHDAY PLAN A

SUPPLIES NEEDED:
- Plate of freshly baked cookies
- Beer
- Cozy sleeping bags

PUT SUPPLIES IN TREE FORT

"HA! We caught you! Come down with your hands up!"

Saturday: HAPPY BIRTHDAY TO ME!

Tuesday, June 11—
Text messages between
Elidee & her mom

MAMA: Go ahead and make spaghetti ok? I'm going to be late

ELIDEE: Do you know how late?

MAMA: Not sure

Everything okay?

ELIDEE: Yeah

I just had kind of a crummy day

MAMA: Those boys after you again?

ELIDEE: Kinda

MAMA: I'll make an appointment to go in and talk to somebody

ELIDEE: Don't do that please

Sorry I know you're busy

It can wait until you get home

MAMA: You sure you're all right?

ELIDEE: I'm ok

MAMA: I'll try not to be too late

Love you to the moon and back

ELIDEE: Love you too

MAMA: You can't do better than that for me?

ELIDEE: Hold on a sec

Love you to Methuselah and back

Technically it's called PSR B1620-26b, but I like the nickname better

They found it in 1993

MAMA: That's my girl!

Dear future Wolf Creek residents,

I probably won't put this letter in the time capsule either (if I include everything, you'll be really sick of me by now), but I can't sleep again, so I'm writing to you.

It's weird. There haven't been any police sirens tonight. No helicopters have flown over. It's not the search keeping me up this time.

It's the rain.

It isn't super loud with thunder or anything, so you'd think it would help me sleep. They even put rain sounds on those sleep-noise machines sometimes.

But this rain is different. It's not soothing. Instead of lulling me to sleep, it's making me wonder what it's covering up. What am I not hearing over the drumming on the roof?

If I were the inmates and I were going to break into a house, I wouldn't do it on a nice, quiet summer night. I'd wait for a night like tonight, so nobody would hear a thing.

Even if they did, they'd think it was just the rain.

Your wide-awake friend from the past,

Nora Tucker

Good morning, Wolf Pack! Please stand for the pledge to the flag.

(Pledge)

Gym classes will be held inside again.

Chess club semifinals are after school in room F-4.

The student council will be giving out more blue ribbons today. Please see Lucy Arnot if you'd like to volunteer.

Happy birthday this morning to Mr. Russell . . . who says the only thing he wants for a present is his library books back. Please return any outstanding titles by the end of the day.

It's rainy out there today, but our quote of the day reminds us to look on the bright side. Helen Keller said, "Optimism is the faith that leads to achievement; nothing can be done without hope."

Also . . . a correction. I've been informed that I mistakenly attributed yesterday's quote to Founding Father Alexander Hamilton when its actual origin is more recent. Wise words, all the same.

That concludes our morning announcements.

Wednesday, June 12—
Letter from
Nora Tucker

Dear future Wolf Creek residents,

It's day five of our prison-break manhunt, and you know what? Having police around is starting to feel normal. The teachers are all finishing their last units and reviewing for finals. Trooper Elliott was eating tater tots in the cafeteria today, and nobody even noticed her until she asked to borrow our ketchup.

I used to watch the news and see stories about countries at war or neighborhoods with gangs and stuff, where kids would have to go through metal detectors at school, and I'd wonder how kids in those places could just go about their lives like that's normal. But I guess you can get used to almost anything.

Your friend from the past,
Nora Tucker

Wednesday, June 12—
Signs outside Wolf Creek
Community Church (I took
these photos when we were
on our way in for the
ham supper.)

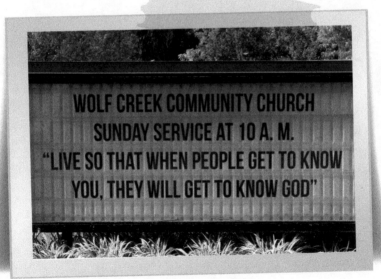

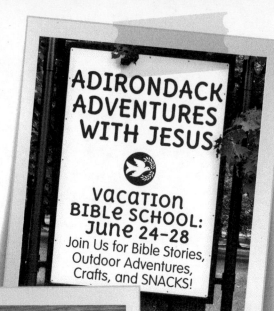

Wednesday, June 12—
Recorded on Lizzie's
WhisperFlash Z190 at
the ham supper

MRS. JABLONSKI: New recruits! Thanks for volunteering, girls. We need another four hundred sets of silverware rolled into napkins.

LIZZIE: Four hundred?

MRS. JABLONSKI: Gotta feed all our boys in blue.

NORA: And girls.

MRS. JABLONSKI: What?

NORA: Women, I mean. There are women out there, too. My aunt Sandy's been running roadblocks.

MRS. JABLONSKI: Of course! Call me old-fashioned, but I think "boys in blue" has a nice ring to it. Here are the napkins, and then . . . Hmph.

NORA: What's wrong?

MRS. JABLONSKI: Nothing. I just don't think it was a good idea to invite all those city reporters. That missy from CNN was on the TV last night saying that some of our COs at the prison were breaking rules about contact with inmates and such. Look at her with her fancy shoes over there. If you ask me, unless you work in a place like that, you have no business criticizing those who do.

NORA: Actually, our social studies teacher says it's kind of the opposite with journalism. That you need people from outside a place to ask hard questions, whether that place is a school or a sports team or the whole government.

MRS. JABLONSKI: Hmph.

MRS. JONES: Hi there! I'm Latanya Jones, and this is my daughter, Elidee. Mary Beth Arnot said you could use some help with the silverware?

MRS. JABLONSKI: No, I think we're fine here.

NORA: Didn't you say we needed another four hundred sets?

LIZZIE: I'd sure like help with that.

MRS. JONES: We're happy to pitch in. Got more napkins?

LIZZIE: Yep. Right here.

MRS. JONES: Are you girls excited about the school field day? I know Elidee's looking forward to it. She says there's a race—

ELIDEE: They know, Mama.

NORA: I love field day. I just hope we get to have it.

LIZZIE: We will. They'll just have police all over.

MRS. JONES: Well, I thank the Lord no one's gotten hurt.

MRS. JABLONSKI: We really do have plenty of silverware help if you and Melody* would like to head home.

MRS. JONES: Goodness, no. We just got here, and we're happy to—

MRS. ARNOT: How are we doing here? Mrs. Gonzalez says they need help with desserts if anyone's free.

MRS. JONES: Perfect timing! We've just been released from silverware duty, and we'd love to help Mrs. G. Lead the way!

LIZZIE'S REFLECTIONS: I don't know what Mrs. Jablonski's problem is, but we still had a TON of silverware left to wrap, and we could have used the help. I recorded this next part after supper while the moms were wrapping leftovers.

ELIDEE: Mama said I should see if you need help drying dishes. Got another towel?

NORA: Sure.

ELIDEE: Thanks.

NORA: Your mom's nice.

ELIDEE: Yeah.

NORA: Hey, can I ask you a question?

ELIDEE: Depends. What is it?

NORA: How come you came tonight?

ELIDEE: To volunteer. How come you came?

NORA: Same. I was just surprised to see you because . . .
you know . . . you didn't work on the sign in class or
anything, so . . .

ELIDEE: We go to church here. Mama says when you're part of
a community, you show up.

LIZZIE: Mine, too. That's kind of a mom thing.

NORA: So, Elidee . . . do you have any brothers or sisters?

LIZZIE: Nora . . .

ELIDEE: I think you know I have a brother. Isn't your dad in
charge of that whole prison?

NORA: Well . . . yeah. But he doesn't talk about stuff like that.

ELIDEE: Neither do I.

LIZZIE'S OTHER REFLECTIONS: So that was awkward. Nora
gets caught up in journalism once in a while and forgets
she's talking to real people with feelings. (Sorry, Nora. I know
you're reading this, but it's true.) Also, I think I agree with
Mrs. Jablonski about having so many reporters poking around.
Everybody's stressed out—Grandma and Nora's dad and all the
officers. The last thing they need are reporters who've never
been inside the prison telling them they're not doing their jobs
right. I liked that sign they had out in front of the ham supper,
though, standing up for people who work at the prison.

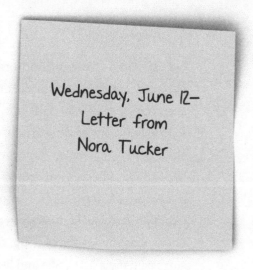

Dear future Wolf Creek residents,

We got back from the ham supper a little while ago, and here's
what I have to report on that.

1. It was crowded. There were hundreds of state
   troopers and corrections guys, still in their muddy
   search clothes, sitting at the church's long fold-up
   tables.
2. There was ham. Lots and lots of ham. Also salad,
   rolls, potatoes, and potluck desserts. I was hoping
   Lizzie's grandma would bring minty brownies, but
   she wasn't there.
3. There were also media people. I heard Mrs. Arnot
   invited them because she wanted the ham supper
   on the news. I wasn't sure how that would work
   out. I figured anybody who doesn't like the subs
   at Joe's Mountain Market! wasn't likely to be
   impressed with ham and scalloped potatoes either,

but Elizabeth Carter Wood from CNN seemed
perfectly happy, sitting in the middle of a bunch of
searchers, eating Mrs. Jablonski's orange-banana
Jell-O. I thought about warning everybody that
she's tricky and was probably just being friendly so
they'd talk to her and she could put it on the news.
But before I had time, Mrs. Arnot showed up with
her clipboard and sent us to wrap silverware.

4. Elidee was there volunteering, too, which
   surprised me a little. She and her mom wrapped
   silverware with us until Mrs. Jablonski fired them,
   which was dumb. We could have used the help.
   And you know what? The more I think about it, the
   more I think she was being a jerk, just like Walker
   and Cole. I should have said something.

Lizzie says I was being a jerk, too, asking Elidee so many
questions. I swear I wasn't trying to be nosy this time. Asking
questions is just sort of my thing. I need to quit doing that.

When Sean got back from the market tonight, I told him
what happened. He said Mrs. Jablonski was being a racist old
biddy, and me speaking up probably wouldn't have helped
anyway. He said I should just try to be friendly and include
Elidee in stuff so she knows not everybody here is a jerk. Maybe
I'll see if she wants to hang out with Lizzie and me at field day on
Friday.

So now we're home, and Lizzie's sleeping over again. Uncle
Tommy's here, too, downstairs with Mom. He was in the woods
searching all day, so Mom gave him a pair of Dad's shorts to

change into while she washes his uniform. She's using tweezers to pull ticks off his legs and arms. Lizzie and I were hanging out with them awhile, but that was too gross to watch, so we went upstairs.

We kept my door open so we could listen, though. Uncle Tommy just told Mom the police found clues in a hunting camp today—bloody socks that they're testing for DNA to see if the blood belongs to one of the escaped inmates or just some hunter with a blister. Uncle Tommy says this could be a huge break, but I'm not so sure. They thought they had a huge break yesterday when a guy on Mallard Road heard a sound in his shed and called the police to report that the inmates were hiding in there. Officers came and broke in to the shed, but all they found was Mrs. Heggleson's cat, Nebula, who ran away a week and a half ago. Mrs. Heggleson was excited to get him back, so it's still a happy ending. Just not the one the police wanted.

But Uncle Tommy is pretty sure those bloody socks are a real lead. Also, he told Mom the police are about to arrest somebody for helping those guys escape. I hope they throw whoever it was in prison, too. Stay tuned . . .

Your friend from the past,

Nora Tucker

Wednesday, June 12—
Letter from Elidee to
her brother, Troy

Dear Troy,

Mama dragged me out to help at a ham supper for the searchers tonight. Apparently, that's a thing they do here. Mama says when folks want to help but can't really do anything, serving up food makes them feel better. So we had to go serve ham to cops.

People here sure do love the police. They want everybody to wear blue ribbons and all that. There's even a sign outside the church warning people not to talk trash about corrections officers. Seriously. I'm not making this up.

"And maybe just remind the few, if ill of us they speak, that we are all that stands between the monsters and the weak."

So apparently, if you're not a corrections officer, you're either weak (that's Mama and me) or a monster (that's you). Made me want to kick that sign right over. But I didn't. I followed Mama into the church to serve ham.

Actually, I didn't serve ham. I folded plastic silverware in napkins until some old white lady decided she didn't want my black hands all over her plastic forks. Then I helped Mama and Mrs. G. with desserts and dried some dishes, and now I'm

writing you a ham-supper rap in the voices of all the church
ladies. (When they did this in the musical I saw, it was Hamilton
and all his buddies from the Revolutionary War introducing
themselves. They're way cooler than the church ladies, but I'm
working with what I have here . . .)

Yo yo yo yo yo!
What time is it?
Ham-supper time!

Well, I'm Latanya Jones in the place to be,
So pleased to be a part of this community.
I'm a busy working mama and a sole breadwinner
But tonight I'm all yours to serve up ham dinners.
You say you need your silverware wrapped up in napkins?
My girl and I'll get it done before I finish rappin'.
Load up a paper plate with those scalloped potatoes
Sliced red tomatoes (even though I hate those).
It's all about community, child, you gotta show up
But if I gotta smile much longer I'ma blow up.

Hey! Hey! Hey! I'm Mary Beth Arnot in the place to be,
You don't have to look far if you're looking for me!
I'm here with my clipboard and you ain't gonna get bored.
When I'm in the house—I got jobs for you, all sorts to do.
If you got the chops, serve some food to these cops!
We got brownies for the townies and ham for state police.
Don't you mind the grease—it's just more fuel for keepin' the
    peace.

I'm Ruth Jablonski in the place to be,
And I welcome you to Wolf Creek Community
Church. We come together in unity
To honor the officers—they get immunity,
Act with impunity at every opportunity.
So we throw a ham supper and
Hope they keep the upper hand.
(If it ain't quite legal, put your head in the sand.)
'Cause we gotta walk the walk, make them monsters talk
On the cellblock and show 'em where they stand.

Pretty sharp, huh? Okay, maybe not. But I'm working on it. I'd keep writing but Mama's calling me downstairs. I never told her any more about those boys in gym class the other day. I thought she forgot, but she didn't. She said we were going to have some pineapple smoothies and a good long talk tonight. Truth is, I'm only looking forward to the smoothies part.

I hope you're doing okay.

Love,
Elidee

Thursday, June 13

Good morning, Wolf Pack! Please stand for the pledge to the flag.

(Pledge)

Gym classes will be held inside again.

Finals in the chess club tournament are after school in room F-4.

We have no birthdays to celebrate this morning, but Mr. Russell says he'd still like to see those missing library books and will consider them a belated birthday gift if you turn them in today.

Our quote of the day is from basketball superstar Michael Jordan. "Always turn a negative situation into a positive situation."

And along those lines, I'm afraid I have some not-so-positive news . . .

On the advice of law-enforcement officials, we've made the difficult decision to cancel tomorrow's field day. We realize this is a favorite end-of-school event, but safety is our top priority. Instead of field day, your teachers will plan some fun indoor activities, and we'll still have our Wolf Pack cookout—actually, I guess it's a cook-*in* now—with pizza and cupcakes in the cafeteria. We'll do our best to turn a negative situation into a positive one, and we appreciate your understanding.

That concludes our morning announcements.

Thursday, June 13—
Handout from
Ms. Morin at the
beginning of English
class

Dear students,

After this morning's announcement about field day, several students requested that today's ELA lesson be focused on the process for crafting a petition. We've talked this year about how persuasive writing can change the world. It is in that spirit that I share today's lesson.

~Ms. Morin

HOW TO WRITE A PETITION

A **petition** is a specific request for action, most often addressed to a government official and signed by numerous individuals. When writing a petition, keep in mind the 3-S guidelines— SPECIFIC and SHORT with SUPPORT.

1. Be specific when you write your petition. Be clear about what you want to happen and who you want to do it.

2. Make your petition short. If you write concisely, it should take less than a page to explain what you want and why it's the best course of action.

3. Support your request with specific facts and details. It's often helpful to acknowledge the other side of the argument to show that you understand it, and then offer a rebuttal to show why your course of action is preferred.

Once you've finished writing a draft of your petition, read it aloud to make sure your argument is clear. Revise as needed to make your case stronger. Before you share your petition, proofread it to make sure it's free from errors in grammar, spelling, and punctuation. (Nothing sinks a student petition faster than poor editing.) Then circulate your petition to get signatures and present the final document to the person or group in charge of making the change you desire.

Please understand that even when petitions do not bring about the results you desire, they do result in your voices being heard and considered.

Dear future Wolf Creek residents,

You guys are probably still talking about "that year they had to cancel field day because of the inmates." They made the announcement this morning. Field day is off. At least for now.

That might change, though, because we're making a petition. Ms. Morin helped us, and Lucy Arnot is typing up the final draft right now in study hall. She's going to take it around to the lunch periods to get signatures and deliver it to Mr. Simmons after seventh period. I think it turned out pretty good. We followed Ms. Morin's guidelines and even used one of Mr. Simmons's own quotes in our argument. That part was my idea. I hope it works.

The other news today is that there might be an arrest in the escape. Not the inmates (because nobody can find them), but somebody who helped them. That's what the police are saying. I can't imagine who would do that, but apparently, somebody did, because Tommy Dunbar's uncle is a detective and Tommy says there's for sure a warrant and whoever's name is on it is getting arrested today.

Lizzie had to leave after first period—her mom picked her up for an appointment or something, but I'm calling her after school so we can go to the market and report on all this. More to come . . .

Your friend from the past,

Nora Tucker

Dear Mr. Simmons and whoever else decided to cancel field day:

Wolf Creek Middle School Field Day has taken place on the second Friday in June for pretty much ever. Our parents and grandparents have fond memories of spending that day outside in the sun with their friends.

   We understand that everyone is worried about the prison break, and we appreciate your concern. However, we think it's very unlikely that the inmates would show up at field day. Seriously, if you were the inmates, would you come running out of the woods into a school soccer field surrounded by state police cars? We don't think so. Therefore, we believe field day would be totally safe.

We look forward to field day all year. Classroom activities are no substitute. Where would we race? How could we have the water-balloon-the-principal prize? Also, serving pizza inside in place of the Wolf Pack cookout is lame.

If you cancel field day, it's like letting the inmates win. Just last week, you shared wise words from Thomas Edison as our quote of the day. Remember that? He said, "Our greatest weakness lies in giving up." We agree with this and are not willing to give up our field day just because there are inmates running around in the woods.

Therefore, we, the undersigned, call on you to reconsider your ill-advised decision to cancel such a proud and important tradition. Please let field day take place as planned, outside and with an outdoor cookout, tomorrow.

Signed,

Lucy Arnot

Rory Burke

Jessica Maynard

Erin Gonyo

Nora Tucker

Ivy Germain

Elidee Jones

Talia Coleman

Lisa Grimmal

Alyssa Beals

Tommy Dunbar

Walker Tremont

The names filled eleven more pages, but you get the idea.

Good afternoon, Wolf Pack.

I'd like to take a moment this afternoon to address the thoughtful petition that was brought to me after lunch.

I am truly impressed with your determination, school spirit, and persuasive writing skills. However, I cannot go against the advice of our officers. Thomas Edison may have said we shouldn't give up, but someone else said, "Better to be safe than sorry." Holding an outdoor event during the manhunt would simply create too great a risk. I'm afraid we must stick with our decision to cancel.

I do applaud you for your well-written petition. I realize that indoor activities can't take the place of our beloved field day, especially the Mad Mile. And given that, I'd like to propose an alternative that addresses the water-balloon-the-principal issue. As you know, our Wolf Creek Firefighters' Carnival is a week from Saturday. One of the carnival traditions is the annual five-kilometer relay. While it's not an official school event, I'd like to invite students to form teams and participate. The winning team of runners will all have the opportunity to . . . uh . . . toss a water balloon at me after the race.

That concludes our announcements—and our school day. Have a good afternoon.

NORA: Hey!

LIZZIE: Hey

NORA: U busy?

LIZZIE: No

NORA: Did u hear about the field day petition?

LIZZIE: I heard Lucy was doing one

NORA: Ms Morin let us write it in class but Mr Simmons said no anyway

LIZZIE: Bummer

NORA: But they're doing a relay at the carnival next week so we have to make a team.

I was thinking we could ask Elidee bc she's fast & we'd be a great team so when I saw her at her locker after school I asked if she might want to run with us but she said no

LIZZIE: Not surprised

NORA: Yeah I know but she could have helped us win . . .

Did you hear somebody's getting arrested today for helping the inmates? . . .

We should go to the market before dinner to see what people are saying . . .

Don't you think?

LIZZIE: Sorry I can't

NORA: How come?

LIZZIE: Have to go somewhere with my mom

NORA: Want to come over later?

. . .

U still there?

Thursday, June 13—
Letter from Lizzie to
her grandma

Dear Grandma,

I didn't get to say good-bye to you because Mom made sure I wasn't home when the police came. All I know is that after I got on the bus this morning, she drove you to the police station to turn yourself in. Then she came back to get me after first period because people were already whispering about you getting arrested even though nobody knew yet it was you.

They will soon, though. Secrets don't last long in Wolf Creek.

Nora hasn't heard yet. I was just texting with her and she wanted to go to the market so we can report on the "new developments."

Yeah. No thanks.

I'm sure she'll find out soon, like everybody else. That makes me want to run away and disappear like those guys they say you helped.

You didn't really help them, right? Mom says you were just too nice, like always. She says you brought those guys minty brownies, even though you technically aren't supposed to do that because it's against prison rules, but you didn't actually help them get away or anything. You'd never do that. Mom says it'll just take some time for the police to figure things out and find out who really helped them escape. I still can't imagine anybody doing that.

Mom also says you'll be arraigned in court tonight. That's when they officially accuse you of helping and that's also when all the reporters will find out your name. Then everybody else will know, too.

I hope it doesn't take long before people find out it's not true. And I hope you can come home soon. I already miss you.

Love,
Lizzie

Thursday, June 13—
Text messages
between Nora &
Lizzie, 5:55 p.m.

NORA: U there?

I'm here if you want to talk ok?

Lizzie?

My mom told me about your grandma bc she knew it was going to be on the news tonight

Are you ok?

LIZZIE: Not really

NORA: Sorry

LIZZIE: Not your fault

NORA: I know

Still sorry

LIZZIE: Yeah

Thanks

It's a mess bc she brought those inmates brownies or something and the police found out and now they think she helped those guys get away

NORA: That's so dumb

How can they arrest her for that??

LIZZIE: Idk

Mom says they'll figure it out and she'll be home soon

NORA: I hope so

Want to come over?

LIZZIE: No thx

NORA: Ok

See you tomorrow

Thursday, June 13—
Letter from Elidee to
her brother, Troy

Dear Troy,

Are you doing all right? I know you can't answer that, because
I can't even send this letter, but I'm writing anyway because it
makes me feel like that wall's not quite so big between us.

I hope you're okay. The newspapers keep talking about how
things inside the prison are bad now. How the guards are in
trouble for this escape, so they're taking it out on you guys. I
hope you're watching your step and minding your temper like
Mama taught you.

I've been minding mine. Mama and I had our smoothies and
our talk last night. She said she could almost see darts coming
out of my eyes when that old white ham-supper lady told us we
should go home. Mama says that woman's got a heart full of fear
and that's her own problem. It's our job to do God's work in the
world, and last night, that meant serving at the church supper
with smiles on our faces. (Personally, I have a hard time believing
that what God wants most in this world is for me to wrap plastic
forks in napkins, but I didn't say that out loud because you and I
both know how well that would have gone over.)

I told Mama what happened at school this week, too. Then I

felt bad because there's really nothing she can do about it. I sure don't want her swooping in to the office. She didn't make that offer again, anyway. I think she knows it wouldn't make anything better. She just told me I have to stand tall and be me.

Before we came to Wolf Creek, Mama explained that it might be tough sometimes. Mrs. G. had told her it's pretty white here—at least outside the prison. Mama says that's why some people in this town are so ignorant. She says I need to keep my chin up and study hard and show them who I am. I'm trying. I am. But sometimes I get thinking about what things would be like if I'd gotten in to that other school. When I visited, I felt like that's where I was supposed to be. Only the people in charge disagreed. Then Mama decided she and I both belonged up here in the middle of nowhere, with you. So here we are.

And you know what? Mama never once asked what I thought about moving. I'm the one who always does fine. Never matters what I want. All her attention's been on you since you first got in trouble. Sometimes I feel like I ought to start ripping off bodegas, so the world could revolve around me once in a while, too.

Anyway, after that ham supper last night, Mama told me I have to keep it together and stay focused. I'm good at that, right?

Then she gave me a big hug, and it was worth that long lecture and then some. I didn't realize how much I miss her now that she's working so much and nobody else is around.

You probably miss her even more than I do. Stay safe in there.

Love you,
Elidee

ELIDEE: Hi mama

MAMA: Hi there!

ELIDEE: Want me to start dinner?

MAMA: Yes please. You can put that chicken in the oven

ELIDEE: Ok

MAMA: How was your day?

ELIDEE: Pretty good

MAMA: I'll be home in about an hour

Love you to Medusa

ELIDEE: ?

MAMA: That planet you told me about

ELIDEE: Methuselah?

MAMA: Yes! That one!

ELIDEE: Ha! Love you too

LEARNING FROM JACQUELINE #4

wolf creek correctional facility
by Elidee Jones

(Inspired by "rikers island" from *Brown Girl
Dreaming* by Jacqueline Woodson)

Jacqueline Woodson's family
got a middle-of-the-night phone call
Just like ours.
Her uncle,
Calling from prison.
Prison.
Feels like it needs a capital P
Because it changes everything.

I was eight years old, asleep
When our first phone call came.
I only remember a little.

Mama's hushed voice full of sad, sad worry,
Oh, Lord. What happened?
Where are you now?
You keep your mouth shut. I'll be right there.
She left me in my pj's with Grandmama
And went to get him.

Our last phone call came two years ago,
The night Troy made his worst choice of all.
In one can't-go-back-and-change-it minute
His life would never be the same.
And neither would mine.

his name is troy
by Elidee Jones

(Inspired by "moving upstate" and "on the bus
to dannemora" from *Brown Girl Dreaming* by
Jacqueline Woodson)

Jacqueline Woodson's uncle got sent to a big prison,
   too.
She rode a bus like we used to ride
Through mountains
Up a long, long highway to the top
Of New York State.
Saw her uncle wearing prison-green shirt and pants
That sound a lot like Troy's,
Number on his pocket
Instead of a name.

I bet she felt like I do
Every time I see him.
Troy.
Sometimes I want to shout,
He has a name, you know.
Troy.
Troy!

When he was nine,
He used to hit baseballs in the shadow of Yankee
    Stadium.
And just up the street,
Across from the fruit cart
And the old guy selling honey-roasted peanuts,
There's a row of metal doors painted with the faces
    of baseball's best—
Roberto Clemente.
Satchel Paige.
Troy would look up, juice from an orange dribbling down
    his chin, and say,
"That's gonna be me someday!"

He's still in there somewhere, you know,
Behind the prison greens,
Tired smile,
Measured words,
Empty eyes.
Troy!

Dear future Wolf Creek residents,

By the time you read this, everything will be straightened out, but things are a mess today. The police think Lizzie's grandma helped those inmates. She's the person who got arrested. The news is saying she brought the inmates a phone and tools and stuff, but Lizzie says all she did is make them her not-so-secret-recipe minty brownies like she makes us. Like she makes everybody.

 If you work at the prison, you're not allowed to do stuff like that. There are a zillion rules meant to keep distance between the inmates and the staff. Dad says that's to protect everybody because some inmates are so smart and sneaky they can talk anybody into anything. They can make you think they're good guys, even when they're not.

 Lizzie didn't want to talk about what happened. I don't know if she saw the news. They showed her grandma handcuffed, walking into the courthouse. The city reporters were sticking microphones in her face and there was nothing she could do except keep walking and ignore them. The crime they say she committed is "promoting prison contraband," which sounds a lot worse than sneaking brownies.

So now Lizzie's grandma is in the county jail, and those two guys are still out of the big prison. Every time a sound drifts in my window at night, I wonder if it's them. My head knows it's probably raccoons in the garbage or a car door slamming in the neighbor's driveway, but my heart speeds up, anyway. Every single time.

Your friend from the past,

Nora Tucker

PS at 11:10 p.m.

OMG, Owen just tried to catch the escaped inmates.

Five minutes ago, somebody knocked on our door, and when I went to the stairs to see what was going on, Mom had just opened the door. Owen was standing there in front of a state trooper, who had a plate of cookies in one hand and a six-pack of Dad's beer in the other.

"Evening, ma'am," the trooper said. "I saw your boy in the yard and wondered if you knew he was out."

"Nope," Mom said, "I sure didn't know that." She grabbed Owen, pulled him into the house, and asked him what he was thinking.

Then Owen started crying and said, "It wasn't for me!"

And then Mom looked at the cookies and beer in the trooper's hand and smiled a little. "Honey," she said, "we're all thankful to the police, but they can't drink beer on duty. The cookies might have been nice, but you can't just go—"

"They weren't for me, ma'am," the trooper said. "They were for the fugitives."

"What?" Mom looked like she might take the trooper's handcuffs and lock Owen up herself.

"To catch them!" Owen said. "I figured they'd be hungry and thirsty, so if I put stuff out, they'd eat the cookies and drink the beer and get all sleepy." Owen's voice got quieter and quieter. He pointed to the trooper. "And then he could catch those guys and I could have my birthday."

"I advised him that wasn't the best idea," the trooper said. He handed Mom the cookies and beer. She gave back the cookies and thanked him again. Then she double-locked the door and sent Owen to bed.

I'm back in bed now, too, but I still can't sleep.

Poor Owen. If we lived in one of his comic books, the good guys would have caught the bad guys a long time ago.

The news tonight said we have a thousand officers searching through the woods for those inmates.

It's *a thousand to two* out there now.

How are the two still winning?

WOLF CREEK
FREE PRESS

LOCAL WOMAN ARRESTED IN PRISON PLOT AS SEARCH CONTINUES

by Vera Hemingway, staff writer

Police have arrested sixty-three-year-old Priscilla Wadsworth of Wolf Creek in connection with last weekend's prison break. Wadsworth is charged with promoting prison contraband, a felony punishable by up to seven years in prison.

Prison officials say Wadsworth has been a civilian employee at the prison for twenty-two years, most recently as a kitchen supervisor, where sources say she supervised inmates, including escapees John Smith and James Young. Wadsworth is accused of providing the inmates with prohibited items, including a cell phone and tools, in the days leading up to their escape.

"At this time, the police are interviewing witnesses both inside and outside the prison," said Wolf Creek Correctional Facility superintendent Bill Tucker. He says it's not clear if Wadsworth knew about the escape plan.

State Police Captain Bradley Mason says Wadsworth is cooperating with investigators. "She's providing us with information that we hope will expedite the capture of the two escaped inmates," Mason said. "Our searchers will be in the woods every day until we find them."

COMMUNITY SHOWS SUPPORT FOR LAW ENFORCEMENT
by Vera Hemingway, staff writer

On Wednesday night, Wolf Creek Community Church held a free ham supper for local and visiting law enforcement. Organizers say more than two hundred officers enjoyed the meal.

"We all pitched in," said volunteer Ruth Jablonski. "And it wasn't just ham. I brought my famous mini-cheesecakes."

Volunteer Maria Gonzalez says the church was happy to help out. "These men and women are guests in our town," she said. "Feeding them a home-cooked meal was our way of doing the Lord's work in Wolf Creek."

"We're grateful to the church and local community," said Sergeant Ted Phelps. "We have many officers who have been away from their families for the better part of a week now. It means the world to our guys to know they're appreciated."

MANHATTAN
DAILY INQUIRER

WANT SOME POWER TOOLS WITH THOSE BROWNIES?

NORTH COUNTRY NANA BUSTED FOR AIDING ESCAPE

Police have arrested an upstate New York grandmother accused of helping two convicted killers escape from Wolf Creek Correctional Facility last weekend. They say Priscilla Wadsworth, 63, made stealthy prison deliveries of everything from baked goods to potentially lethal tools. Confidential sources tell the *Daily Inquirer* that Wadsworth regularly ignored prison rules.

"She was always bringing them brownies and all," said an inmate who worked in the kitchen under Wadsworth's supervision. He spoke on the condition of anonymity, fearing retribution. This remote prison has long been known as a place where inmate complaints can lead to severe punishment at the hands of guards, while prison administrators look the other way. Prison superintendent Bill Tucker did not respond to an interview request for this report, other than to share a press release saying: "The prison is obviously cooperating with police. As far as any other allegations, our officers are held to the highest standards and are working diligently to keep their community safe."

If a jury finds Wadsworth guilty of the charges she faces, the over-friendly baker could find herself trading in her apron for jailbird stripes. She's accused of a felony that could land her in prison for up to seven years.

Good morning, Wolf Pack! Please stand for the pledge to the flag.

(Pledge)

We'll be running a regular class schedule today, but as you know, your teachers have some fun field-day alternatives planned.

Congratulations to Mia Tunbridge, who is our chess club tournament champion! We'd also like to recognize runner-up Amy Ordway. Great job, ladies!

Also, a special shout-out to Ms. Morin for her excellent instruction in persuasive writing. I've received a couple of new petitions this morning, following yesterday's field-day request. Again, these were thoughtful and well written, but I'm afraid we are not able to purchase a climbing wall for the gym or install a sundae bar in the cafeteria at this time. I'll pass your documents on to the school board, however, for consideration at their summer meeting.

Let's all wish a happy birthday to Riley Porter and . . . how am I supposed to say that? Okay . . . and feliz cumpleaños to Señora Luck!

Our quote of the day is from Abraham Lincoln, who said, "Most folks are about as happy as they make up their minds to be." Let's all keep that in mind as we enjoy indoor field day.

That concludes our morning announcements.

Dear future Wolf Creek residents,

I feel awful for Lizzie. Her grandma is in all the newspapers, and everybody's talking about it, but nobody knows what to say to Lizzie. They get quiet whenever she's around, but it's not like she doesn't know they're talking about it when she walks into class and everybody shuts up all at once. She's mostly ignoring people and working on a new parody or something.

Those city newspapers are going after everybody. Dad, too. I don't know if he's seen the one that talks about his prison being a place where guards punish inmates for complaining. I'd never heard that before. I can't believe Dad wouldn't fix that if it were true.

I wish they'd catch those guys.

Today is so dumb. It's beautiful and sunny out, so everybody's twice as grouchy about field day being canceled. Even the teachers. They're supposed to be outside, too, wearing shorts and T-shirts and drinking coffee while we run around.

Instead, we're all trapped inside looking out the window at the stupid, perfect weather.

Mr. Simmons ended announcements with a quote from Abraham Lincoln about being happy even when everything stinks, but it didn't help anybody's attitude. I wonder if Lincoln even said that. Earlier this week, Mr. Simmons told us Alexander Hamilton said something, only then he had to make a correction because somebody called him out and told him it wasn't true. I'm going to stop by the library at lunch to check on this Lincoln situation.

I have to go now because we're playing mandatory MATH BINGO in place of field day. It's extra sad because usually Lizzie loves math bingo, but today, she's barely paying attention. If math bingo ends early, we get to watch an episode of *Quadratic Magic*. I'm not sure I'll be able to stand all this fun.

Your friend from the past,

Nora Tucker

Just so you know, I don't think this is funny, but I'm including it because journalists look at all sides of an issue and try to be fair and inclusive. Even when that includes sharing parodies that say mean things about their dads. ~Nora

BUSTED FOR BROWNIES

by Lizzie Bruno

Yesterday local police proudly announced that they arrested an old lady for baking brownies.

"We're working hard to keep the public safe," said Officer Stu Pitt. "Wolf Creek can sleep easy tonight, knowing that this dangerous criminal won't be baking anymore."

At press time, two convicted killers who recently escaped from the prison were hanging out in some hunting camp, not being bothered by anyone. Police say they're not too worried about that but have launched a new investigation into another lady who might be baking chocolate chip cookies.

PRISON OFFICIALS DEFEND GUARDS BUT DON'T CARE ABOUT ANYBODY ELSE

Local prison officials responded to the arrest of a loyal kitchen worker today by not defending her even a little. "Whatever," said prison superintendent Bill S. Tucker-Dout. "It's been a rough week, so I'll totally blame her if it keeps people off my back."

Tucker-Dout refused to respond to criticism that prison rules aren't being followed and that inmates who complain are being treated unfairly. "Nah, we're keeping everyone safe," he said. "Really, pretty much everything is that kitchen lady's fault."

Tucker-Dout was also questioned about his own role in prison security breaches that might have led to the inmates' recent escape.

"We're all working hard except that kitchen lady. None of this would have happened if she'd followed the rules," Tucker-Dout said. "And hey! Would you like some minty brownies? Someone left them in the break room . . ."

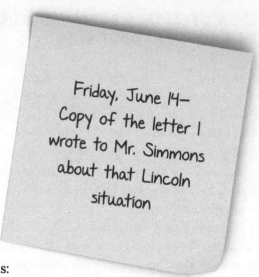

Friday, June 14—
Copy of the letter I
wrote to Mr. Simmons
about that Lincoln
situation

Dear Mr. Simmons:

At the end of announcements today, you shared a quote you said
was from Abraham Lincoln: "Most folks are about as happy as
they make up their minds to be." I'm guessing you chose that one
so we'd feel bad about complaining that field day got canceled.
But Abraham Lincoln never said that.

I looked it up. That quote was first mentioned in 1914, and
LINCOLN WAS ALREADY DEAD THEN. Because field day was
canceled, I had plenty of time to read about how quotes get
misattributed, and it seems to happen to poor Lincoln the most.
Here are some other things Lincoln didn't say, just in case you
were planning to use these fake quotes, too:

"Whatever you are, be a good one."

A guy named Laurence Hutton says another guy named
William Makepeace Thackeray said this. The Internet says
nobody's really sure about that, but it definitely wasn't Lincoln.

"Better to remain silent and be thought a fool than to speak and remove all doubt."

Lincoln didn't say this. God did. Or something like it, anyway. It's in the Bible. Unless somebody misquoted God, too, which is possible.

"Here I stand—warts and all."

Vice President George Bush said in a speech that Lincoln said this, but it's not true. It's actually a mash-up of two quotes from Martin Luther and Oliver Cromwell.

There are plenty of other things Lincoln did say, so the next time you quote him, you should try to choose one of those. Also, no offense, but you should probably be more careful about quotes because this is the second time in a week this has happened. The morning announcements are sort of like journalism, and journalists need to be careful to say what's true. Not rumors and not just things that fit their arguments.

Sincerely,

Nora Tucker

Friday, June 14—
Letter from
Nora Tucker

Dear future Wolf Creek residents,

This is another thrilling update from field day. We're watching
Dora the Explorer in Spanish as our AMAZING FUN ACTIVITY to
make up for not being outside. Lizzie just passed me a note that
said "Es estupido."

    Normally, I'd write back, but I'm mad about that thing she
wrote about my dad. Seriously, it's not his fault her grandmother
did whatever she did. What's he supposed to do about it?

Your friend from the past,
Nora Tucker

(Lizzie & I were writing
back and forth here
during the *Dora* video.
I labeled everything N
or L so you know who
wrote what.)

L: Are you mad at me?

N: Kinda. That was a jerky parody.

L: I know. Sorry. I feel like everybody's blaming my
grandma for everything and she didn't even do
anything that wrong.

N: Well she did something. And it's not like my dad
can just jump in and fix it.

L: I thought he'd stand up for her. She's worked there
forever. And you know she's a good person.

N: So is he. And everybody's on his case about this too.

L: Sorry. I'm having an awful day.

N: I know.

L: I won't put that one in the time capsule. I'm really sorry.

N: It's okay.

L: Everybody's whispering.

N: I know. Except Dora. She's talking REALLY REALLY LOUD!

L: Es still really estupido.

N: Muy estupido.

Dear future Wolf Creek residents,

Our sad substitute for field day is finally over. I did not die of
boredom, so I'm on the bus home now. Also, Lizzie and I made
up. Mostly. I still think what she wrote was mean, but she's really
upset about her grandma. I spent the rest of the day trying to
distract her by talking about other stuff.

I told her how Owen tried to catch the inmates himself, and
that made her laugh. Then we decided maybe Owen has the right
idea. Not the cookies-and-beer trap, but about looking at the
escape from angles that the police haven't considered. Maybe if
we can figure out what really happened, they'll find out sooner
that it wasn't Lizzie's grandma's fault.

Our social studies teacher Mr. Langdon always says history
repeats itself, so we have to learn from the past. But in this
case, the police are too busy searching to do research on historical
escape attempts, even though there might be some details that
could give them ideas about how to solve this one. So instead
of watching the Bill Nye: Science Guy movie in science and
The Magic School Bus video in social studies, Lizzie and I got

permission to go on the computers to do research. During study hall, we wrote a letter with highlights to give to the police. We're going to make them cookies later, too. To make sure they pay attention to the letter.

In other news, I'm still hoping to be the first Tucker to water-balloon Mr. Simmons, but I'm not sure that's going to work out. Lizzie and I will be on a relay team together, but she's kind of slow, so if fast people like Talia and Tara and Madison get together, they'll probably win. Lizzie offered to not be on my team, but I'd never do that, especially with everything going on with her grandma, so I said it was all fine and we'd do our best. I really wish Elidee would do it. I wonder if she knows about the water-balloon-Mr.-Simmons prize. I'm going to ask again in case that makes a difference.

Your friend from the past,
Nora Tucker

Friday, June 14—
Copy of the letter
Lizzie & I wrote to
the police

Dear police,

Our social studies teacher says the best way for leaders to solve a problem is to study how people dealt with similar challenges in the past. If that rings a bell, it's probably because Mr. Langdon has been around forever, and lots of you must have had him, too. But right now, you're probably busy tromping through the woods, so we've gathered some information about past escape attempts from other prisons, in case there are any clues there.

ALCATRAZ ESCAPE ATTEMPTS

1936 Bowers—tried to escape while he was out burning trash at the incinerator. Didn't even make it over fence.

1937 Cole & Roe—filed through iron bars, climbed out window, went down to water & believed to be swept out to sea. So that didn't work out.

1938 Limerick, Lucas & Franklin—tried to escape by overpowering guards on roof. Failed.

1939 Five guys sawed through bars, went down to water & were going to jump in but decided that was a dumb idea (the water around the island is super cold, with sharks), so then they got caught.

1941 Bayless—escaped while out on garbage detail. Got in water
      & it was too cold, so he gave up.
1941 Four inmates took corrections officers hostage while
      they were working in the prison industries area. Officers
      somehow convinced them the escape plan wasn't going
      to work, so the inmates gave up. (One of those officers, by
      the way, went on to become warden of Alcatraz. Probably
      because he was so good at convincing inmates to stay put.)
1943 Four guys took officers hostage in prison work area and
      escaped into water, but guards started shooting at them.
      Two got caught. One drowned. One got away and was
      hiding in a cave near shore for two days. Must have gotten
      cold and hungry, so he gave up and went back to the work
      area.
1943 Another guy disappeared from laundry building, caught by
      shore.

(Are you noticing that lots of these guys escape while they're on
some kind of work duty? Maybe you should stop letting inmates
do laundry and take out the garbage and stuff.)

And finally, 1962 Morris, Anglin & Anglin—they dug out of cells
      with spoons, made a raft & drowned in the bay. (Probably—
      but that's not for sure because their bodies were never
      found. If you want to know more about this one, you can
      watch the movie they made about it, *Escape from Alcatraz*.
      Clint Eastwood plays Frank Morris.)

Here are two other interesting escape attempts that didn't happen at Alcatraz:

Louisiana, 2006 Inmate who had the job of repairing prison mailbags escaped by sneaking out with the mailbags. He got caught in Canada. Same guy escaped two other times, once by sneaking through a ventilation duct and once by putting lip balm on his wrists to slip out of handcuffs. This probably doesn't relate to our inmates, but you may want to consider banning lip balm at the prison from now on.

Stillwater Prison in Sydney, Australia, 1999 Some inmate's girlfriend watched a movie about a prison break with a helicopter, so then she signed herself up for a helicopter ride, pulled a gun on the pilot, and made him land in the prison exercise yard where her inmate was waiting and jumped in. The guards shot at the helicopter, but they got away—even with a bunch of other prisoners trying to grab on to hitch a ride. They got caught forty-five days later. If our inmates' escape lasts that long, summer will be over and we'll miss all our chances to go camping and have bonfires, so we really hope this is helpful.

Sincerely,
Nora Tucker
Investigative Journalist

Lizzie Bruno
Not an investigative journalist. (I'm just helping Nora.)

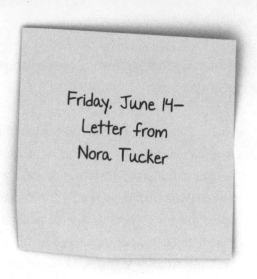

Dear future Wolf Creek residents,

First, let it be known that pizza was as crummy a substitute for the Wolf Pack cookout as everybody thought it would be. They ran out of pepperoni.

Second, I told Elidee about the water-balloon prize and she actually smiled a little, so I asked her again if she'd be on our relay team. She said she'd think about it! I gave her my number and am keeping my fingers crossed.

I wonder what they'll do if the inmates aren't caught by then. Uncle Tommy says they're testing DNA from that bloody sock but don't know yet if it's from the inmates or someone else who left it there. The police still say they don't think those guys have gone far. But they've said lots of things that turned out to be wrong.

At first, they thought they'd catch the inmates within hours. They didn't.

Then everybody hoped they'd catch them the next day. They didn't.

We hoped they'd catch the inmates before field day. (Nope.)

Before Owen's birthday. (Which is tomorrow night, so that's not looking good. Also, this just reminded me that I need to wrap his wand.)

What if they don't catch them before the carnival? Or the Fourth of July? Will we still have fireworks?

Sometimes it feels like we'll be hoping forever. Summer will pass, and we'll hope they get caught before school starts. When that doesn't happen, we'll add Thanksgiving and Christmas to our hope-they-get-caught-by list.

At least when winter comes, the inmates will leave tracks in the snow.

But I can't imagine sitting around the tree on Christmas Eve, singing "Silent Night," looking out the window at the falling snow and still not feeling safe.

Your friend from the past,

Nora Tucker

Friday, June 14—
Letter from Lizzie to
her grandma

Dear Grandma,

After school today, Mom came into my room and told me what happened, what the court papers said. So I know now it wasn't just brownies you gave them. I thought all the newspapers were lying. But they were telling the truth about it being more than that.

Mom says you felt bad for one of those guys and let him use your cell phone so he could call his little daughter. That's what he told you. But the police got your phone records and found out he was really calling other people. Bad guys, who might be helping him hide now. I get that you didn't know that, but why would you break the rules for someone you know killed a person?

You gave them tools, too. Drill bits and a screwdriver or something. Mom says when they asked for the tools, you said no at first. You must have known that was dangerous. But that was after you'd already broken rules with the brownies and the phone, and they said if you didn't get them tools, they'd tell your bosses about the other rules you broke and you'd lose your job and probably get arrested. So you did it.

They told you they needed those things to adjust their bed frames, so they'd be high enough to store stuff underneath. Did you really believe that? Did you not think about all the other things they could have done? They could have attacked a guard with that screwdriver. They could have stabbed Uncle Mike or Paul's dad or Lucy's dad. Did you ever think of that?

Mom says the reason you had to go to the hospital last weekend was because you were having some kind of breakdown. She says you need help. So I probably won't send this letter or the one I wrote yesterday. I'm not going to make it worse by telling you how mad I am.

But I am. Those guys are out there and if they hurt or kill someone, it will be partly your fault.

You know what else is your fault? Everybody whispering about our family. I was making up excuses for you in my head all day. I even wrote these parody articles blaming everybody else for what happened to you and got in a fight with my best friend because I said jerky things about her dad in one of them, but really, it was your fault the whole time. I was just so angry about what people were saying. Here are some of the things they whispered in the halls when they thought I couldn't hear:

I told you. It's Lizzie's grandma.
My dad says she's going to prison and then she'll be sorry.
She'll never survive in there.
I heard she gave the inmates a phone.
She gave them tools.
She gave them guns.
They totally conned her.

Only an idiot would do that.

No, she knew what she was doing. She knew.

I hope she never gets out of jail.

I hope she does, and then the escaped inmates find her.

I hope they find her and kill her.

It would serve her right.

I don't want you to get hurt or anything. I love you. And I hope you'll be okay. But I don't understand how you could do this to us.

Lizzie

P.S. You might think it's selfish of me to be talking about all the gossip when you obviously have bigger problems. But if you've never walked down the 7th-grade hallway with everybody whispering about you, you can't understand how awful school is for me right now. I don't know if it'll ever go back to being the way it was before.

Friday, June 14—
Text messages between
Elidee & Nora

917-555-0192: Hey

NORA: Hey

917-555-0192: What's up

NORA: Not much

Who is this?

917-555-0192: Sorry it's Elidee

NORA: Oh hi!

Sorry

Didn't recognize the number

What's up?

917-555-0192: I'll run with you guys

NORA: Really?

917-555-0192: Yeah

NORA: Cool!!

Thanks

917-555-0192: It'll be fun

NORA: Night

Friday, June 14—
Text messages between
Lizzie & Nora

NORA: Guess what?!

LIZZIE: What

NORA: Elidee texted and said she'll run the relay with us

LIZZIE: Wow

Why'd she change her mind?

NORA: Idk but I'm psyched

LIZZIE: That's good I guess

NORA: How are you doing?

LIZZIE: Ok

NORA: Really?

LIZZIE: Nah but I don't want to talk about it

NORA: Ok

We should practice for the relay

LIZZIE: Ugh

NORA: At least handoffs

We're not running in gym anymore

LIZZIE: I like not running

NORA: But we have to stay in shape

LIZZIE: I'm working out right now

NORA: ??

LIZZIE: Lifting chips to my mouth

NORA: Haha

Maybe we can run in the morning

LIZZIE: No way the moms will let us out

NORA: Maybe if we're all together

Hold on and I'll ask

Mom says we can go!

LIZZIE: Noooo! I was counting on your mom to save me from running

NORA: Nope!

We can go but she's making Sean follow us in the car

LIZZIE: That's awkward

NORA: Can u meet at my house at ten? We can't go later bc sean has to work

LIZZIE: Ten's ok

NORA: I'll call Elidee and let her know

LIZZIE: Sounds good

Friday, June 14—
Letter from Elidee to
her brother, Troy

Dear Troy,

They have something here called a firefighters' carnival, which sounds like a block party only on a field and with some kind of fire-hose battle instead of dance contests. There's also a relay race, and this girl Nora asked me to run with her and her friend Lizzie. I told her no at first, but then I thought about how I promised Mama I'd make an effort, so I said I'd do it. Nora just called back, and we're going to practice tomorrow.

Mama was so happy she ran out and got stuff to make cookies so those girls can come over after we run. I haven't asked yet, so I don't know if they'll come or not. We're not friends or anything. I know they only asked me because I'm fast and they want to win some water-balloon prize. I mostly said yes because of Mama. Also, that girl Lizzie's getting all kinds of grief because her grandmama just got arrested. You hear about that? They say she helped those guys get out. I don't know if it's true, but part of me feels bad for that girl. People whisper about me, too, but at least I'm kind of used to it by now.

This race at the carnival is some kind of substitute for the field day they usually have here in June. That was supposed to be today, but it got called off because they can't catch those inmates. Some girl who seems to be in charge of everything at school launched a petition, and she was racing around telling everybody to sign it. Like it was gonna save the world or something.

It didn't work. Sometimes you can write whatever you want and it doesn't matter. I hope that won't be the situation with your appeal, but I know it might be. You should keep working on it anyway. I've decided that I'm going to start working on something, too.

Love you,
Elidee

PS Here's a little rap battle I wrote that might be part of the thing I'm working on. In the *Hamilton* musical, they called this "Cabinet Battle #1," and it was Jefferson and Hamilton arguing. My version is about the school student council vice president and the principal, but I think it's still pretty cool.

Ladies and gentlemen, you could be
anywhere in the world right now,
but you're here with us at Wolf Creek Middle School!
Are you ready for the morning announcements?

The issue on the table:
End-of-School Field Day.
Principal Simmons? Take it away . . .

MR. SIMMONS:

Due to the inmates who escaped from the jail
(And the searchers who have searched for them to no avail),
I've been forced to take an unpopular position:
Field day is canceled. That's my final decision.

STUDENT COUNCIL GIRL:

Wait! We have a petition!
Dear Mr. Simmons,
The field day competition is a decades-long tradition!
We set up this coalition and now we're on a mission
To get you to change your mind. Don't give us any line
About keeping us safe—it's all fine because you see,
A field full of cops is the *last* place those killers wanna be.

MR. SIMMONS:

I appreciate your position, but police have new suspicions
That the inmates have acquired guns and maybe
      ammunition.
We can't be too cautious.

STUDENTS:

Quit tryin' to brainwash us!

MR. SIMMONS:

Students, please! Settle down. Don't frown
Just because the playground's
Off limits. You'll see—here's field day Plan B!

Our indoor feast'll put old cookouts to shame!
We'll have pizza! Brownies! Movies and games!

STUDENTS:
That is so incredibly lame.

MR. SIMMONS:
My decision remains the same. This is a final
    pronouncement,
And that concludes your morning announcements.
Please pass now to your first-period class
And if you don't like the news, you can ~~kiss my~~
Take it up with the school board later if you choose.

PPS See what I did there at the end? I think Lin-Manuel Miranda
would be proud of that one.

There's a big break today in the case of two inmates who escaped from an upstate New York prison a week ago. Police say DNA from a bloody sock found in a hunting cabin is a match for James Young, one of the inmates who escaped from Wolf Creek Correctional Facility. Young's fingerprints were also found on a doorknob inside the cabin, and police believe the evidence was relatively fresh—not more than a day or two old when they found it. That means the two escapees are likely still in the area.

Officers are still operating under the belief that the two inmates are traveling together. That's helpful to searchers because two men together are easier to spot, especially since one of the inmates is black and one is white, and this is not a particularly diverse part of the state. If the men have split up, police say they've given up the advantage of traveling as a team—taking turns sleeping or keeping watch—and that could make them more vulnerable.

Also new in the case today, the state has launched an independent investigation to look into policies and supervision at the prison. Questions have been swirling about whether a serious lapse in security paved the way for the brazen escape. Corrections sources tell CNN it's likely that at least some prison officials will pay for that lapse in security with their jobs.

Saturday, June 15—
Text messages between
Elidee and Nora

ELIDEE: Hey it's Elidee

NORA: I know

I put your # in my phone

ELIDEE: Do you & lizzie want to come over after we run?

My mom's making pb chocolate chip cookies

NORA: Sure! I'll check with my mom but I'm sure it's fine

ELIDEE: We're meeting at school at 10:15 right?

NORA: Yep

ELIDEE: See you then

MASTER PLAN
TO CATCH BAD
GUYS BEFORE MY
BIRTHDAY PARTY
TONIGHT . . .

Saturday, June 15—
From Owen's Master
Plans & Evil Plots
notebook

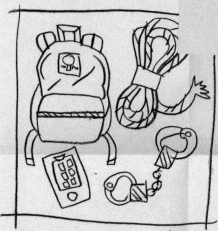

Supplies needed:
Backpack
Handcuffs
Rope
Cell phone

Two heroes head into the woods.

Owen says in a super deep voice,

Hey, James! It's me, John!

Time to set our trap. Be sure to leave a little slack in the rope.

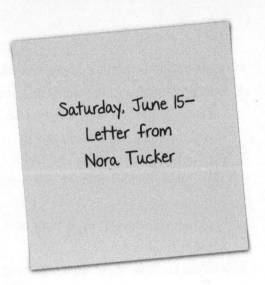

Dear future Wolf Creek residents,

I'm waiting for Lizzie to come so Sean can drive us to school to meet Elidee, and I have to say it again—I wish they'd catch those inmates. It stinks being a kid while they're out there. Mom made us go over every tiny detail of our plan for this morning:

> We're meeting at school at 10:15.
> Sean's driving behind us.
> We won't get more than a block ahead of him.
> Or go on any trails in the woods.
> We'll keep our eyes open and be smart and come straight
>   home if anything feels unsafe.
> Yes, we have sunscreen.
> We'll stay hydrated, too.

Also, Mom was weird when I told her we were going to Elidee's for cookies after our run. I gave all the usual details— where she lives (right up on Porter St.) and whether a parent would be home (yes). Mom said I should ask them to come here instead. I told her Elidee asked first and her mom already made cookies, so that would be totally rude. Then Mom got mad and said she didn't know Elidee's family, so she wasn't comfortable with us going. I told her to call Elidee's mom. That's what she always does if I have to work on a project at somebody's house with someone she doesn't know. I thought that was reasonable, but Mom said she was tired of my back talk, so we have to come home right after we run.

You know what I'm tired of? Living with all these rules. I'm tired of not having freedom. I'm tired of having only one parent because Dad's at meetings about shifts and schedules and inmate bed checks and whether they were done or not. I'm tired of fighting with Mom over dumb stuff like going to Elidee's and why she can't find her cell phone. She just accused me of moving it off the counter, but then she called it and found it in Owen's room, shoved in his backpack with a pair of toy handcuffs and a bunch of rope from the garage.

At least that got Mom off my case. Now she's upstairs yelling at Owen about how he absolutely positively cannot try to catch the inmates again and needs to make a plan B for his indoor birthday party tonight.

Inmates ruin everything.

Your friend from the past,

Nora Tucker

STINKY
NEW PLAN
FOR CRUMMY
BIRTHDAY
COOKOUT

Saturday, June 15—
From Owen's Master
Plans & Evil Plots
notebook

STUPID FAKE BATCAVE IN LIVING ROOM
Boring pizza
Indoor brownies
Indoor Rice krispies Treats
Lame s'mores cooked over dumb fireplace

Saturday, June 15—
Recorded on Lizzie's
WhisperFlash Z190
during our run

SEAN: Okay, you guys can start your run and I'll follow.

LIZZIE: Great. If the run doesn't kill me, I might die of embarrassment. Nora, do you have a pocket for this recorder?

NORA: Yep, I'll take it. Let's go!

SEAN'S RADIO: And now another Nashville favorite from your station for music in the mountains. Here's Big Ben the Rambler with "Ain't Never Gettin' Over You."

ELIDEE: What station is this?

NORA: 95-MOS: Moose Country.

SEAN'S RADIO:

> WELL I SNIFFLED AND SNEEZED
> I COUGHED AND I WHEEZED
> AND I FINALLY GOT OVER THE FLU . . .
> BUT THIS PAIN THAT I'M FEELIN'
> DON'T SEEM LIKE IT'S HEALIN'
> 'CAUSE I AIN'T GETTIN' OVER YOU . . .

ELIDEE: We gotta listen to this for three miles?

NORA: Two and a half. We have to skip part of the route because my mom won't let us run through the woods.

LIZZIE: I can't believe she made Sean follow us. He's like a giant car-turtle stalking us at eight miles an hour.

NORA: I know, it's—hey, did you see that?

ELIDEE: What?

NORA: There's a guy running on the bike path by the river. I just saw through the trees.

LIZZIE: There!

NORA: Ohmygosh, is that the inmate?

LIZZIE: If it is, where's the other one?

NORA: Didn't you see the news? They found DNA but only from one of them, so maybe they split up, and that guy. . . Sean!

SEAN: What's up?

NORA: There's a guy on the bike path!

SEAN: Where? Whoa! That—wait . . . no. That's Kayla and Paul Washington's dad.

NORA: Oh yeah . . . it is.

SEAN: He's always out running. Kayla says he's training for one of those Spartan Races.

NORA: Oh . . . I thought . . . never mind.

SEAN: You gonna get moving? I have to be at work by noon.

SEAN'S RADIO:

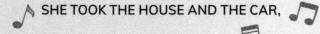 SHE TOOK THE HOUSE AND THE CAR,

SO I'M HITTING THE BAR FOR A COUPLE OF
BREAKUP BREWS . . .

SHE TOOK THE DOG AND THE TRUCK

AND I FEEL LIKE A SCHMUCK JUST SINGING THESE
BROKE-UP BLUES . . .

ELIDEE: Let's see if we can outrun this music.

NORA: Lizzie, you okay back there?

LIZZIE: I can't keep up with your pace, but go ahead. I'll keep
Sean and the lonely cowboy singer company back here.

NORA: All right, but holler if we get too far ahead.

LIZZIE: Okay!

NORA: So aside from Sean's music, how do you like Wolf Creek
so far?

ELIDEE: It's okay.

NORA: Do you miss New York City?

ELIDEE: Yeah, like a ton.

NORA: Like what?

ELIDEE: Friends. Family. My cousins and my aunt and
Grandmama. Just everything. Taking the subway to
midtown. The cat at the bodega on my street. Going
there for chopped cheese sandwiches.

NORA: Guess they don't have those at Joe's Mountain Market.

ELIDEE: Nope.

NORA: But they have great subs. There are a few good things
about living here, you know.

ELIDEE: Yeah?

NORA: It's quiet. And safe.

ELIDEE: Safe? Ha!

NORA: Well, now is weird. I meant that we don't have gangs or anything.

ELIDEE: You see that in a movie about New York City once?

NORA: Well. Yeah. But isn't it, like, a thing?

ELIDEE: In a few places, sure. But not everywhere. I have more rules here than I ever had at home.

NORA: We all have dumb rules now. Once they catch those guys—

ELIDEE: That won't fix anything.

NORA: What do you mean?

ELIDEE: Different people have to follow different rules in a place like this. Mama's always on me to watch my step, watch my mouth. She says you only have one shot to make a first impression.

NORA: So that's why you came to help at the ham supper.

ELIDEE: Yeah.

NORA: Why didn't you sign that banner for the police then?

ELIDEE: Thank you, law enforcement?

NORA: Yeah. So?

ELIDEE: I just . . . Look, when the police showed up in my old neighborhood, they weren't always there to hold open the school door for us. One of them beat the snot out of my friend's brother, and you know what her brother had done? Nothing. Except look a little like a guy who robbed a convenience store. He was all kinds of bruised up. Mama says Troy's lucky he's in prison and not dead. He could've been just like Tamir Rice.

NORA: Who's that?

ELIDEE: Seriously?

NORA: Who is it? Can't you just tell me?

ELIDEE: Do I look like your teacher? Go look it up.

NORA: Sorry. I just—

SEAN: Nora! Get in the car! Now!!

LIZZIE'S REFLECTIONS:
I'm kind of glad I fell behind and missed part of this conversation because Elidee sounded pretty ticked off at Nora. I don't blame her. She must get tired of people asking her about stuff. I'm pretty sick of people whispering about my grandma, too.

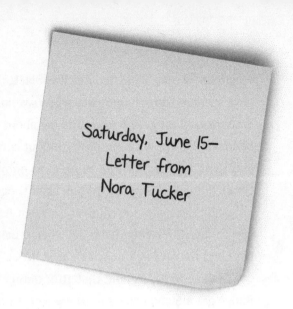

Dear future Wolf Creek residents,

I'm grounded. Mom says it's indefinite, so I may still be grounded when you read this. She won't listen to my side of the story. Here it is, in case you care. No one in my time period does.

First, our run got interrupted when Mom called Sean. She heard that police searching for evidence by the river saw an inmate running into the woods and were calling in backup to surround him. Lizzie and Elidee and I had to pile into Sean's car, but then Mom called back and said never mind because after they surrounded the inmate with their guns drawn and everything, they figured out it was just Mr. Washington.

And you know what? Unless you're *really* far away like we were, Mr. Washington looks nothing like that inmate. He's like a foot taller, he has a beard, and he was wearing running clothes— the fancy, expensive kind that pro athletes wear. Also, Mr. Washington has lived here forever. He's a corrections officer, but Sean says the out-of-town searchers wouldn't know that. They would know one of the inmates was black, though, so they must have assumed any running black guy would be the escapee. That is so messed up. I can't stop thinking about what it must have been like for Mr. Washington—to be out running like we were and all of a sudden have all those guns pointed at him. I bet Wolf Creek didn't feel very safe to him right then.

And that makes me think about what Elidee said. How she saw things differently than I did when it came to that thank-you banner. I think I get it now. At least a little.

I talked to Sean about that after dinner tonight. I told him Elidee got all mad at me for asking who Tamir Rice is.

First, Sean told me I need to ask him about stuff like that and not keep bothering Elidee. Then he told me about Tamir. He was a kid who got shot by the police in Cleveland because he had a toy gun and they saw him as a threat. They didn't know the gun wasn't real.

Tamir was only twelve years old. Sean says Ms. Madora talked about that as an example of police bias—assuming the worst about black boys. She said that never would have happened if Tamir had been a white kid with a toy gun.

I keep thinking about that. Like, what if Owen had his BB gun at the park one day? Mom would never let him do that because she never lets him use it without Dad around. But what if he did? I can't imagine the police shooting him. They'd march him home to Mom, but they'd never hurt him.

I told Sean that. And I told him Elidee's story about her friend's brother, too. And Sean started talking about how Owen has white privilege and how the thing with Elidee's friend's brother was racial profiling and how that happens all the time and how he and Emily talk about this a lot because she's been to some Black Lives Matter protests at her college. When I asked Sean why he never talked about it at our house, with our family, he just raised his eyebrow.

"You think that'd go over well at the dinner table?"

I guess not. Adults get so weird when you talk about this stuff, and Sean's already arguing with Mom and Dad about whether he'll go away to Syracuse for college or stay here. If they think he's just going so he can hang out at protests with Emily, he'll be enrolled in Wolf Creek Community College before he knows what hit him. But I'm glad he told me, at least. I wish I knew more about all of this.

It's weird. When I think about the police officers I know— Uncle Tommy and those guys— I can't imagine them being so unfair. I've never heard of anything like that happening here. At least not until today. That's making me wonder if that kind of attitude is new, since the inmates broke out, or if it was always here, just sort of hiding.

Anyway, after the whole situation with Mr. Washington was over, Lizzie and Elidee and I got to finish our run. Elidee and I raced the last block. She won by a bunch. And then she asked if we were still coming over.

I was supposed to say no. I was supposed to go straight home after we ran. But I stood there thinking about what had just happened to Mr. Washington. Even before I talked to Sean, I knew nobody would have bothered my dad or Sean if they'd gone out for a run today, even though one of those escaped inmates is white. Then I thought about how Walker and Cole and Mrs. Roy and Mrs. Jablonski had treated Elidee. My mom was doing pretty much the same thing. And moms are supposed to be better than that. I know she's all stressed out because of the prison break and Dad's work, but still. She was *wrong*.

So I said yes. Because Mom's decision wasn't fair. She'd never kept me from going to somebody's house before, even if they lived in the not-so-nice part of town. Mom always said that people are people and it doesn't matter what their houses look like. The only thing different with Elidee is that she's black. And that her brother is an inmate. I wasn't sure if Mom was being racist or prison-inmate-family-ist, but neither one was okay.

So I went. And you know what? It was great. Elidee and Lizzie and I hung out and talked and played Uno. The cookies were amazing and warm and peanut buttery. Elidee's mom was nice. She and Elidee must have read the same book Mom and I used to read together about the bunny who loves his mom to the moon and back, because when Elidee's mom was going upstairs, she kissed Elidee on the head and said, "Love you to Andromeda galaxy and back." That totally embarrassed Elidee, which proves her mom and my mom would get along fine.

I thought Mom would realize that. She was stressed about the inmates, like all of us. But I thought if I went to Elidee's house, Mom would see later that it was the right thing to do.

I still think I was right about going, but I was wrong about Mom's reaction. I'm including her text messages because you can SEE how mad she was. I don't know how Mom manages that with the same 26 letters everybody else gets, but she does.

Your grounded friend from the past,

Nora Tucker

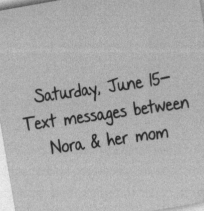

Saturday, June 15—
Text messages between
Nora & her mom

MOM: Where are you?

NORA: Just finished running

MOM: Sean texted and said you were done an hour ago

NORA: We're just hanging out

I'll come home now

MOM: Where are you right now?

NORA: Elidee's house

MOM: Address?

NORA: 15 Porter St

MOM: Stay there. I'm coming to pick you up.

Dear future Wolf Creek residents,

So here's the rest of the deal . . . Mom picked me up and smiled
and told Mrs. Jones it was nice of her to have us over, as if she'd
never said I couldn't go. Then we left and Mom dropped Lizzie
off at her house and headed for home.

I could tell she was mad and I was waiting for her to yell, but
she didn't say anything, so I looked out the window and thought
about Elidee's house. The living room table was full of pictures
in little frames. Elidee said they were her cousins—Emmie and
Brian and Cecelia and Marcus, and her aunt Maya and uncle Joe.
Then I picked up a picture of a skinny teenage boy and a younger
girl who looked just like Elidee. I asked if they were her cousins,
too, and Elidee said no. That was her and Troy, back when he
was fourteen and she was seven. Before he got in trouble. (Elidee
didn't say that—I just thought it in my head.)

In the photo, he looked like such a good brother, laughing
with his arm around her. He looked nice. Elidee must have
thought so, too, because she poked her finger at Troy's blue-and-
yellow-striped shirt in the photo, as if she could reach back and
touch the way he was before.

I bet Elidee wishes she could take herself back in time, too. Back to New York City. She seems homesick. And you know what? I've lived in Wolf Creek my whole life, so I can't imagine not feeling at home here, but it's weird. We talk all the time about being a friendly, welcoming community, but Elidee doesn't see us that way at all. And if people don't *feel* welcome, then maybe we're not as welcoming as we think. That's part of why I went to Elidee's house. I didn't want to be like Mrs. Jablonski or Mrs. Roy or the people who whisper about Elidee at school. It didn't work out the way I thought it would, though.

When Mom and I got home, she finally let me have it. She was all "What were you thinking?" and "How dare you go over there when I told you not to." I had answers to all her questions, but when Mom is mad, there's no right answer, so I kept quiet, and now I'm grounded in my room. Which is kind of pointless, actually. Since those inmates got out, being grounded isn't much different from not being grounded.

Except that Lizzie and Elidee and I were going to get together again tomorrow to practice our relay handoffs, and then Lizzie and I were going to bake cookies to give to the police with our research letter. But one of those is kind of a school-related activity, and one is totally community service, so I'm hoping we'll get to do them anyway. Once Mom calms down, I'll ask about that. Can you have a petition if there's only one person to sign it?

Your friend from the past,

Nora Tucker

Saturday, June 15—
Petition from
Nora Tucker

PETITION FOR REDRESS:
Submitted to Mom from Nora—
June 15, 7:40 p.m.

Dear Mom:

Civil disobedience is a well-respected strategy for protesting unjust rules and laws, like when black people sat down at whites-only lunch counters during the Civil Rights Movement and refused to leave. We talked about this in social studies. Those protesters knew the lunch counter law was stupid and unfair, so they broke it. It was a leadership moment for them.

My decision to go to Elidee's house also falls under the category of civil disobedience because I felt like your rule about me not going there was unfair. You've never cared if I went to a friend's house before. Even a new friend. It never mattered who they were or where they lived. You've always just called the mom and found out an adult would be home and then it was fine. So how come it wasn't fine with Elidee?

You didn't say whether you were making that different rule for her because she's black or because her brother is in prison or because she's new, but I don't believe any of those reasons are good ones. As a result, I was compelled to break the rule and do what I felt was right. I was engaging in civil disobedience just like Henry David Thoreau, Mahatma Gandhi, and Martin Luther King Jr., but on a slightly smaller scale.

Therefore, we, the undersigned, call on you to reconsider your decision to punish me for making this choice. Please cancel my grounding (because let's face it—there's not much I'm allowed to do right now anyway) or at the very least, make an exception so Lizzie and Elidee and I can practice our baton handoffs tomorrow and so Lizzie and I can get the stuff we need to make cookies for the searchers like you said we could.

Signed,

Nora Tucker

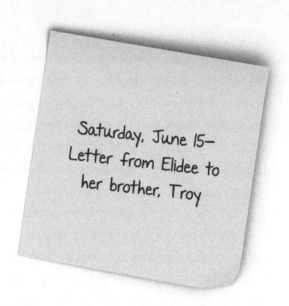

Saturday, June 15—
Letter from Elidee to
her brother, Troy

Dear Troy,

Those girls came over today. It went okay except when Mama
decided to kiss my head like I was five years old and announce
to everybody that she loves me to who-knows-what galaxy and
back. You better hope she never does that to you in front of the
prison guys.

After Mama went upstairs, Nora and Lizzie saw that
picture of you and me. You know which one I mean? You were
all scrawny, and you had on that too-big striped shirt. I think
it was from Grandmama's birthday cookout, early in the day
before we were all wet. Remember how we had all those water
balloons after supper? You thought you were so smart hiding
them behind the building, only then the little cousins found
your stash and absolutely soaked you. Remember that? When I
looked at that picture today, I could almost hear your voice, back
when it was starting to get deep but still squeaked and squawked
sometimes. You were already starting to hang around those

guys, but we didn't know it yet, Mama and me. We didn't see you changing until it was too late. It was that fast. Seems it anyway.

When we used to come from the Bronx to visit you, before everything got locked down, we never talked about what happened. Any time Mama asked, you said it wasn't worth talking about because if we weren't there on the street that day, we could never understand. So eventually she gave up and stopped asking.

People ask me sometimes. These two boys at school are always bugging me, and I bet they'd be surprised to know the truth. That I'm not even sure I know what happened. What the truth is. You say you didn't have a choice, but you did. Maybe not at the very end, the way you saw it, but I'm talking about before. We always have choices. Doesn't feel that way, but we always do. Even when we feel so stuck we pretend we don't.

Love,
Elidee

PS I meant to tell you I went running with those girls before we had Mama's cookies, and it was the best part of my day. After the incident, it was, anyway.

Just a little while after we started, we had to pile into Nora's brother's car because the police were all over this guy down by the river. They thought it was one of the inmates, but it was actually one of the corrections officers out for a run. They were pointing guns all around him. He didn't look anything like that escapee on the news, but you know how white cops are with telling black people apart. They figured it out pretty quick, so he didn't get hurt, which is good. Nora said his kid goes to our school. I don't know what that guy was thinking, going for a run with this going on. Mama would have lectured you up one side and down the other if you did that.

The other bad part of the afternoon was when I made a mistake and told Nora why I didn't want to wear that "thank you, police" ribbon. She didn't get it even a little, and I just couldn't deal anymore. She'd already gone off on how unsafe it must have been for me back home because of gangs roaming the streets. Like we lived in some Spike Lee movie or something. Mama was so excited about me making friends here, but she never told me that with white friends, you have to keep teaching them how not to be racist.

Anyway, after all that was over, we got to finish our run. It wasn't like running at the park at home, but it was pretty sweet, and I felt a whole lot better at the end. Running today felt like flying instead of feeling stuck in one spot.

Writing's starting to make me feel that way, too. Here's another "Learning from Lin-Manuel" rap. It's based on "History Has Its Eyes on You." If you ever get a chance to hear the *Hamilton* soundtrack, you should check that one out.

Late at night when it's all dark
I see a man in the trees surrounded
Blue shirts pouring into the park
Guns drawn circled all around him.
He holds his hands to the sky
And I hear Mama's prayers for me.
Lifting me way up high
To a future waiting there for me . . .

Let me tell you now what I know
About this place where I don't belong.
You don't have to be home to grow
And my anger's making me strong.
I found my voice
In this town that don't care for me
And I'll take my choice
Of futures waiting there for me.

PPS Mama has the rest of the day off, too, so we're going to pick
strawberries now. I wish we could bring you some.

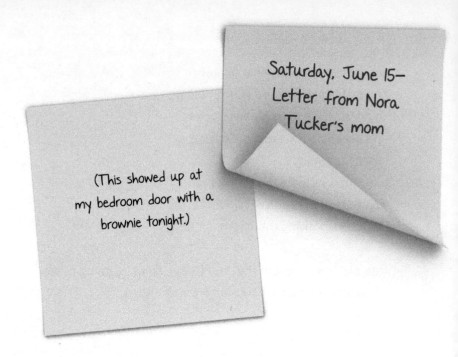

Saturday, June 15— Letter from Nora Tucker's mom

(This showed up at my bedroom door with a brownie tonight.)

Dear Nora:

Thank you for your petition. I was disappointed in you today. I told you clearly not to go to Elidee's house, and you went anyway. You chose to do this, even after the family made arrangements for you girls to run safely this morning.

Please understand that I like both Elidee and her mother. My decision had nothing to do with race or her brother or anything other than the fact that there is too much going on right now. I didn't need one more thing to worry about.

While I appreciate your historical perspective on civil disobedience, Dad and I are not an unjust government. We are your parents. We make rules to keep you safe, and breaking those rules has consequences. As you may know from your excellent social studies class, accepting consequences for one's actions is an important part of civil disobedience. In his Letter from a Birmingham Jail, Martin Luther King Jr. wrote, "One who breaks an unjust law must do so openly, lovingly, and with a willingness to accept the penalty." When Thoreau ignored the Fugitive Slave Law in 1850, he said, "Under a government which imprisons any unjustly, the true place for a just man is also a prison." Thoreau, Gandhi, and King all willingly spent time in jail for their decisions to break the law.

I trust that you are noble enough to accept the consequences of your decision today as well. However, as you point out, there is not much to ground you from at the moment, given how often we've had to be inside lately. Therefore, your new consequence will be two weeks of doing dishes after dinner and limited out-of-the-house activities, including preparing for your relay and community service such as baking cookies for the police.

We, the undersigned, ask that you accept your punishment in the spirit of all the civilly disobedient people you mentioned in your letter. We also ask that you accept this brownie as a token of our love.

Signed,
Mom

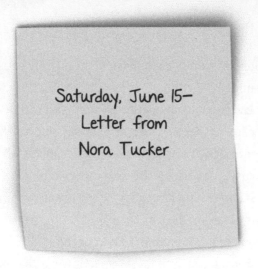

Saturday, June 15—
Letter from
Nora Tucker

Dear future Wolf Creek residents,

I need to talk with Mr. Langdon about civil disobedience on Monday. When you're teaching kids about cool people who break laws in the name of justice, it seems important not to leave out the fact that they got thrown in jail. You future people should know that there are penalties for civil disobedience, in case it still works that way when you read this.

No one bothered to share that information with me, so now I'm in dish-jail for two weeks. Actually, it wouldn't have mattered even if someone had told me ahead of time. I would have gone to Elidee's anyway.

I ate the brownie Mom left with her return petition, but I still think her decision was wrong. And I'm not sure I believe that it had nothing to do with Elidee or her brother.

Your friend from the past,
Nora Tucker

"my own Saturday
morning"
by Elidee Jones

**LEARNING FROM
JACQUELINE #6**

(Inspired by "saturday morning" in *Brown Girl
Dreaming* by Jacqueline Woodson)

Today in this new place there are strawberries.
Bigger and fatter than we grew
In the community garden back home,
Sweetest I've ever tasted.
Mama didn't have to work so we went out picking
With Mrs. G., who knew a place
Where you get a wagon ride back to the fields.
Old white man in a green baseball cap helped us up
Then climbed onto the tractor and we were off,
Bumping over a rutted dirt road
Past knee-high cornfields and trees with baby apples
Out to the strawberries.
Rows and rows and rows beyond rows.
College girl in cutoff blue jeans weighed our baskets
And sent us with a man darker than Mama and me
    put together.

He was from Jamaica, just like Grandmama's daddy,
But he comes here to work in summer and fall.

So he showed us where to pick and
I squatted down in the straw between the plants.
Started filling my basket but then I found one
So perfect and warm from the sun
I wanted to eat it right then.
I held it, scratchy seeds in my palm,
And caught Mama's eye.
She shook her head.
"Not until we pay for them."
But then someone said, "Nah, go right ahead."
Jean-shorts girl was grinning down at us.
"Grandpa Bob says everybody should enjoy a few while
    they pick.
It's part of the deal."
Mama smiled back at the girl and nodded
So I popped that strawberry into my mouth
Before she could change her mind.
It was so warm and sweet and full of sunshine
It almost made me cry,
And I thought just maybe
Grandpa Bob would be the sort of person
To loan you an egg if you needed one.
Maybe the Wolf Creek Mrs. G. talked about
Wasn't a total lie
After all.

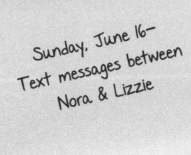

Sunday, June 16—
Text messages between
Nora & Lizzie

LIZZIE: You awake?

NORA: Kinda what's up

LIZZIE: I'm on my way over

NORA: Now? I thought we were meeting after church

LIZZIE: We were but it's crazy here so my mom just talked to your mom and she's bringing me now

NORA: Everything ok?

LIZZIE: Yeah

Really no

I'll talk to u when I get there

NORA: Ok see u soon

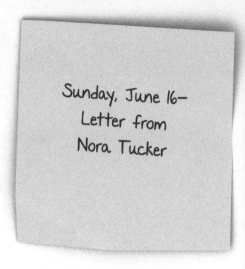

Dear future Wolf Creek residents,

Lizzie texted me awake early, and when I went downstairs, Dad was drinking coffee and talking with Mom at the kitchen table. For a second, I thought he came home because they finally caught those guys, but he didn't look happy enough for that. He smiled and hugged me, though, and said he's missed his girls. (I'm sure he missed Sean & Owen, too, but they weren't there.) He came by to give Mom a quick update before he goes back for more meetings.

I'll tell you this much. Dad is steamed about all the news reports talking about the prison. He says if you've never been in the yard with six hundred inmates and eight officers, knowing that you're only okay because the inmates *let* you be okay, then you can't really understand what working in a prison is like.

That might be true, but I still think it's important to have journalists to report on everything. I didn't tell Dad that. Instead, I told him about our relay plans and how we were going to practice baton handoffs today. He wasn't really listening, though, I could tell. Ever since those guys escaped, even when he's here (which is not very often), he's not really here. I'm pretty sure he didn't hear a word I said.

But at least now you future Wolf Creek residents know my plans for the day. I'm taking my peanut butter toast into the living room to watch TV.

Your friend from the past,

Nora Tucker

Sunday, June 16—
CNN morning news
report (This was all
on TV, but I printed
this from CNN.com)

It's day nine in the massive manhunt for two inmates who escaped from Wolf Creek Correctional Facility, and there are several new developments.

Yesterday's big lead in the case, a man running near the river, turned out to be a false alarm. However, searchers have returned to a wooded area not far from the prison today. They say last night, helicopters picked up an infrared image of what may have been someone in the trees.

Meanwhile, investigators continue to search for answers about how the escape happened. They say accused prison-break accomplice Priscilla Wadsworth is cooperating and will have another meeting with police investigators today. Her family members declined to comment on the situation.

Meanwhile, an investigative team from Albany is due at the prison this afternoon to conduct more internal interviews about just what happened in the days leading up to the escape.

Sunday, June 16—
Letter from
Nora Tucker

Dear future Wolf Creek residents,

I know I just wrote, but now I know why Lizzie's coming over.
CNN just showed video of her house when they said family
members didn't want to be interviewed. There are like twenty
reporters buzzing around the driveway.

I bet I know what Dad's whispering about, too. The state's
sending investigators to his prison today. You can learn a lot
watching CNN.

In other news, I'd like to apologize to whoever owns our
house in the future because the fireplace is probably still
covered in burned marshmallow drips. Owen had his not-a-
cookout birthday party last night, and Mom let them make
s'mores in the living room. Owen and Noah are out in his
tree fort now. (Mom is standing guard on the porch to make
sure no inmates show up.) They're casting spells with his

new wand, writing plots and plans, and eating all the leftover marshmallows. It's amazing what you can get away with when people feel bad that inmates ruined your birthday.

Speaking of inmates, there are two police cars parked on our road now. CNN says it's because police in helicopters might have seen something.

In the first days after the escape, everybody got excited every time there was a development. There'd be a reported sighting, and we'd all think, This is it! But it always turned out to be nothing. Two days ago, Bud Kalman over on Trudeau Road was sure he saw two men running through his field in the rain, so the police went screaming over there. They couldn't find anybody or even any sign anybody had been there. The only tracks in the muddy field were from Mr. Kalman's cows. You have to be pretty paranoid to mistake cows for inmates.

Uncle Tommy says the officers are starting to feel like they're chasing ghosts.

The police cars just left, heading toward the river. No lights or sirens, but they left pretty fast. Maybe somebody saw another ghost.

Your friend from the past,

Nora Tucker

OWEN AND NOAH'S
MASTER PLAN TO
DEFEND THE
BACKYARD FROM
BAD GUYS

Sunday, June 16—
From Owen's Master
Plans & Evil Plots
notebook

LIST OF SUPPLIES:

- Binoculars
- Catapult stuff
- Sticks
- Giant rubber bands (or
something else that's super stretchy)

- Rocks
- Cell phone
- Wand
- Brownies

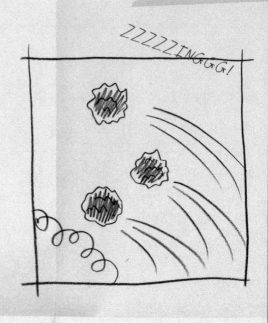

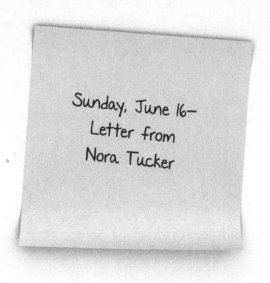

Dear future Wolf Creek residents,

I'm sneaking in this letter even though Lizzie and Elidee are here because we're just hanging out in the kitchen now, drinking lemonade. They came over so we could make our relay plan. I'm running the first leg of the race to give us a good head start. Lizzie's doing the second leg, and Elidee's our anchor (that's what you call the last person in a relay), so she'll do any catching up that needs to be done. She really is fast, which is going to be great for our cross-country team in the fall. I told her she needs to join.

Anyway, we practiced relay handoffs in the yard while Owen and Noah hung out in the tree fort. They built this weird, enormous slingshot with Mom's pantyhose and bungee cords and were flinging rocks around. I thought she'd be mad when she saw it, but she just laughed. Owen's milking this ruined birthday for all it's worth and was having a great day until a state trooper drove up and told us to go inside because the search was close to our house again.

I think all of Owen's birthday frustration came crashing down on him then, because he started crying and couldn't stop. Poor Noah didn't know what to do, so he just sat in our kitchen eating leftover marshmallows. Mom tried to distract Owen with Monopoly but he just kept saying "I hate this!" and crying harder.

Nothing helped until Elidee sat down next to him and handed him a napkin. He blew his nose on it. Then she told him that her mom always says helping somebody else is the best way to get over being upset yourself.

Owen made a face and said that was dumb. Mom told him that wasn't nice and to apologize to Elidee, but Elidee just laughed. What she said reminded me that Lizzie and I were going to make cookies today, so I told Owen he could help with that. He was happy for a second until Mom figured out that when the police said "stay inside," that meant nobody could go to the store for chocolate chips. So Owen started crying again.

But then Mom said, "Hold on!"

She's all excited now, but I have no idea why, so you're getting an in-the-moment play-by-play here . . .

She's riffling through the cupboards, taking stuff out: tomato paste . . . hot sauce . . .

She just got an onion out of the fridge.

Now she's poking around in the freezer.

She just thunked a bunch of frozen ground beef on the counter.

She's flipping through her recipe file. Index cards are flying everywhere . . . Wait . . . She's got one & is putting the rest back.

I have to go because she just told us all to go wash our hands so we can help with Operation Michigan. I have no clue what Operation Michigan is, but I doubt it's as exciting as Owen thinks. He's jumping up and down like he's about to go off on some great secret spy mission. I'll get back to you on this later.

Your friend from the past,

Nora Tucker

ELIDEE: Are you home yet?

MAMA: Yes need a ride?

ELIDEE: I don't think you can pick me up right now bc there's a roadblock here

MAMA: Ok just stay inside for now then

ELIDEE: Don't worry nora's mom is a safety freak

MAMA: You okay waiting a little while?

ELIDEE: Yeah

I'm going to help them make chili or something so maybe come in an hour if it's all clear by then?

MAMA: Sounds good

ELIDEE: Love you to Uranus & back

MAMA: Ewww

ELIDEE: Ha!

MAMA: I love you to Galaxy MACS0647-JD and back.

ELIDEE: I should never leave that book home with you.

MAMA: It's 13.3 billion light-years away

I AM THE CHAMPION

ELIDEE: See you in a while

MAMA: Ok have fun

Sunday, June 16—
This is a copy of
Great-Aunt Hilda's
Secret* Michigan
Sauce recipe

* Great-Aunt Hilda has been
dead for a long time, so
Mom says it's fine to share
now.

Recipe

Great-Aunt Hilda's Secret Michigan Sauce Recipe

(You can go ahead and double or triple this if you're cooking for an army. Just make sure the pot's big enough or it'll spatter all over your stovetop.)

2 pounds lean ground beef
24 ounces tomato sauce
2 teaspoons minced onion
1 tablespoon hot sauce
4 teaspoons chili powder
2 teaspoons cumin
2 teaspoons red pepper flakes
2 teaspoons black pepper

Heat up a pot on the stove, and once it's plenty hot, dump in the ground beef. Brown it just a little to get some flavor. DO NOT cook it all the way through because you don't want the meat getting all chunky on you.

Dump in the tomato sauce, onion (make sure it's minced up real small or it'll mess up the texture of your sauce), hot sauce, and spices, and stir it around real good. Then mash it all down with a potato masher, stir it again, turn the burner down to low, and let it simmer for a good hour or so. Remember to stir it every once in a while so it doesn't stick to the bottom of the pan.

Sunday, June 16—
Letter from Elidee to
her brother, Troy

Dear Troy,

Remember that time you were in sixth grade and I was in
preschool and Mama let us set up that lemonade stand outside
the youth center? And remember how Marcus and Rachel and
Brian came to help, and we were all squeezing lemons and
flicking seeds everywhere and laughing? Something happened
today that reminded me of that.

Mama dropped me off at that girl Nora's house after church
so we could practice for the relay race, only then we got sent
inside because the search was going on. Nora's little brother was
all upset, and I told him what Mama always says about helpful
hands making a happy heart (I didn't say it that way exactly
because that's corny, but he got the idea) and then they decided
to make Michigans. I thought Michigan was just a state, but
apparently, here it's a blinged-out chili dog—a hot dog covered
with a meat sauce that Nora's mom claims her great-aunt
invented. They have mustard and sometimes onions, and if you
ask for the onions buried, they get put on first and then covered
in meat sauce. We were locked in that house awhile, so I learned
a lot about Michigans.

We all helped. I opened the cans of tomatoes. Nora put a pan on the stove. Her mom dumped in the ground beef, added spices, and then sizzled the meat all around so it could brown. We took turns stirring, then dumped in the tomatoes and stirred some more, and it smelled pretty amazing—all sweet and meaty and spicy, like Grandmama's jollof rice.

They boiled a pile of hot dogs, and then we got an assembly line going. This is what reminded me of our lemonade stand. Lizzie held the rolls open. Nora used grabby tongs to put a hot dog in each one. I ladled the sauce. Owen and Noah took turns squirting mustard. We skipped the onions because Nora's mom said she'd be crying for a week if she chopped up fifty dogs' worth of onions, so folks would have to do with just mustard.

Nora's mom wrapped the Michigans in waxed paper and lined them up in a cardboard box to deliver to the police working out on the roadblocks.

I didn't really want to help with that part, which worked out fine because they had to wait until the search area was cleared to go outside anyway. As soon as it was, Mama came and picked me up, and they went off to deliver their Michigans. It wasn't too bad a day, though.

Love,
Elidee

PS I'd bring you a Michigan if I could. I tried one. Everybody here talks about them like they're the greatest thing ever, and they're no chopped cheese, but they're pretty good.

Sunday, June 16—
Letter from
Nora Tucker

Dear future Wolf Creek residents,

I'm back with details on Operation Michigan. We made a zillion Michigans, and as soon as we could go outside, we delivered them. Elidee had to go home, which stinks because she missed the best part.

I guess the police must still think the inmates are nearby, because they have officers stationed every thirty yards or so on our street tonight. At first, it felt weird driving up to these super serious guys with guns, asking if they wanted hot dogs, but then Owen rolled down his window and started shouting, "Michigans! Get your fresh, hot Michigans here!"

The first officer we met was from somewhere else and had no idea what a Michigan was. But the guy next to him was from here. He came running over and said, "It's a local thing. Trust me, buddy, you want one." So Lizzie handed them Michigans out the car window, and we drove on to the next guy, and the next, until we gave away every last one.

It was the best day since this whole escape started. Except when we got back, Mom reminded me that it was also the first day of my two-week sentence for civil disobedience, so I had to wash all the Michigan dishes.

Lizzie and Mom ended up helping, though. Sean got home and pitched in drying dishes. We put on music and all danced around and flicked soapsuds at one another. I said something about Elidee leaving before cleanup and missing out on a crucial part of her first-ever Michigan experience, and Mom said Elidee was kind to reach out and talk to Owen like that. She said Elidee was really articulate, and then Sean said, "Jeez, Mom. You don't have to sound so surprised." And then Mom got all flustered and said, "I'm not. She's just very well spoken and a nice kid. That's all I meant." Sean rolled his eyes.

I wanted Mom to say more. Like that she was sorry she wouldn't let me go over to Elidee's house. Or that it would be fine if I went another time.

But she didn't.

Your friend from the past,

Nora Tucker

PS I just went to Sean's room and asked why he was so bent out of shape about what Mom said, because being articulate is a good thing. I looked it up just to make sure, and the Google definition says it means "having or showing the ability to speak fluently and coherently." Sean asked if I'd ever heard Mom call any of my other friends articulate. I couldn't think of a time she had, even though Elidee pretty much talks like the rest of us. Sean says the fact Mom said that shows she didn't expect Elidee to be so smart or well spoken. So it's kind of like saying, "Hey, you speak really well for a black person," which is awful. I know Mom would never say something like that, but it bothers me that she might have even been thinking it.

To be honest, it also bothers me that I have to think about all this stuff now. It feels so complicated and overwhelming, and I'm getting tired of trying to understand and not say the wrong thing. I told Sean that. He said I should stop whining and suck it up because people like Elidee and her mom don't have the luxury of tuning this stuff out. They have to deal with it all the time no matter what, and I should try to imagine what that would be like.

I hope this doesn't make me a bad person, but I'm getting a little tired of Sean, too.

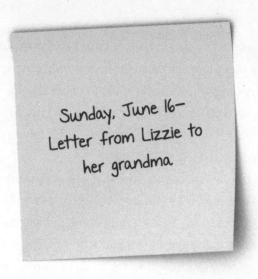

Sunday, June 16—
Letter from Lizzie to
her grandma

Dear Grandma,

I helped deliver Michigans to the searchers tonight. It was dark
out when we went, so I don't think any of them recognized me or
knew I was related to you. Lots of them aren't from here anyway.
It felt good to help out. Like maybe I was making up for what you
did, at least a little.

There were reporters and TV people all over our yard today.
They wanted to talk to Mom about what you did, like it's her fault
or something.

I saw you on the news again, too. The reporters were
pushing microphones at you, but you didn't say anything. I
wonder if you'll talk to us about all this when it's over, because I
still can't understand what you were thinking.

Lizzie

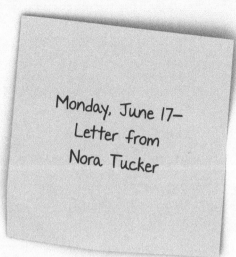

Monday, June 17—
Letter from
Nora Tucker

Dear future Wolf Creek residents,

Just so you know, I didn't forget to print the morning
announcements today. They don't have them during finals week.
Real school is over now, so all we have left are five days of exams
and picking up portfolios and stuff.

The police didn't get on our bus on the way to school today.
And when Mom got stopped at a roadblock after school, they all
seemed kind of bored. They're still opening trunks, but not like
they expect to find anything interesting.

After so many days of frantic searching and maybe-we-saw-
them reports and today-could-be-the-day feelings, it's quiet
now. Like maybe the inmates are just gone. Maybe they got away.

Is it awful that part of me hopes so? Part of me hopes they're
somewhere far from here, hiding in somebody else's woods.
Blending into some big city or celebrating on a beach or wherever.
I don't care as long as I don't have to keep worrying they're here.

Your friend from the past,
Nora Tucker

Tuesday, June 18—
Recorded on Lizzie's
WhisperFlash Z190 at a
roadblock on the way
home from school

STATE TROOPER: Afternoon, ma'am.

MY MOM: Hi there. Need me to open my trunk?

STATE TROOPER: No, you're all set. Have a good day.

LIZZIE'S REFLECTIONS: I'm not sure the police still believe in the inmates. They're like Bigfoot or the Loch Ness Monster—some weird, scary thing that people love to whisper about but nobody ever sees, so nobody knows for certain if they're out there or not.

I'm not even sure the officers are still searching. The state police said on the news tonight that the search is still going on, but it's "expanding in scope and might be less visible." I think that sounds like code for "We can't find them, so we're calling it a day."

The newspeople are starting to fade away, too. They only camped out in our driveway that one day. It kind of feels like everybody's decided to give it up and go on with their regular lives. Everybody except Nora's mom, anyway. She's still making Sean follow us in the car if we go running. We're going after school again tomorrow.

Wednesday, June 19—
Letter from Elidee to
her brother, Troy

Dear Troy,

They say they're reopening the prison for visitors soon. I should probably write you a letter I actually plan to give you now. We have to get you more Starbursts, too. I'll remind Mama to stop by the market. Or maybe I'll do it myself after I run today. I'm practicing for the carnival relay with Nora and Lizzie again after school. So that should be pretty cool.

Funny how now that I know you might get to read my letters, I don't have so much to say anymore.

Love,
Elidee

Wednesday, June 19—
Recorded on Lizzie's
WhisperFlash Z190 after
our run

ELIDEE: That was a sweet run!

NORA: I know, right?

LIZZIE: Wrong. M&M's are sweet. Ice cream is sweet. That run was miserable.

NORA: You did great, though! We're going to be an unbeatable relay team. Want to stop at the market to get a drink?

ELIDEE: Sure—I have to pick something up anyway.

LIZZIE: I'm in. I'm dying for a Gatorade.

(MARKET DOOR JINGLES)

LIZZIE: I hope they have the blue kind.

MARTHA: Backpacks behind the counter, ladies!

NORA: What?

MARTHA: Backpacks need to be left behind the counter. Store policy.

NORA: Since when?

MARTHA: Since always. There's a sign right on the door.

NORA: But you never have people do that.

MARTHA: I'm busy, girls. Do you want to follow the rule or do you want to leave?

NORA: I'm just asking why—

ELIDEE: Let it go, Nora.

NORA: But that's so dumb. We're just—

ELIDEE: Let's just leave them and get our drinks and go.

NORA: Okay . . .

MARTHA: Need anything at the deli?

NORA: No, we're just getting Gatorade.

MARTHA: Sounds like a plan. You can grab your bags on the way out.

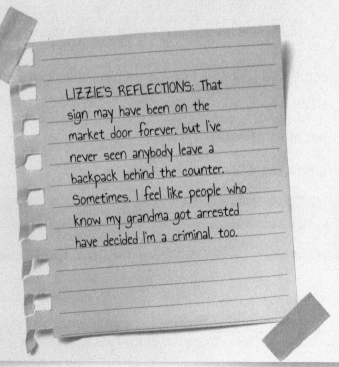

LIZZIE'S REFLECTIONS: That sign may have been on the market door forever, but I've never seen anybody leave a backpack behind the counter. Sometimes, I feel like people who know my grandma got arrested have decided I'm a criminal, too.

Wednesday, June 19—
Letter from
Nora Tucker

Dear future Wolf Creek residents,

This is another one of those letters I might not send you, but I need to talk about something that happened.

Back at the beginning of the school year, we read a story in English class. I don't remember the title, but the narrator was a black kid talking about how he and his friends got followed around in stores when they weren't doing anything wrong. I remember thinking that story wasn't realistic, because who would do that? Who would follow somebody around a store, thinking that they might steal things just because they're black? I sure didn't know anybody like that.

Only now I think maybe I do.

Lizzie and Elidee and I stopped at the market after we ran today. Martha told us to leave our backpacks at the counter. She was looking right at Elidee when she said it. When I asked where that rule came from, Martha said it was store policy and there was a sign saying so. That's true, but I've been in that store a thousand times and never left my backpack anywhere. I think she made us leave them because of Elidee. I know that's why. I'm pretty sure Elidee knew, too.

So we left our backpacks and got our drinks and then went home, and nobody said anything else about it. But now I feel like I missed a leadership moment. Like I should have said something else. I just don't know what. I don't want to talk to Sean about this because he works there and I'm afraid he'll get mad and say something like he did with Mom and then lose his job, and it'll be my fault.

Is Joe's Mountain Market still open when you're reading this? If it is, you should check the door to see if there's a sign about backpacks and find out if they really make everybody leave them at the counter, or if only certain kinds of people have to do that.

Your friend from the past,

Nora Tucker

Wednesday, June 19—
Letter from Elidee to
her brother, Troy

Dear Troy,

You know what? Sometimes I feel jealous of you because even
though you're in there, at least you're around some other people
who look like you. I know that's dumb. But I bet you don't have to
listen to some old MOOSE country station while you're working
out in the yard. Or maybe you do. The guards probably play it
just to mess with you.

Shoot. I was at the market today but forgot your Starbursts.
I was too busy putting my backpack behind the counter so
the white lady in charge could make sure I wasn't stealing her
Gatorade. You remember that old guy at the store on the corner
at home? The one who used to wander up and down the aisles
anytime we were in his store? She was just like that.

Anyway, sorry about your Starbursts. I'll remind Mama to
pick some up before we come to see you.

Love you,
Elidee

PS Here's another take on *Hamilton*'s "Cabinet Battle #1." I call this one "The Backpack Battle."

MARKET LADY:

May I call your attention to the sign on the door?

It's clear—no backpacks are allowed in my store.

You can leave 'em behind the counter over there.

NORA:

Hold on a second—how is that fair?

That sign's been on your door as long as I've been around.

I've never left my backpack, so I'm not backin' down.

ME:

Hold on . . . take it down . . .

See, I know a thing or two about choosing battles,

And, white girl, I can see you getting ten kinds of rattled.

So take it from your friend with the dark brown skin.

You're not gonna win this one living in this town, kid.

NORA:

But wait! Isn't that discrimination?

I'm gonna take a stand!

I read about this in my history class and—

MARKET LADY:

I don't appreciate that allegation.

You want your lemonade and Gatorade?

That's the price you're gonna pay.

Now take your drinks, be on your way.

One more thing—thanks for stopping by after school.

You're always welcome here if you follow my rules.

Thursday, June 20—
Recorded on Lizzie's
WhisperFlash Z190 after
our run

NORA: I really think we're ready for Saturday.

LIZZIE: You guys are, anyway.

ELIDEE: You kept up pretty good today.

NORA: I'm thirsty.

LIZZIE: Me too, but I don't feel like getting shaken down for my backpack.

NORA: We can leave them on the lawn outside. Nobody will take them.

ELIDEE: I have to get home. See you tomorrow.

NORA: Let's do one last practice run after school, okay?

LIZZIE: Noooooo . . .

ELIDEE: Sounds good!

(MARKET DOOR JINGLES OPEN)

MARTHA: You girls hear the news? Somebody spotted the inmates downstate!

LIZZIE: Really?

MARTHA: Yep. Officer came in for a ham sub half an hour ago and said somebody saw 'em by a railroad tunnel. Thinks they hopped a freight train in the middle of the night. Our boys are headed out now to help.

NORA: So they moved the search down there?

MARTHA: Yep. Let's see if I can get that county on my scanner app. Here we go . . .

SCANNER: (static) Captain says that's a negative.

MARTHA: Wouldn't it be great if they got 'em today? I got a good feeling.

SCANNER: Beep! Beep! Beeeeep! All units to Fordham Road and Route 28. Caller reports two men walking along railroad tracks behind her barn.

LIZZIE: Whoa!

NORA: It could be them!

SCANNER: Subjects are headed south along Fordham Road.

MARTHA: This might be it!

NORA: I wonder if it's on the news yet.

MARTHA: Tony! Turn on that TV!

CNN: Breaking news now on the New York prison break . . .

MARTHA: Look! They got choppers up there!

CNN: Police are investigating a possible sighting of the two escapees, and teams are arriving now to search. There are reports . . . wait . . . I'm being told that one of the helicopters now has a confirmed sighting of at least one of the inmates at this time.

MARTHA: Go get 'em, boys!

LIZZIE'S REFLECTIONS: Sounds like this might be it! I really hope so. It feels like Wolf Creek is stuck in time right now, like we're all in some bad TV science fiction movie and things can't move forward again until those guys get caught.

MOM: Where are you?

NORA: Market

MOM: Head home now please

NORA: Be there soon. We're listening to Martha's scanner bc there's stuff going on

MOM: NOW

NORA: Ok

Thursday, June 20—
Letter from Nora
Tucker

Dear future Wolf Creek residents,

I think the inmates are going to get caught tonight!! Police in another part of the state have them surrounded, and we've been watching the news all night. Helicopters keep flying around and the reporters say the police are closing in, only they haven't caught them yet and Mom says we have to turn off the TV because it's freaking Owen out. She says it'll probably all be over by morning.

I hope so.

You know what's kind of funny? It feels weird not having police sounds outside anymore. My window is open. All I hear are crickets. The inmates aren't here, and I'm so happy, I feel a little guilty. Some other kids in another town are closed up in their stuffy rooms tonight, while Uncle Tommy and the other officers stand guard on their road, staring into the woods. Waiting.

I hope nobody gets hurt.

Your friend from the past,

Nora Tucker

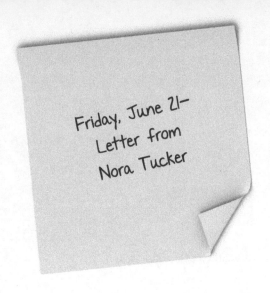

Friday, June 21—
Letter from
Nora Tucker

Dear future Wolf Creek residents,

It's official. Those inmates really are ghosts. They were surrounded downstate last night but didn't get caught. Now nobody knows where they are.

Some people are saying they were never surrounded at all. Some people say they were, but they got away. Nobody knows the real deal.

We only had ten-minute classes at school today to pick up report cards and turn in books. (I finally gave up my Alcatraz book now that I don't need it to keep my mind off worrying about inmates in our woods.) Our teachers spent the whole time we were at school poking at their phones, looking for news. There were three more reported sightings of the escapees downstate. Also one in Pennsylvania and one in Maine.

But no one's seen them around here, which means we get to have the carnival and relay race tomorrow! Elidee and Lizzie and I went for one last practice run—an easy one because you're mostly supposed to rest the day before a race. Elidee had to go home right after we ran, but Lizzie and I stopped at the market for drinks, just the two of us. Nobody asked us to leave our backpacks anywhere. I wanted to ask Martha why not, but she was busy with a Pepsi delivery guy, and it felt awkward to wait around to ask that. Maybe I'll talk to her about it next time.

We're all meeting at the carnival at ten tomorrow morning. Sean's taking us because Dad is working and Mom has a hair appointment she's had to cancel three times because of manhunt-related roadblocks, and she says she'll have to run away and live in the woods, too, if she doesn't get it trimmed soon. I invited Lizzie and Elidee over for pancakes before the race, but Lizzie wants to sleep in, and Elidee is going to the prison. She says they finally reopened it to visitors, so she and her mom are going to see her brother. That's weird to think about—her being inside the wall and then coming to run with us. I wonder if she'll tell Troy about her race and Lizzie and me. That's even weirder to think about.

I'll write a news story for you after the race tomorrow so you'll know how we did, even though you'll probably have read all about our famous victory in your history books (ha-ha!).

Your friend from the past,

Nora Tucker

Friday, June 21—
Letter from Elidee to
her brother, Troy

Dear Troy,

I've been writing you letters this whole time that we haven't been
able to see you, but most of that news is pretty old now, so I'm
just going to bring you this new one when we come tomorrow.

Today was our last day of school. It went pretty well for me,
even though it was tough starting classes so close to the end of
the year. There's only one other black kid in our grade (maybe in
the whole school—I keep looking but haven't seen anybody else),
but I haven't talked to him because every time I've seen him, he's
hanging around with these two boys who are jerks. I did meet a
couple of girls who are okay, Nora and Lizzie. I'm running with
them in a relay race right after we visit you. It's part of the town's
firefighters' carnival. I wish you could be there to see me run. I'll
try to get some pictures to show you.

Mama's been praying for you every night, and I always think
about you, too. I hope you're doing okay, taking care of yourself
and keeping out of trouble, and I hope you'll take all the classes
you can whenever they start up again. Thirteen more years may
sound like a long time, but you'll still have a future waiting for

you if you do things right. You need to make that choice, okay? Because I miss you almost as much as Mama does.

Love you,
Elidee

PS You should be getting your Starbursts soon. Mama got you those and some nuts and stuff. She followed all the package rules really close, but if you don't get them, that means they got taken away and we'll have to try again.

45TH ANNUAL
WOLF CREEK
FIREFIGHTERS'

CARNIVAL

SATURDAY, JUNE 22

ADMISSION ★ $3—ADULTS ★ $1—STUDENTS & SENIORS ★ **FREE**—KIDS UNDER 5

SCHEDULE:

10 A.M.–10 P.M. Games & food booths open

10 A.M.–12 P.M. Wolf Den craft area open

10 A.M. Water Ball Fight Round 1

11 A.M. Carnival Relay!

1 P.M. Children's bike parade

2 P.M. Water Ball Fight Round 2

3 P.M. Giant Slip 'N Slide on the soccer field

4 P.M. Water Ball Fight Finals

5 P.M.–7 P.M. Chicken Barbecue to benefit the Wolf Creek Lions Club

8 P.M. Annie and the Shenanigals perform in the band shell

9:30 P.M. Fireworks over the soccer field

Dear future Wolf Creek residents,

We're in the car on the way to the carnival, and I am SO excited!
I brought my notebook to write down our race times. It turns
out only two teams ended up registering for the relay—us and
Walker, Cole, and Josh. We're going to obliterate them.

After the race, we're getting pizza from Mama Maria's food
truck for lunch, and then Owen and Noah are doing the kids' bike
parade. They're connecting their two bikes to make them look
like the Batmobile. After that, we're going to watch the water
ball finals and then Mom's meeting us for the chicken barbecue
and our neighbor's band (they're terrible) and fireworks. Dad said
he's hoping to come over after he's done at work, too, but Mom
said don't count on it so I'm not. I guess even though the escaped
inmates are far away, Dad still has a ton of work to do. I'm just
glad they're not around here anymore. This is the first day that's
felt like a normal, awesome Wolf Creek summer.

I hope you still have the firefighters' carnival in the future
because if not, you're seriously missing out.

Your friend from the past,

Nora Tucker

NORA: You're still gonna interview us before the race, right?

LIZZIE: Yes, I'm recording now. Are you guys ready?

NORA: Yep.

ELIDEE: Sure thing.

LIZZIE: What do you think about the race?

NORA: Lizzie, you need to be more reportery! Do a cool introduction so it sounds official . . .

LIZZIE: Okay then . . .

Breaking news! Archenemy runners join forces at annual carnival!

In an unprecedented move, two speedy and fierce rivals will combine their efforts on a Wolf Creek carnival relay team this morning. Sources say Nora "I'm So Fast My Shadow Can't Keep Up" Tucker will run the first leg of the race, while Elidee "Gone Before You See Me Coming" Jones will be the team's anchor. Lizzie "I'm Only Here Because They Made Me" Bruno will run the middle segment.

NORA: Lizzie! Come on . . . We should have a more serious report on this for the time capsule.

ELIDEE: I thought that was pretty funny.

LIZZIE: Thanks! I like to do comedy stuff. I just haven't in a while, I guess. But okay . . . Sorry, Nora. Here we go . . .

Good morning! I'm here with carnival relay athletes Nora Tucker and Elidee Jones, who are preparing for the big race. How are you feeling, ladies?

ELIDEE: Pretty good.

NORA: Excellent! We've been training hard, we're in great shape, and we're going to kick some boy-runner butt.

LIZZIE: What's your strategy for the race?

NORA: I'm going to start out and get us a nice lead, hopefully. You're going to run the second leg, Lizzie, as you know.

LIZZIE: I'll try not to die halfway through.

ELIDEE: And I'm going to wrap things up. Straight to the finish so we can win this thing!

LIZZIE: Great! I see that the water ball fights are about to start. Let's go over there and check in.

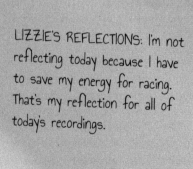

LIZZIE'S REFLECTIONS: I'm not reflecting today because I have to save my energy for racing. That's my reflection for all of today's recordings.

Saturday, June 22—
Recorded on Lizzie's
WhisperFlash Z190 at
the water ball fight

LIZZIE: All right, people, you are in for a treat! We're at the annual Wolf Creek Firefighters' Carnival, where the sweet scent of fried dough is already making me drool and the water ball tournament is about to get under way. I'm told that the competition is fierce this year!

NORA: You're really getting into it now, Lizzie! This is going to be so great for the time capsule.

LIZZIE: It's kinda fun. All right now . . . The teams are lined up and ready to go. The famous Wolf Creek Rainbow Beach ball lies between them, ready for action. And I see that fire chief Paula Labray is about ready to begin the competition. Let's listen in . . .

MRS. LABRAY: Remember our rules, ladies and gentlemen. Your water pressure is to be ninety pounds, and your nozzle man or nozzle woman cannot cross the white line spray-painted on the grass. When I raise my arm, you'll turn on the water and begin with streams crossed over the beach ball. When I lower my arm, you may lower your stream and begin. Ready?

LIZZIE: It's a tense moment, ladies and gentlemen. The teams have both turned on the water. The streams are crossed, waiting for the official signal . . . and . . . there! The competition is on!

LITTLE KID IN CROWD: Come on, Uncle Ronnie! Don't give 'em an inch!

ELIDEE: What exactly is the point of this?

NORA: Each team has to try and spray the ball over the other team's line. It's like a training thing, to help their aim.

LIZZIE: Let's get back to the action here. We had a little movement early on. It looks like the blue team connected first and got the ball moving toward the reds just a bit, but red has come back strong. They've gained a few feet, but no . . . wait! They lost the connection, and it's blue! Blue is gaining ground . . . Just a few feet left to cross the line now and . . . Yes! Ladies and gentlemen . . . let's hear it for the blue team! Your round one water ball champs!

LIZZIE: All right, ladies and gentlemen, it's just about race time, so I'm going to step back as your master of ceremonies. I'll keep the recorder running so you don't miss any of the action. I see that Mr. Simmons has his bullhorn out— he really, *really* loves his bullhorn . . .

MR. SIMMONS: Attention, Wolf Creek runners. Our carnival relay is about to begin. Please report to the starting line immediately . . .

Let's go over the route. Your first runner will begin at the starting line, run across the field and through this small stretch of trees along the school nature trail. Then you'll come out of the woods to Madison Street, run over the bridge and up Spruce Street. You'll turn right onto Main Street, run past the prison, and turn right again to return to school. At that point, you'll enter the drop-off circle, where your second runner will be waiting, and that's where you'll pass the baton. That second runner will take off into the woods and complete the same loop before passing it off to your third runner, who has an extra tenth of a mile to run. He or she will run the same loop but then continue across the soccer field to the finish line. Are there any questions?

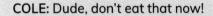

COLE: Dude, don't eat that now!

WALKER: But I'm hungry.

COLE: We're about to run, and you're scarfing down sausage from the Mr. Piggy Truck?

WALKER: I'm second. I'll be fine by then.

MR. SIMMONS: Does anyone have questions?

WALKER: Do we water-balloon you right after the race or later?

MR. SIMMONS: We have the winner's prize scheduled for right after the race. All right, let's get organized. Once you have your numbers on, see me to pick up a baton, and head to your spots for the relay. We want to start right at eleven, so you need to be ready when the gun goes off. Now . . . uh . . . who has the starting gun?

MR. PORTER: We've been asked not to use that, remember?

MR. SIMMONS: Right. Never mind. Also . . . I should mention that you'll see police officers along your entire relay route today, and that is nothing more than a precaution. There's no reason to believe we'll have any problems, but you will see officers, particularly in the wooded area. Are we all set?

NORA: Lizzie, you're not running with that recorder thing, are you?

LIZZIE: It's okay—it fits in the pocket of my shorts. Look!

NORA: It's gonna fall out and break. Besides, all you'll get is breathing.

LIZZIE: Good point. I'll turn it off when you start and leave it here.

NORA: We better get to our spots. Ohmygosh, my hands are all sweaty already.

COLE: Ready to eat our dust?

ELIDEE: Not planning on it.

COLE: Ohhh . . . look who's getting all mouthy.

WALKER: We're gonna waste you guys.

NORA: Fat chance, sausage breath.

COLE: Oh, burn!!

NORA: Good luck, Lizzie! Good luck, Elidee!

ELIDEE: You too! We got this.

LIZZIE: Yep. Let's do it.

MR. SIMMONS: Runners . . . on your marks . . . Get set . . . Go!!

Saturday, June 22—
Text messages between
Nora & Sean, 11:35 a.m.

SEAN: You ok?

NORA: Yes

SEAN: Where r u?

NORA: Library

Where r u? Do you have Owen??

SEAN: Yeah

I got Noah too

They put us in the gym

NORA: How's Owen?

SEAN: Terrified

NORA: I'd come but they won't let us leave

SEAN: Wait there when they give the all clear and I'll find you ok?

NORA: Ok

I hope it's soon

Mom's gonna freak out

SEAN: I'll text her so she knows we're ok

Saturday, June 22—
Text messages between
Nora & Lizzie,
11:38 a.m.

NORA: Where r u?

LIZZIE: Gym where r u?

NORA: Library

I wish u were here

LIZZIE: Me too

NORA: I'm scared

LIZZIE: Me too

Saturday, June 22—
Text messages between
Elidee & her mom

ELIDEE: Hey mama you busy?

MAMA: Yes but what's up?

ELIDEE: I'm at school & we got a lockdown thing because they're searching the woods

Just want you to know I'm safe

MAMA: Are you with nora and lizzie?

ELIDEE: They're here somewhere but I don't see them

It's ok

I'll get a ride whenever it's over

MAMA: My shift goes until 5 but I'll call nora's mother when I get a break

ELIDEE: Thanks

MAMA: Love you to the moon and back

ELIDEE: I can't remember any of the new galaxies I read about but I love you too

MAMA: Be safe

SEAN: Hey just so you know we're ok

MOM: ??

SEAN: Possible inmate sighting near the carnival so we're on lockdown in the school

MOM: You're safe?

SEAN: We're safe

MOM: I'll be right there.

SEAN: I don't think you can get us yet bc they're not letting anybody leave

MOM: Are you all together?

SEAN: Owen's with me in the gym and Nora's in the library

NORA: Hi mom

MOM: Hi. You're ok?

NORA: Yeah

MOM: How's Owen?

SEAN: Scared

NORA: Does anybody around u have paper or a notebook?

SEAN: Some people had backpacks so they've got stuff. Why?

NORA: See if you can borrow paper and a pencil and tell owen to do one of his evil plots

SEAN: Now?

NORA: It'll help

SEAN: Ok I'll ask him

MOM: I'm on my way

SEAN: You'll probably get a roadblock

MOM: I know, see you soon

I love you

SEAN: Love you too

NORA: Me too

Dear future Wolf Creek residents,

My hands are shaking and my heart won't slow down, and I'm writing to you because I have to do something besides listen to police scanners and helicopters outside and people crying here in the library.

I'm going to go back to when the race started and write everything that happened. I'm going to write every tiny detail, like Ms. Morin told us to do in our personal narratives, with dialogue and everything, so it'll take a really long time and by the time I write my way back to now, hopefully everything will be okay.

So . . .

Cole and Walker were trash-talking us and by the time the race started, I was so ready to waste them. There was no starting gun because the police thought it might scare people, so Mr. Simmons just shouted, "Go!" and we took off. The grass was all

OMG, somebody's banging on the library door and even Mr. Simmons looks freaked out. He's on his phone . . . Okay, he just opened the door and it's two state troopers. They're standing there with their hands on their guns like they expect the inmates to come busting in here any second. I want to go home so bad right now. I want to go to the gym, where Sean and Owen and Lizzie are. I want to get away from here. How could the inmates be back?

Okay . . . I was going to talk about the grass. It was wet from the water ball fight, so it was hard to dig in. I was wishing I'd brought spikes, but it was okay because nobody else thought of that either.

Josh started out ahead of me, but he almost wiped out in the mud, so I caught up halfway across the field and we were even for a while. Everybody was shouting all at once, but I could hear Lizzie screaming, "Come on, Nora!" and Elidee: "Get on out ahead of him! You go, girl!"

I'm going to draw the course for the race here, so you have a better idea what I'm talking about.

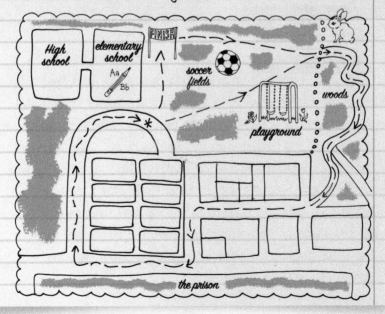

Okay. Now, do you see where the nature trail starts? That path is super narrow and I knew whoever got there first would stay in the lead through the woods, so I blasted ahead of Josh and darted into the trees.

I could still hear Lizzie cheering from the drop-off circle: "Let's go, Nora!"

Sean, too: "Head up, Nora! Eyes ahead! Run your race!"

And Elidee: "Come on, Nora! You got this!"

I tried to run even faster for them.

They told us there would be police in the woods, and I don't know if I forgot or what, but when I took a curve and saw a trooper there in the trees, it surprised me so much I tripped on a root and went flying. But I caught myself, and the trooper guy called, "Nice save there, runner!"

And then more voices came booming out of the trees:

"Way to go!"

"Great job!"

"Stay strong!"

The police were cheering for me. Cheering for everybody, I guess, but I pretended it was all for me, and I think that made me faster because by the time I got out of the woods, I couldn't even hear Josh breathing behind me anymore. I snuck a peek over my shoulder even though you're not supposed to do that, and I saw that he'd fallen back a little.

I didn't look back again. I pretended Josh wasn't even there. I tipped my chin up and pumped my legs and thudded over the old bridge across the river. I raced down the street and pretended the state troopers lining the road were just race fans like everybody else, only with guns.

I focused on getting around the loop to Lizzie so she could take the baton and stay ahead, and even if she didn't, she'd keep up enough for Elidee to run us home.

I focused on my breathing and the pounding of my running shoes on the asphalt, and then I turned onto Main Street and felt the cool shadow of the prison wall. I didn't look up at the guard tower. I didn't think about Dad working inside or Elidee's brother or the other inmates or anything. I kept running until I was back in the sun.

Sweat dripped into my eyes as I turned the corner. I swept it away and saw Lizzie waiting way down the block, jumping up and down in her orange shorts and yellow T-shirt, and when I got closer I heard her screaming, "Come on, Nora!" And then she started to run.

I didn't slow down. I raced beside her and planted the baton in her hand. I held on and kept running until I felt her tug it away. Finally, when I knew she had it, I let myself slow down. I stopped and bent over with my hands on my knees so I could breathe. People were still shouting, but my heart in my ears was louder.

I stared down at the pavement and sucked in big gulps of hot air until I felt a hand on my back and looked up. It was Elidee.

"You wasted him!" she said.

"Lizzie . . ." I still hadn't caught my breath. "Lizzie had a good lead to start?"

Elidee nodded. "At least ten or fifteen yards."

That was good, but I knew it might not be enough because Walker was fast. "You ready to make up time if you need to?"

Elidee looked over at Cole, who was shaking his hands and

bouncing on his feet, looking all cocky. Then she looked back at me. "I am so ready."

She took a deep breath, and I got out of the way because I knew it wouldn't be long before somebody turned the corner and came sprinting at us. I so wanted it to be Lizzie.

But it was Walker.

"Shoot," Elidee whispered. Then she said, "That's okay. Here she comes . . . We still got this."

Lizzie had turned the corner about half a block behind Walker, coming faster than I'd ever seen her run. Walker was out straight, though, and pulling ahead.

Elidee and I screamed, "Come on, Lizzie! Come on!"

Cole stepped in front of me and shouted, "You got her, Walker!" He held out his hand for the baton, but I kept shouting, "Go, Lizzie!" right in Cole's ear. I didn't stop until he grabbed the baton and took off toward the nature trail.

Elidee stepped up, hand stretched out behind her. Her fingers twitched, and when Lizzie got closer, she started to run.

"Great job, Lizzie! Finish strong!" I shouted her in until Elidee's hand closed around the baton and she took off, and then I yelled, "Go, Elidee! You can do this!"

She was hauling. I cheered after her until she disappeared into the trees, and then all I could do was hope.

Lizzie collapsed in a heap on the grass, and you're not supposed to do that after you run, so I tapped her on the shoulder. "You did great, but you gotta get up." I tugged her hand. "Come on . . . I'll walk you around to cool down."

I pulled Lizzie up and walked her around the circle while we waited for the runners to loop around. Pretty soon it would be over and we'd know if we won and got to water-balloon Mr. Simmons, but you know what's weird? I didn't really care about being the first Tucker to water-balloon him anymore. I just wanted to win. I wanted Lizzie to be happy. I wanted Elidee to beat Cole. And win. I wanted that more with every second that ticked by on my watch.

When they'd been out four minutes, Lizzie had finally caught her breath and found her recorder. We picked up our backpacks and were about to head for the finish line, but we remembered that the last runner had to do one more lap around the field, so if we waited in the drop-off circle, we'd be able to cheer for her there and then race to the end to see the finish.

"Here they come!" Lizzie pointed, and I whirled around to look down the street. Elidee and Cole had just turned the corner— tiny figures, way down the block. They were racing side by side, sprinting all out as if everything in the world depended on who got to that finish line first.

It was going to be close.

Saturday, June 22—
Letter from Elidee to
her brother, Troy

Dear Troy,

This is another one of those letters I'm not sending you, but I'm writing anyway because I'm locked in the school library since they all of a sudden think those two inmates might be in the woods we just ran through on our relay race. The course went right through the nature trail, and there were cops behind every tree. You'd think that'd be scary as heck, running down a chute full of police, but it was okay. They cheered when I ran through. "Way to go!" and "Great pace, runner! Keep it up!" Loud, too. Like they meant it.

We won the race. Me and Nora and Lizzie. There only ended up being two teams but the other one was made up of those jerk boys, and we didn't know if we'd be able to keep up, but we did. I had some ground to make up in the last leg, and I almost lost it slipping in the grass at the end, but I kicked hard and blew past that boy so fast he didn't even know what went down. It was pretty sweet. I wish Mama could have seen it but she's at work today. Wish you could've been there, too.

I don't know what's going down outside now, but none of it sounds good. I'm going to write some lines so I don't have to keep listening and wondering. In that *Hamilton* musical I saw there was a song called "Ten Duel Commandments," and races are kind of like duels, so . . .
Love you,
Elidee

The Ten Race Commandments

One, two, three, four, five,
Six, seven, eight, nine!
We're counting down
the ten race commandments!

NUMBER TEN!
Find yourself a team—
a couple other athletes who can run like a dream.

NUMBER NINE!
Figure out your spots.
Save your fastest for the anchor
If you wanna have a shot.

NUMBER EIGHT!
The day before the race if you wanna be a winner
You gotta start hydratin' and eat a solid dinner,
Then get yourself to bed and start countin' sheep.
You ain't gonna own the course without a good night's sleep.

NUMBER SEVEN!
Wake up before dawn,
Practice once more handin' off that baton.

NUMBER SIX!
When the sun creeps up and starts shinin'
Head on over to the start so you can sign in.

NUMBER FIVE!
Get your spikes inspected.
Listen to directions,
Where you'll hit a straightaway and where you gotta
   turn.
Don't give anything away! Push it hard! Feel the burn!

NUMBER FOUR!
Hold fast to that baton till it's really time to swap it.
You're out of the race if anybody drops it.

NUMBER THREE!
Ain't no room on this course for attitude.
You start throwin' elbows and you're gonna get DQ'd.
You gotta keep it cool when the competition's crass.
Don't get yourself distracted by some losers talking
   trash.
Keep your eye on the prize cause it's all a head game.
Just focus on that finish line and take deadly aim.

NUMBER TWO!
The whole thing ends right here in the park.
So keep to your lane,
No pain (no pain)
No gain (no gain)
Runners . . . take your marks.

NUMBER ONE!

Set . . .

Is there gonna be a gun?

No.

We opted not to take any chances.
People might be scared under the circumstances.

Oh.

Ready then? Go!

PS I'm done & they still have us locked in here. At
least I have my phone. Wish you had one so I could
talk to you.

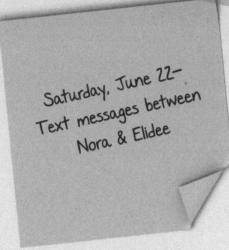

Saturday, June 22—
Text messages between
Nora & Elidee

ELIDEE: Hey

NORA: Hey

You okay?

ELIDEE: Yeah

This is going on forever

NORA: Where r u?

ELIDEE: Library

NORA: Where?

ELIDEE: By the computers

NORA: I'm on the floor by the new books display

ELIDEE: I'll come find you

NORA: They said not to move around

ELIDEE: I'll be stealthy

It may take a while

NORA: I'll be here

Thanks

Anyway . . .

Lizzie and I screamed down the street at Elidee with every bit of voice we had left. Cole's friends had all gone to the finish line, so we were the only ones left.

"You can do this, Elidee!" I shouted when she was close enough to hear. "You're stronger than he is! Come on!!"

I don't know if Elidee heard me, but Cole did. His face was already clenched up from running so hard, but his eyes locked on me and he ran even harder.

So did Elidee.

They were even when they turned into the circle. They flew past Lizzie and me and started down the edge of the field.

"Lizzie, come on! We have to book if we want to see the end!" I grabbed my backpack, cut across the field, and ran for the finish line like I was racing, too. We made it just as Elidee and Cole turned into the final stretch.

"Get her, Cole!" Walker shouted. His face was all red. "Come on, man! Don't let a girl beat you!"

"Come on, Elidee! You can do this!" I screamed.

Right then, Elidee's running shoe slid on the wet grass. She didn't fall, but it was enough to break her stride, and Cole pulled ahead.

"Yeah!" Josh shouted and pumped his fist. "Yeah, man! You got this!"

For a second, it looked like he did.

But Elidee had one last kick left. She blew past Cole and crossed the finish line first.

Cole didn't stop to shake hands or anything. He turned and walked toward the woods. You could tell he was too mad to even look at anybody. Walker followed him.

I didn't care where they went to cry, because Elidee won. We all did.

"Yes!" I screamed.

And that's when tires screeched out by the road. Sirens started wailing, and all at once, four police cars peeled out of the school parking lot and raced over the bridge toward town.

"What's going on?" I asked Mr. Simmons because he was right there at the finish line, holding the Carnival relay trophy. But he looked surprised and confused, too.

Our nature-trail state troopers all came running out of the woods with their hands on their guns, and Mr. Simmons waved one of them over. "Is everything all right?" he asked. "Should we—do we need to get people inside?"

The trooper pulled a radio from his belt and talked into it. "School administration is asking if a shelter in place is necessary at this time. What should I advise?"

He waited. We all did. The sirens got quieter.

Then the radio squawked, "Not at this time. Over."

I let out my breath. I didn't even know I'd been holding it.

"You're fine," the trooper told Mr. Simmons. "We had a report—unconfirmed—of a hunting camp broken into recently with guns and ammunition missing. But that's five miles east of here, so you can stand by for now."

"All right. Thank you, officer." Mr. Simmons turned in a circle. Everybody had gathered around him, and he looked like he didn't know quite what to do now. "So . . . ah . . . if we could all stay nearby for now, that would be great. Once we know that all is well, we'll go ahead with the . . . ah . . . what's next? The bike parade." He gave a kind of weak smile. "And of course, I have a date with some water balloons as well."

Mr. Simmons stepped away to make a phone call, and Elidee walked up to Lizzie and me.

"Hey," she said.

"Hey? That's all you have to say after the most amazing race in the history of races?" I gave her a fist bump.

"That was awesome," Lizzie said.

Elidee smiled. "It was pretty fun at the end there."

"You obliterated him. I hope somebody was videotaping because—"

"May I have your attention, please?" Mr. Simmons had found his bullhorn. "State police are requesting that we evacuate school grounds at this time. There is not a current threat. However, they've requested that everyone go home in order to facilitate the investigation. We'll open up the school building for those of you who need to call and wait for rides. In the meantime, please stay nearby."

Josh walked up to Mr. Simmons. "I gotta find Cole and Walker, okay? I'm getting a ride with Cole's dad."

"Where are they?" asked Mr. Simmons.

"Down the nature trail."

"Fine. Run up and holler for them to come back, please. We need everyone to start heading home."

But before Josh could run anywhere, Cole and Walker came busting out of the trees. I couldn't believe they had anything left after the way we beat them, but they were running even faster than they had been in the race.

"Inmates!" Cole shouted in between gulps of air. He kept running toward us, flailing one arm back at the trees. "They're . . ." He bent over coughing.

Mr. Simmons ran up to him, pulled him up to stand, and said, "What?"

"They're in there! In the woods!" Cole spit out a mouth full of whatever he'd coughed up. "It was them! They had on green prison pants and everything. We saw them!" He looked at Walker.

Walker nodded. His eyes were huge. "They saw us, too."

Then everything got chaotic and awful. People ran and pushed, and we got herded into the school. I got separated from Lizzie and Elidee, and I couldn't find Sean or Owen or anybody, so I just kept moving. The water I drank after the race was churning around in my stomach while I got shoved down the hall and hurried into the library to sit down in a corner with my sweaty backpack pressed against a bookshelf. I took it off and pulled out my notebook.

And now I'm back to the now. Writing to you. The helicopters are still circling.

We have to wait here until the area is secure. Until police are sure we can leave without inmates coming after us in the parking lot.

It was supposed to be over by the time I finished telling you this story, but it's not.

Elidee's in the library somewhere, too. She texted and was going to come find me, but she hasn't yet. I hope she's still trying. I hope she doesn't get in trouble.

It's weird. With everything that just happened—the race and the shouting and confusion and pushing—the one thing I can't stop thinking about is Walker's face. Every bit of his cockiness was gone. He looked pale and sweaty and terrified.

Like he'd just seen a ghost.

I guess he did in a way. After all those days. They're still here.

Outside our school.

Hiding.

Waiting.

And now that I'm done telling the story so far, I'm really scared again.

Your friend from the past,
Nora Tucker

Saturday, June 22—
Notebook conversation
between Nora & Elidee

(We weren't allowed to talk
in the library, so we wrote
back and forth. I labeled
everything with N or E so
you know who wrote what.)

N: I'm not talking b/c we'll get yelled at if we're not quiet but
I'm so glad you found me.

E: I had to wait until Mr. Simmons got on the phone
again to crawl over.

N: I can't believe this.

E: They were _in there_ when we ran through the woods.
They probably saw us.

N: I know. I was thinking that too. But it's making me more scared. Can we talk about something else?

E: Yeah. The race was cool except for the whole thing at the end, wasn't it?

N: SO great. Josh kept trying to pass me, but I'd speed up and he was getting so mad.

E: I could tell. I thought his face was going to explode.

N: That would have been fun.

E: Also kind of gross.

N: Ha! Did you get to go see your brother today?

E: Yeah but only for 15 minutes. It was good though.

N: Is he doing okay? It must be weird in there with everything going on.

E: He's ok. I guess the lockdown was pretty awful. The inmates weren't allowed to leave their cells at all. It was a whole week before they were even allowed out to take a shower. It's like they all got punished for what those two guys did. But that's all Troy said about the escape. He doesn't like to talk about what happens inside. Mostly now, Mama just asks what he wants us to send him.

N: Like what?

E: Food. Mixed nuts and snack stuff like that. He always wants Starbursts. When we were little, we used to trade colors so he got all the reds and I got all the oranges.

N: That makes me think of the photo I saw at your house. He looked really nice in that picture.

E: He is. He was anyway. It's hard to know who he is now. That picture's from right when he started hanging out with these guys, Will and J. P.

N: It's just that it's hard to see him in that picture and imagine him doing something to get into prison.

E: Troy was small. People used to mess with him on the way to school until he got to be friends with those two. They looked out for him. Only then they started making him do stuff. Stupid stuff at first, like stealing beef jerky from the bodega or whatever. But then it got bigger and worse and they said if he didn't do what they wanted, they'd hurt him.

N: That's awful. God, I'm so sorry, Elidee.

E: Yeah. They said they'd hurt us, too. Mama and me. So you know . . . He did stuff.

N: When will he get out?

E: 13 more years.

N: Wow—we'll be 25 then.

E: Finished with college and everything.

N: You thought about what you want to go to school for?

E: Maybe law. Maybe something with science. I'm not sure yet. But I've been thinking about stuff lately. I have some plans.

MOM: I'm here. Are you allowed to leave?

SEAN: They're just starting to let people sign out now

NORA: Finally! did they catch the inmates?

SEAN: Nope

Heard they cleared the woods but didn't find them

NORA: Oh

MOM: I'm picking up Lizzie and Elidee too. Are they with you?

SEAN: I've got Lizzie

NORA: Elidee's with me in the library

SEAN: Wait there and I'll come get you after I sign out from the gym ok?

NORA: Ok

SEAN: Also Owen's been drawing for like an hour so thx for the suggestion

NORA: Cool glad he's ok

SEAN: See you in a few

OWEN AND NOAH'S
SUPER SMART
GOOD-GUY PLAN
FOR CATCHING
THE BAD GUYS
OUTSIDE THE
SCHOOL

Saturday, June 22—
Owen and Noah's
master plan of the day

The Problem, Part I:
Bad guys are hiding
in the woods outside.

The Problem,
Part II: We
are locked
inside.

THE SOLUTION:

Step 1: Everybody gets all the balls and weights and other heavy things in a big pile.

Step 2: Cut the cargo net down from the gym ceiling.

Step 3: Open gym window above bleachers and push cargo net out window. Hold on to ends of net really tight so it doesn't just fall out the window.

Step 4: Fill cargo net with balls and very heavy things. Keep holding on to ends really tight. Bring more people to help hold if needed.

Step 5: Wait until dark.

Step 6: Watch for inmates to come out of the woods and go past the school. (They will do this because they will want to steal a car from the parking lot, and they will have to walk by the gym windows to get there.)

Step 7: When inmates are underneath gym window, let go of ends of net!

Victory!

THE END

Good evening. The search is back on tonight in the mountain town where two inmates escaped from a maximum security prison two weeks ago.

Earlier this week, a reported sighting downstate sent search teams south, where police believed at one point that they had the inmates surrounded. But that lead turned out to be a dead end, and while the hunt continued, police began to wonder if they were searching in the wrong place. Their answer came today, with a new hunting camp break-in not far from the prison and then a sighting of the inmates within yards of a local carnival packed with schoolchildren.

Police say everyone got to safety. School grounds were evacuated and cleared, but there are no solid answers tonight. Police made a complete sweep of the woods where the inmates were spotted, but despite the soft ground and mud, there were no tracks or signs that anyone had been off the main trail. Investigators say they went over the area several times and found nothing but hoofprints from a cow that must have broken out of its fence from a nearby farm.

Despite that, sources tell CNN they believe the inmates are still nearby. Police are in the woods at this hour, convinced this will be the lead that finally brings this fifteen-day manhunt to an end.

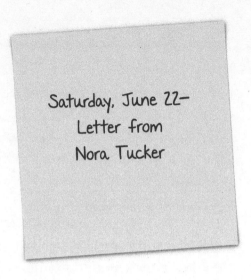

Dear future Wolf Creek residents,

This might sound dumb, but I think Lizzie and Elidee and I figured something out tonight. I really, really hope so. We were sitting around my room, wishing we could do something to help because the police are still out searching, but it's starting to look like those inmates got away. Again.

Lizzie and I told Elidee about the research we put together so the police could learn about past escapes. We showed her our information and Lizzie's Venn diagram. Elidee laughed at how nerdy we are. She told us that her family's like that, too. Especially Troy. He used to be, anyway. She told us about a report he did in eighth grade about Prohibition, the time in America when alcohol was illegal. I guess Troy was really into it. He made a big poster and everything.

I was only half listening because Lizzie and I started adding more stuff to her charts, based on everything that happened since she made them. We got in an argument over whether today's sighting was a false alarm or not. Lizzie thought Walker and Cole were lying about seeing the inmates, but Elidee said they looked too scared. I think she's right. Those guys just aren't that good at acting. But then Lizzie said that's impossible because there were no tracks. It was super muddy all through the woods today, and there were no tracks anywhere off the trail except for hoofprints from some cow.

That's when Elidee got all excited and started talking about her brother's Prohibition report again. I couldn't figure out what she meant until she asked to use our computer and pulled up an old newspaper article archived online that explains EVERYTHING. At least it might.

You'll see what I'm talking about when you read it. So Lizzie and Elidee and I wrote a letter, and now they've gone home and I'm trying to sleep but I can't because I'm waiting to see what happens.

Your friend from the past,

Nora Tucker

The Evening Independent
Tampa, May 27, 1922

SHINERS WEAR "COW SHOES"

Prohi Director Allen has Latest Trick Device of Still Tenders.

Tampa, May 27—A new method of evading prohibition agents was revealed here today by A. L. Allen, state prohibition enforcement director, who displayed what he called a "cow shoe" as the latest thing from the haunts of moonshiners.

The cow shoe is a strip of metal to which is tacked a wooden block carved to resemble the hoof of a cow, which may be strapped to the human foot. A man shod with a pair of them would leave a trail resembling that of a cow.

The shoe found was picked up near Port Tampa where a still was located some time ago. It will be sent to the prohibition department at Washington. Officers believe the inventor got his idea from a Sherlock Holmes story in which the villain shod his horse with shoes, the imprint of which resembled those of a cow's hoof.

Saturday, June 22—
Picture of a cow shoe
that we found at the
Library of Congress

Prohibition Unit Cow Shoes,
6/28/24. Photograph. Retrieved from
the Library of Congress, https://www
.loc.gov/item/2016849213/

Dear police,

We know you're busy tonight, checking on the latest inmate sighting, but we have something for you to consider. It might be nothing, but you guys always say you want to "leave no stone unturned," so we've printed an article that we think might explain why you didn't find any inmate tracks after those guys were seen in the woods. We think the inmates might be wearing cow shoes.

If you read the attached article, you'll see that this is actually a thing. During Prohibition, when alcohol was illegal in our country, smugglers used to wear these shoes so officers wouldn't follow their tracks to the stills, where they made moonshine, which is illegal alcohol. The Prohibition officers would be running around the woods looking for human smuggler tracks but probably didn't worry about cow tracks.

We're guessing you guys probably haven't considered that either. We don't know if the inmates have cow shoes or not, but it's worth checking out. Our inmates could have read the same article we read about the Prohibition guys, or maybe they read the Sherlock Holmes story and got the idea.

Anyway, we think you should look into this. We hope you find those guys and get to go home soon.

Sincerely,
Nora Tucker
Lizzie Bruno
Elidee Jones

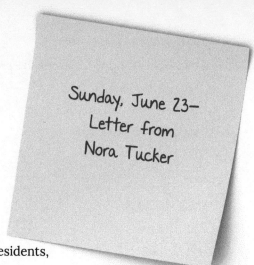

Dear future Wolf Creek residents,

It's super early in the morning, but I can't sleep anymore. I think this whole inmate thing is about to end. I know everybody keeps saying that, but it feels real this time.

After we finished writing our letter last night, Elidee and Lizzie went home, and I waited for everybody to go to bed. I'm sneakier than Owen, so I got all the way out to the trooper on the street, gave him the letter and our article, and snuck back in without getting caught. The trooper didn't rat me out to Mom either. I gave him a super quick summary, and then he looked at the article and looked back at me and sent me inside. But I could see him in the streetlights from my window when I went back upstairs. He was on his phone, and I'm hoping that means he told somebody and they thought it was important enough to check.

It's pretty quiet outside now. I looked out the window, and the trooper from last night is gone.

I'll let you know if anything happens.

Your friend from the past,
Nora Tucker

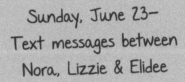

Sunday, June 23—
Text messages between
Nora, Lizzie & Elidee

NORA: Hey team

ELIDEE: Hey

LIZZIE: Hey what's up

NORA: Not much

Lizzie u left ur recorder-thing here last night

LIZZIE: Shoot

I'll pick it up later ok?

NORA: Ok

ELIDEE: Did you deliver that letter?

NORA: Yep haven't heard anything though

It's super quiet right now

ELIDEE: Here too

LIZZIE: Here too

Make sure you record if anything good happens

NORA: I will

Sunday, June 23—
Recorded on Lizzie's
WhisperFlash Z190 at
Nora's house, 7:25 a.m.

(Lizzie left her recorder at my house, so I decided to record this phone call in case it was something good. I thought it would be Dad, but it was Aunt Sandy.)

MOM: Hi, Sandy . . .

No, we're all home except Bill—how come?

Whoa.

Okay.

When?

Wow. Okay.

Yep—love you, too.

NORA: What's up?

MOM: Uncle Tommy texted a few minutes ago and told her the searchers just found fresh footprints. Seems like they might finally have them.

NORA: Where?

MOM: The woods near school.

NORA: Whoa! Did they say anything about . . . Did they say why they decided to look there again?

MOM: Another lead that came in overnight I guess.

NORA: Yes! We were right!

MOM: About what?

NORA: Nothing . . . just . . . Uncle Tommy's out on the search now?

MOM: Yeah. Aunt Sandy says she'll call when there's news

NORA: Can we turn on the police scanner? Owen's not up yet.

MOM: Okay.

SCANNER LADY: Unit five three one, please stand by.

MOM: God, I hope Tommy's okay out there.

SCANNER LADY: All units, be advised the subjects are moving east toward Trudeau Road. Units along the perimeter, stand by.

NORA: Where's Uncle Tommy?

MOM: I don't know.

NORA: Is he near Trudeau Road?

MOM: I don't know, Nora. Shhh!

SCANNER LADY: Captain's calling for radio silence.

. . .

. . .

. . .

. . .

SCANNER LADY: All units, be advised, shots fired in the woods near the intersection of Route 72 and Homer Trombly Road. Stand by.

MOM: Oh no . . .

NORA: Who got shot?

MOM: Hopefully no one, but . . .

NORA: Why aren't they saying anything else? How come—

MOM: Shhhh!

. . .

. . .

SCANNER LADY: Captain Moore, please contact command.

. . .

. . .

. . .

Wolf Creek Fire Dispatch . . . An ambulance is needed at the intersection of Route 72 and Homer Trombly Road for a subject with a gunshot wound to the torso.

MOM: Oh, Lord.

ME: What subject? Mom . . . Why won't they say who?

MOM: That's not how it works, Nora.

NORA: What if it's Uncle Tommy?

MOM: Shhh . . . It's not.

NORA: How do you know?

MOM: Because if it were one of the searchers, there's a different radio call for that. Officer down.

ME: Oh . . .
So does that mean they shot one of the inmates?

MOM: I don't know.
    Maybe . . . Probably.

SCANNER LADY: Attention all units, please observe radio
        silence.

. . .

. . .

NORA: What does that mean?

MOM: It means . . . I don't know . . . They don't want chatter . . .
    Maybe . . .

NORA: Does it mean something went wrong? Why aren't they
    saying anything?

MOM: Nora, please!

SCANNER LADY: All units, stand by . . .

NORA: Mom, what if—

MOM: Shhhh!

. . .

. . .

SCANNER LADY: All units, be advised . . . The first subject is
        deceased. Second subject is in custody.

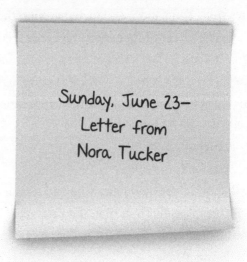

Sunday, June 23—
Letter from
Nora Tucker

Dear future Wolf Creek residents,

It's over. I held my breath while I was listening to the scanner.
Mom did, too. She let it all out in a big whoosh when they said
the second suspect was in custody. About an hour later, Dad
called and gave us the whole story.

The police found the inmates hiding in a tree stand in the
woods as the sun was coming up, but there were only two
officers there, so they had to call for backup. While they did that,
the inmates jumped down and ran for it. The police chased them,
and one ended up surrendering. They shot the other one. And
killed him.

So it's over. Dad's waiting at work because the governor is
coming for another big news conference. Lizzie and I are going,
and nobody's worried about us walking there, because there are
no bad guys in the woods anymore. It really is over.

Owen cheered when Mom told him. He made up a "Good

guys rule!" song and was dancing around the kitchen table. It felt so good to see him happy and not scared that I danced with him. He sang, "They got 'em! They got 'em!" and we high-fived and cheered some more. Mom was standing by the fridge, just looking at us, and when I saw the expression on her face—all tired and sad—I stopped.

Somebody got killed.

Somebody got *killed*.

I know it was an inmate who had escaped. I know he'd done awful things aside from that. But probably he had people who loved him anyway, who kept hoping for him.

He was gone now.

And we were *cheering*.

I told Owen to stop. He got all quiet and then looked up at Mom and whispered, "I'm glad. Does that make me a bad guy, too? Because I can't help it. I'm not sad. I'm glad."

Mom hugged Owen. She told him it was okay to feel relieved when you've been scared a long time. That made me feel a little better, too.

You can think whatever you want about me. But try to keep in mind that you haven't been living through all this like we have. You haven't been staying awake in your room every night, looking out into the dark and wondering where the inmates were and if they were going to break through your window. You haven't been checking under your little brother's bed every night or watching your uncle go to work in his uniform, worried that some inmate hiding behind a shed might take a shot at him. You haven't gone two weeks without seeing your dad because everybody decided that what happened was his fault. You haven't seen the circles under his eyes when he does come home, and the worry that maybe they're right.

And yeah, I know that two weeks isn't really all that long, but it sure felt like a long time.

You can think whatever you want, but you weren't here. So you can't really understand.

Your friend from the past,

Nora Tucker

Sunday, June 23—
News conference
recorded on Lizzie's
WhisperFlash Z190, 11 a.m.

GOVERNOR RAMOS: Good morning. As you know by now, the search for the two prisoners who escaped from Wolf Creek Correctional Facility two weeks ago has come to an end. I'd like to thank all the officers who put themselves in harm's way to keep our community safe. I'm going to turn the podium over to State Police Captain Mason now. He'll brief you on how the situation was resolved early this morning.

CAPTAIN MASON: At approximately 5:30 this morning, Trooper Rebecca Fairlee and Trooper Jason Boyer were in the woods near Wolf Creek Middle School checking on a tip from a community member when they became aware that two individuals were taking shelter in a tree stand near the edge of the woods. Following procedure, the officers called for backup. While additional cars were en route to the scene, the two individuals were observed jumping from the tree stand and fleeing. Our officers gave chase and caught up to the men in an area with dense brush. Trooper Boyer reported that one of the individuals raised what appeared to be a shotgun, and at that point, our officer discharged his weapon, shooting John Smith in the torso. He was pronounced dead at the scene of the incident. The second escapee, James Young, surrendered at that time and has been taken into custody. At this point, we'll take your questions.

NORA: Huh. I guess my dad's not talking at this one.

LIZZIE: Probably because none of today's stuff happened at the prison.

NORA: Maybe. I still thought he'd say he's glad it's over and thank his officers.

ELIZABETH CARTER WOOD: Were there witnesses to the shooting?

CAPTAIN MASON: Only Troopers Boyer and Fairlee. The backup units had not arrived at that time.

ELIZABETH CARTER WOOD: Will there be an investigation into the use of deadly force?

CAPTAIN MASON: Of course. But at this time, we have no reason to believe the use of force was inappropriate. Trooper Boyer was staring down a shotgun. All indications are that he acted to protect his life and the life of his partner.

NY TIMES GUY: Can you comment on the internal investigation at the prison?

CAPTAIN MASON: I'll let the governor address that.

GOVERNOR RAMOS: That investigation continues. We take prison security and protocol seriously, and it does appear that there were breaches in this situation. Beyond that, all I can say is that we plan to hold a news conference in Albany on Monday with an update.

NY TIMES GUY: Will that update include changes at the prison?

GOVERNOR RAMOS: That is a very likely scenario.

LOCAL REPORTER: Can you tell us about the tip that led to today's break? Wasn't that area searched before?

CAPTAIN MASON: It was. And you may recall that the initial search failed to produce evidence that the inmates had been in the area. However, there were a number of tracks from what we believed at the time to be a cow that had broken through a fence at a nearby farm. The tip we received suggested that perhaps those tracks had been . . . ah . . . doctored, and we did indeed find that to be the case.

LOCAL REPORTER: Doctored how?

CAPTAIN MASON: Evidence was collected from the tree stand, including what appears to be a homemade shoe attachment that would cause a man's footprint to resemble that of a cow.

LOCAL REPORTER: So they had . . . cow shoes?

CAPTAIN MASON: It would appear that way, yes.

ELIZABETH CARTER WOOD: Is James Young talking to police?

CAPTAIN MASON: He is cooperating, but we don't have information on the results of his interview. I should add that Ms. Wadsworth, the prison employee arrested for aiding the inmates in the escape, has also provided investigators with useful information.

ELIZABETH CARTER WOOD: One last question! I heard there's a thank-you celebration being held to honor law enforcement?

CAPTAIN MASON: We're not in charge of that, but yes. We hear community members are organizing some kind of gathering for tomorrow, but we don't have further details. Our work continues, and we need to get back to it. Thank you.

LIZZIE'S REFLECTIONS:
It's finally over. So there you go, future Wolf Creek People.

The End.

Dear Grandma,

They said at the news conference that you've been helping the
police. That's good. Mom says it might help you get a lighter
sentence. It's so awful to imagine you in prison. Just a couple of
weeks ago, I made a joke about prison food in my letter to the
future residents of Wolf Creek. It doesn't seem funny at all now.

But Mom says we're hoping for the best with your sentence.
She says you're lucky nobody got hurt. Nobody except the
inmate they shot, anyway.

I still don't understand how you could have broken those
rules to help them escape. You said you didn't know what they
were planning, but that seems kind of stupid. And it doesn't
matter, really. You broke the rules. That's why all those hundreds
of searchers were in danger every day for two weeks. You've
probably had lots of time to think about that in the county jail
by now. You put everybody in danger, including Mom and me.

Knowing that is probably worse than any other punishment they could give you. I know it would be for me.

Mom says we might never really understand. She says we'll never forget what you did, but maybe we can forgive a little bit. She says we should try anyway. Because she's only got one mom and I've only got one grandmother and that's still you. So I'm going to try. I'll come see you next time we're allowed. We don't have to talk about all this. I think I'd rather talk about something else. But I'll come.

Love,
Lizzie

Sunday, June 23—
Letter from Elidee to
her brother, Troy

Dear Troy,

I'm back to writing letters I'm not going to send you because I'm
not sure you'd want to hear what I have to say in this one. You
know that tip that helped the cops find them two guys? It came
from you.

I was talking with Nora and Lizzie and somebody mentioned
there were no tracks in the school woods. The inmates
disappeared without leaving any trace. All police found was a
bunch of cow tracks. You know what comes next, right?

Remember that report you wrote about the rumrunners in
8th grade? I told Nora and Lizzie about that, and we looked it up
and wrote a letter to the police and then everything happened.
Everybody's so relieved it's over now. But I've got a twist in my
stomach that won't go away.

Did you know who John Smith was? That place is huge so
you probably didn't. I sure didn't know him. I read what the news
said, about all the things he did and those people he killed. But

they never said on TV if he had a mama or a sister or brother. And I keep wondering. I know that doesn't do any good now. When he broke out of there, he had to have a good idea how that story was going to end. But I think about stuff, anyway.

I know a lot's happened since you wrote that report in 8th grade. When I looked at you yesterday, sitting there in your green shirt with your brush cut and hard eyes, I couldn't even see that boy anymore. But I'm going to keep hoping he's still in there. I bet he is, just waiting out his time. Waiting to come back.

Your story needs a better ending, Troy. You have to make that happen, and I know you can. Be strong, okay?

I'm going to be strong, too. Just you watch.

And you know what? Maybe I'll send you these letters after all.

I'm sending out some of my other writing today, too, because it turns out I have more things to say than I thought.

Love you,
Elidee

**what I believe
today**
by Elidee Jones

**LEARNING FROM
JACQUELINE #7**

(Inspired by "what I believe" from *Brown Girl
Dreaming* by Jacqueline Woodson)

I believe in God (I'm pretty sure) and family.
I believe in poetry—haikus and cabinet battles.
I believe in Nikkis and Gwendolyn, Jacqueline, and
Lin-Manuel.
I believe words have power and
You can write your way out of anything.
Almost.

I believe in jollof rice and Michigans,
Starburst and chopped cheese,
Block parties and water-ball fights and
Relay races with breathless finish lines.

I believe people are never as perfect as their
   best days

But always more than their worst.
I believe in second chances.
I believe prison inmates are still
Boys in too-big striped T-shirts selling lemonade
And dreaming baseball dreams
Somewhere deep inside.

I believe in moments and light-years.
I believe in planets out past Pluto—
Epsilon Eridani b and Methuselah.
And love that's bigger than all of them.

I believe in revolutions—
Alexander Hamilton's kind, and mine.
I believe in wearing masks when you need them
And taking them off when you don't.
I believe in Truth in Time Capsules
And telling your own story,

So that's what I'm doing now.

Sunday, June 23—
Copy of a letter
from Elidee Jones to
the Morgan Academy
of NY

Elidee Kendall Jones
15 Porter St.
Wolf Creek, NY 12802

The Morgan Academy of New York
2345 North Westminster Avenue
Brooklyn, NY 11230

Dear Admissions Committee:

Thomas Edison once said, "Our greatest weakness lies in giving up. The most certain way to succeed is always to try just one more time." It is in that spirit that I write today to ask that you reconsider my recent application for admission to Morgan Academy.

In my original application, I worked hard on the essays introducing myself to the committee. But looking back, I think

I wrote them in the voice of the sort of student I thought you'd want, instead of the voice that really belongs to me.

But I've been finding that other voice lately, writing lots of different kinds of poetry. Please read the attached updated writing samples, based on my recent experience of leaving the city and starting school in a small town a couple weeks before the end of the school year. You may have heard about the prison break in Wolf Creek on the news. Living here taught me a lot about police manhunts and life in small towns. It also taught me a lot about myself. That's why I'd like to give this another shot.

Yo yo yo yo yo!
What time is it?
Showtime!

Welcome to our hood. It's a fine afternoon!
Ignore the killers in our woods. (We'll shoot 'em real soon.)
We love our community. There ain't no doubt.
It's pretty and it's safe—that's what we're all about.
When we see a black man runnin', we point a gun at him.
Racist? Nah . . . We got black friends. (Well . . . one of 'em.)
So make a good impression now you've come to Wolf Creek.
Our school might be in session only two more weeks,
But that's plenty of days for you to learn our ways.
Be on time. Tell the truth. Pledge allegiance to the flag.
Salute our boys in blue. Wear a ribbon. Make a bag.
Keep your voice down. Leave your bag at the door
'Cause we don't need you stuffing nothin'
In there right before you leave our store.

Hey, wait . . . You wanna be on our relay team?
You're fast so you're invited!
Whoa—is this a dream?
What a blast! I'd be delighted.

So we ran with the baton through the afternoon sun
And we passed off the baton when each leg was done.
You can whisper all you want about why I'm fast.
By the time you finish talking, I'll have run right past.
I'll outrace you, outpace you,
Wipe that smirk off your face, you
Slow-walking, trash-talking jerk.
I hate this place.

I'm sorry. I forget myself.
How did I ever let myself
Break the fine rules of this community?
It's all about community.
I appreciate the opportunity
You've given me here.

'Cause a long, long time ago
I promised that I'd grow
Up to be somebody. Somebody free.
I'ma make a name for myself—
Change the game for myself.
Decide who I'm gonna be.
I'ma write my way out
Like that dude in the play.

(Did you see that one? You should
If you got time to get away.)
I know what I'm about,
I ain't gonna be defeated.
I'ma write my way out
Just the way he did.
An island's like a prison with a sea instead of walls,
Like this place walled around by mountains so tall.
You can't see past to see anything at all.
But I'ma rise up on the power of my voice.
I'ma rise up and claim another choice
I am the E-L-I-D-E-E-J . . .
O-N-E-S. What you gonna say?
I'ma rise up just like Mama's Messiah
On the power of a voice that's mine.
I'ma rise up higher and higher.
And hope *you* make a different choice this time.

So . . .
By the power of this petition
I respectfully request permission
To appeal your first decision.
I'm on a mission to have you recognize
My ambition—try this on for size—
An addition to my original application.
A dissertation—a tale of the times, a pile of rhymes
About everything that happened to me
In a place I didn't even wanna be.
Ham suppers and races,

School petitions and decisions,
People getting all up in my face.
Together, these verses do a better job, in my estimation
Of showing who I am, where I stand with my education.

I thank you very much for your thoughtful consideration.
And I promise you this voice is no phony. This one's my own.

The one and the only,
Elidee Jones

Dear future Wolf Creek residents,

We had a parade today. To celebrate. It sounds wrong to say that when somebody's dead, but really, we were celebrating not being afraid anymore.

At noon, all of Wolf Creek lined the sidewalks of Main Street with banners and signs. Owen made a thank-you poster out of a cardboard box we pulled apart in the garage. Lucy Arnot and her mom gave out blue ribbons. Mrs. Jablonski had a big Mylar birthday balloon with a Thanks to Our Boys in Blue sign taped over the Happy Birthday. I didn't see Elidee or her mom, but I'm pretty sure I said hi or waved to every other person I know.

Once the sidewalks were full, we waited for the police and corrections officers and border-patrol guys to arrive in a big parade. But apparently, they never got the details on when everybody would be lined up to thank them. Or maybe they were still busy or home sleeping or something, but whatever it was, almost none of them came. We cheered for a couple sheriff's cars but that was about it. Some people started cheering for regular cars and trucks. I guess we'd been cooped up so long we needed to cheer for something.

After the not-quite-a-parade, we wandered back to the school yard, where the carnival had been before it got interrupted. Everything was still set up from before everybody had to run away, so people opened the game booths and cleaned the damp cotton candy out of the machines and fired them up again, and the carnival went on like nothing had ever happened.

Like none of it had happened at all.

But somehow, things are different in Wolf Creek than they were before. At least to me. I'm not quite sure what it is. Lizzie is coming over tomorrow, and now that we're finally allowed outside, we're going to hike down to the creek and go swimming. Maybe things will start to feel normal again.

Your friend from the past,

Nora Tucker

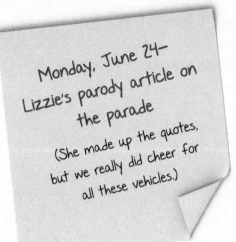

WOLF CREEK HONORS RANDOM VEHICLES ON MAIN STREET

by Lizzie Bruno

Residents of Wolf Creek lined Main Street for a parade today, intended to honor officers who assisted in the recent manhunt. However, nobody told the officers they had to show up and be honored.

Undeterred, people held their thank-you signs high and saluted whatever vehicles happened to drive by.

"Woo-hoo!!! Oh my gosh, I LOVE their salt and vinegar variety!" said one resident as he applauded a Lay's potato chip truck.

Residents also cheered for an NBC News car, a logging truck, and a large green tractor trailer, which honked its horn as it passed Bob's Hardware, prompting another wild round of applause.

"We really should come together to show our gratitude more often," said one woman, waving pom-poms over her head as she cheered for a Bug-Off Pest Control Services van. "This is what makes Wolf Creek so special."

THE MORGAN ACADEMY OF NEW YORK

2345 NORTH WESTMINSTER AVENUE • BROOKLYN, NY 11230

Letter from the Morgan Academy, received by Elidee Jones on July 2

Elidee Kendall Jones
15 Porter St.
Wolf Creek, NY 12802

Dear Ms. Jones:

Thank you very much for your letter and writing sample. As you
surely know, the Morgan Academy is a highly selective school that
receives thousands of applications for admissions each year. As a
result, it is highly unusual for us to read more than one submission
from any prospective student.

However, your letter caught my attention. I happened to see
the same show you did and thought it was excellent. I was intrigued
by your additional writing samples and shared them with my
colleagues, who, upon reflection, voted to offer you admittance
for the coming semester.

I realize that this is short notice, but we will hold an open house for admitted students on Friday, July 5, and hope that you might be able to attend. Please feel free to reach out with any questions.

Very sincerely yours,
Eloise P. Harrington

Eloise P. Harrington

Headmistress, The Morgan Academy of New York

ELIDEE: Hey

LIZZIE: Hi!

NORA: Hey!! I was going to call to see if u guys wanted to run this week

LIZZIE: Sorry but I'm on vacation from running

ELIDEE: I'm home this week

NORA: Cool! What day's good to run?

ELIDEE: I meant real home. NYC home!

NORA: Oh! That's cool too

Visiting your grandma?

ELIDEE: And checking out my new school

NORA: ??

ELIDEE: Can't remember if I told you guys but last year I applied to this private school and didn't get in but then I tried again and they said yes!

LIZZIE: So you're moving again?

ELIDEE: Yeah next week

Mama's going back to her old job, so we're just coming back up there for a day to get our stuff

NORA: Geez that's fast

You're going to miss the centennial celebration

Did u already turn in your time capsule stuff?

ELIDEE: No

NORA: I can submit it with mine if u want

I'm going to get a bunch of other stuff together like news transcripts and text messages

LIZZIE: Dude, why would she bother when she's not going to be here in 8th grade ELA to get the points?

ELIDEE: Ha!

Pretty sure Wolf Creek will be ok without my story

NORA: What about xc? We were going to have the best team ever this fall!

ELIDEE: I'm going to run at home.

NORA: Nyc home

ELIDEE: Yeah

NORA: Wow

Well congrats!

Will you come visit?

ELIDEE: Uh yeah. My brother's gonna be around awhile

NORA: Oh duh

Sorry

ELIDEE: It's ok

Gotta go bc we're having a bbq with my cousins

LIZZIE: Have fun!

ELIDEE: Thx bye

NORA: Bye

Thursday, July 25—
This came in the mail
with all of Elidee's
other stuff for the
time capsule

Hey, Nora!

Hope you're having a good summer. Have you been running?
Practices here don't start for another month, but I've been
running with friends at the park.

I'm writing because I changed my mind about the time-
capsule thing. I was thinking I didn't want to be part of your
town's story, only then I realized that I am anyway. It's just a
matter of who gets to tell my part of it. I decided I want to do
that myself.

So I wrote one more letter to the future Wolf Creek
people. It's in the envelope with some other things I wrote this
summer. I included text messages and letters and stuff, too,
like you said you were doing. Can you take it to the library for
me and make sure it all gets in there? You can just submit it
with your stuff and Lizzie's if you want.

Thanks. And thanks for inviting me to run with you guys.
That relay was pretty sweet even though we never got to water-
balloon Mr. Simmons. You and Lizzie ought to call him out on

that at the first-day-of-school picnic or something. I bet he thinks everybody forgot. If you get to do it, throw one for me.

I'll text you next time Mama and I are coming up to see Troy, and I might see you at some meets, too. The coach at Morgan Academy says we go to a few invitational meets with kids from all over the state, so maybe we'll get to race together at one of those. That'd be pretty cool.

Elidee

PS You can read the stuff in the envelope if you want. I wrote some of it before I really knew you, which I think you'll understand because I got the feeling you didn't like me much at first either. But you and Lizzie both turned out to be okay.

Tuesday, July 30—
Copy of a letter from
Nora Tucker to Joe's
Mountain Market!

Dear market staff:

I am writing to express my concerns about the backpack policy at Joe's Mountain Market. I know the sign posted on the door says, "Welcome to the Adirondacks! Please leave backpacks & large bags at the counter." However, I have noticed that this policy is not enforced consistently. I stop by the market lots of days after school, and I had never been asked to leave my backpack at the counter until one day this June when I was there with my friend Elidee, who is black. On that day, Martha made us leave our bags at the counter while we went to get our Gatorade. But that same week, when I came back with just my friend Lizzie, who is white, we were not asked to leave our backpacks.

It's wrong to make assumptions about who might steal things from you based on what a person looks like. That's called racial profiling, and not only is it unfair, it doesn't work anyway.

But people still do it because of the racism that's built into our society. I've been talking about this with my brother Sean, who's read more about it than I have.

I can't fix all that, but I've decided I don't want to shop at a market that treats people differently based on the color of their skin, so that's what this letter is for.

Please either take down that old sign on the market door and get rid of the backpack rule, or start to be fair about it. Personally, I'm not a fan of leaving my backpack at the counter because it makes a quick stop for gum or Gatorade take longer. But if you feel like you need to have that rule, it should be enforced consistently. You shouldn't say "Welcome to the Adirondacks" unless you really mean it. For everybody.

Thanks for reading this. I look forward to your response.

Sincerely,

Nora Tucker

July 30

Dear future Wolf Creek residents,

When I started writing to you this June, I figured I'd be talking about sleepovers and Fourth of July fireworks and lemonade and swimming. Then those two inmates escaped, and I was pretty psyched at first because there was finally something exciting to write about. Only then it went on and on and it was awful, but I kept writing because this was all that kept me from staring out the window, wondering who was out there in the dark.

This story was supposed to end with inmates getting caught and me winning a race. Those things happened, but the story doesn't feel over so it's weird to be writing this last letter.

It used to be simpler in Wolf Creek than it is now. I know I haven't been writing to you for very long, but a lot has changed since the day those guys broke out of Dad's prison.

It's not Dad's prison anymore, for starters. He decided

to retire early. Only really it wasn't his decision. The state investigators said it was either that or he'd get fired. Dad doesn't like to talk about it much, but he says he made some mistakes along the way and then tried to protect his officers by covering for them. Making a circle of support, I guess. Sean says this is all tied in to those bigger problems with the criminal justice system. I hate thinking that my dad was a part of that, but I'm trying to remember what Sean told Owen at the table—that we can support Dad *and* want things to change.

Anyway, the state investigators decided Dad was partly responsible for the escape and the stuff that came after that, too. I thought Dad would be mad about that, but he says when a problem happens in a prison, the superintendent owns it. That's just how it is.

He seems a lot less stressed out now, so the other night at dinner, I went back to that conversation that we had to stop having when we were making our circle of support last month. I asked Dad if he thought Sean was right about the criminal justice system being broken and racially biased.

Dad picked up a carrot stick and sort of twirled it around for a few seconds, and I thought he was going to change the subject, but he didn't. I didn't have Lizzie's recorder, so I'm going to write what he said, as best I can remember.

"Is the system broken? Maybe it is, Nora. Are there inmates in that prison who are probably innocent or serving unfair sentences? I'm sure there probably are. But I'm not the judge or the jury, and there was no room for personal beliefs in my job. My job was the care, custody, and security of the inmates assigned to me. And I did the best I could."

Dad looked a little sad when he said that, like maybe he'd decided his best wasn't good enough after all. It sure wasn't good enough for the people in charge in Albany.

And Dad's not the only one who got in trouble. A few officers are being investigated for maybe beating up inmates who wouldn't talk.

I know a couple of those officers. I've seen them at the carnival and the grocery store, at our holiday concerts at school, watching their kids. I can't imagine they'd do something like that. Only then I think about how people were talking during the manhunt, how much some people hated those escaped inmates. Maybe it bled over to all the inmates—the ones who got out and all the ones who didn't.

Some people say it doesn't matter. They say inmates wouldn't be in prison if they weren't awful people, so they get what they deserve. But Elidee's brother is in there. I know from her stories that there are good parts of him, even if they're tough to see right now. I know Lizzie's grandma isn't awful, even though she did a terrible thing. She admitted it in court, but Lizzie doesn't know yet what her grandma's sentence will be. They're hoping it won't be too long.

We like to talk about good guys and bad guys around here. But even good guys do bad things sometimes. And I think people who do bad things—no matter how bad—have to be more than the awful things they did.

It's complicated.

This escape reminds me of one summer when I was little and we had a huge thunderstorm with really strong winds. When it ended and we finally went outside, the whole neighborhood looked different. Trees were uprooted and siding was blown off houses so you could see what was underneath. It was all pretty ugly.

This manhunt has been like that, too. It brought out some good things. Like the way all the searchers pitched in and helped day after day. The way people came together to throw the ham supper. The way we made and served fifty Michigans in a night. The way Owen developed super comic skills that let him be a little braver.

But there was other stuff, too.

Like the mean way Cole and Walker talked to Elidee.

The way Mom wouldn't let me go to her house.

The way those police surrounded Mr. Washington on the bike path because to them, he looked like one of the escaped inmates.

The way that old backpack sign on the market door suddenly turned into a thing.

And you know what? I was just reading over my very first entry for this time capsule, and two of the things in it aren't entirely true. Not everybody in town works at the prison. Lots of people in town live in the prison. I just left them out before, but they count, too.

I also told you that Wolf Creek is safe and friendly, but that's only partly true. It feels safe for people like me. But I know it doesn't feel that way for everybody.

Until this June, I'd never heard anyone say racist things, and I always thought people weren't like that here.

But now I'm not sure.

I've been talking with Sean about a lot of this. His last day at the market was last week, so I finally told him about what happened with Martha and the backpacks. He asked me what I did about that situation, and I had to tell him I didn't do anything.

But this morning, I wrote a letter. I'm going to drop it off when I go out to deliver this stuff to the library. At least it's something.

See, this is why I'll probably never finish writing my Alcatraz book. Endings are hard. They're supposed to be satisfying, all wrapped up so people have a new understanding of life. And I don't. So this is my last letter, but I don't think it's very satisfying.

What happens when you finish with more questions than when you started? Is it even an ending at all?

I guess it has to be, because this stuff is due at the library by noon.

I always thought life here was pretty perfect. I was happy jumping on my trampoline and eating Popsicles and swimming in the creek all summer. I'm still looking forward to that. Lizzie's coming over for a bonfire later tonight.

But I can't help feeling like when those two guys busted out of Dad's prison, they stirred up dust that's still swirling everywhere, even now.

After that storm we had a long time ago, things were a mess for a while. Eventually, guys came with chainsaws and cut up the fallen trees and hauled them away. People replaced their siding and planted new shrubs, and everybody mostly forgot it had happened. But things weren't exactly the same. Some people redid their houses so they were nicer than before. Some people just patched them up so there are still scars from what happened. You can still see open spaces where trees used to be.

I feel like all of that's happening now, too. It's complicated.

I'm not sure, but I'm guessing that once you're the kind of person who thinks about all this stuff, you don't go back to being the kind of person who doesn't.

And that's okay.

It's harder, but I think I'd rather be the kind of person who does.

Good luck with the future and everything. Maybe by the time you open our time capsule, it won't be so uncomfortable to talk about stuff like this. Maybe by then, you'll have figured some of it out.

Your friend from the past,

Nora Tucker

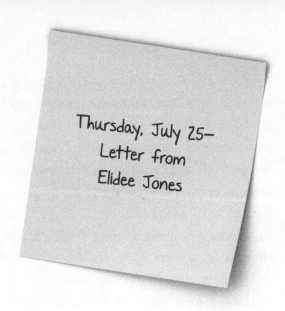

Thursday, July 25—
Letter from
Elidee Jones

Dear future Wolf Creek residents,

I don't know what the other people in this time capsule are telling you it was like here this June. I can guess, though. You're probably reading stories about the prison break and how your good guys caught the bad guys after your awesome community rallied together with blue ribbons and ham.

Some of that's true. Two inmates did escape, and even though you don't know everything about a person just because they're in prison, these two were pretty bad news from what I could tell. They hid in the woods and ran around on cow shoes until one got caught and a cop shot the other one. He said the inmate aimed a gun at him.

Only two people know for sure if that's what really happened—the one who said that and the one who's dead, and the person left alive is the one who gets to tell the story.

I'm not saying that's not what happened. I have no idea. I just think it's worth remembering.

Some of your cops around here are okay. Trooper Elliott will probably be retired by the time you read this, but she's pretty cool. And did you hear about the guys who were on patrol along the school nature trail the day we raced at the carnival? They cheered for us. I don't know if that's a normal thing where you live, but it was pretty great. Made me run faster.

I came in first with Lizzie and Nora in that race, by the way. Here are some other things you should know about me.

I lived on Porter Street for 26 days.

I was in Ms. Morin's seventh-grade homeroom.

I didn't wear my blue ribbon.

But I made a lunch bag for Trooper Elliott.

I helped at the ham supper.

I got a library card.

I made a couple friends.

I'm not perfect. I don't have to talk or write like I am.

I'm pretty good at some kinds of poetry, but I need to keep working on my hip-hop lyrics.

That's about all, I guess. That's my story.

You were also supposed to get stories from the prison inmates in this time capsule, but I bet you never found those. They called that part of the project off when the inmates broke out, and I'm guessing they never got around to it after that. But those guys all have stories, too. My brother's in that prison. His name is Troy.

I didn't live in your town very long because I wrote my way out. I wasn't planning to send you any of this stuff—not even the dumb letters I wrote for extra credit. I was pretty happy about being erased from Wolf Creek. But I changed my mind about that and decided I wanted to tell my own story.

I bet your mountains are still pretty. Other than that, I don't know what Wolf Creek will look like by the time you're reading this. Right now, though, it doesn't look much like me. And the truth is, you aren't as welcoming as that church likes to think you are. Some of you mean pretty well but you say stupid things. Some of you don't mean well at all. But some of you do. And this is mostly for you. In case you want to read this and decide to do something about it.

So here's all my stuff from this summer. The rest is on you.

The one and the only,
Elidee Jones

A note from
the author . . .

Breakout is a made-up story, with fictional characters set in a fictional mountain town, but it was inspired by the real-life manhunt that took place when two inmates broke out of Clinton Correctional Facility in June 2015. That June, I found myself stopped at police roadblocks almost every day, caught in the middle of a search that went on for three weeks and involved more than one thousand law enforcement officers. Suddenly, my sleepy upstate New York town felt less safe. We checked locks on our doors and checked them again. We called off hiking and camping trips. We stayed awake at night listening to police helicopters circle overhead.

I was as nervous as anyone else, but as a former journalist, I was also fascinated by the details of what happened—and how people were reacting to it—so I spent the better part of a week in a coffee shop and market near the prison, talking with people and listening to their stories. We all react differently to fear, so situations like this can bring out the best and the worst in people. They can make us turn to one another, or turn against one another. When we truly listen, we learn that no two people see any situation in exactly the same way, and yet we can almost always find common ground. These were the ideas that I wanted to explore in *Breakout*.

This was a puzzle of a book to piece together, and I'm incredibly grateful to the people who offered help and feedback of all different sorts. Thanks to Sara Kelly Johns, who offered up her old family Michigan recipe, and to my friends Martha and Abby Breyette, who live even closer to the prison than I do and shared their reflections on living at the epicenter of a manhunt. I'm grateful to former Clinton Correctional Facility Superintendent Steve Racette, for taking the time to talk with me about his experiences in the days that followed the escape. Students at Saranac Middle School talked with me when I visited their classroom, even as the police patrolled the parking lot and fields outside. They were thoughtful and honest, and I so appreciate the stories they shared.

J. W. Wiley, director of the Center for Diversity, Pluralism, and Inclusion at SUNY Plattsburgh, took time out of his schedule to talk with me about this project and welcomed me into his class, African American Culture from 1965 to the Present, to listen in on important conversations. Dr. Wiley's writing and teaching were the inspiration for Nora's thoughts on her own "leadership moments."

Autumn Wiley, a talented writer herself, talked with me about her experiences being one of the only black students in a nearly all-white rural school and graciously answered my questions about how Elidee might have reacted to certain situations.

I had the good fortune of being seated next to Kaaren Pringle on an airplane one day while I was working on this story. Our serendipitous conversation about the connection between her life and Elidee's gave me goose bumps. Kaaren has been beyond generous in talking with me and reading an early version of this book, and I'm grateful to have met her.

I'm thankful for the work of Langston Hughes, Paul Laurence Dunbar, Gwendolyn Brooks, Nikki Giovanni, Nikki Grimes, Jacqueline Woodson, and Lin-Manuel Miranda, whose words inspire Elidee in this story just as they've inspired me.

Dhonielle Clayton, Olugbemisola Rhuday-Perkovich, Linda Urban, Bethany Morrow, Allie Jane Bruce, Leo Ward, Loree Griffin Burns, Eric Luper, Liza Martz, Meghan Germain, and Michelle Germain all served as thoughtful early readers for this book. I'm so grateful to them and to the other early readers who were instrumental in my work crafting the best parts of this book. Where I've fallen short, the responsibility rests with me.

Thanks to my agent, Jennifer Laughran, and to the amazing team at Bloomsbury—my wonderful, patient editor Mary Kate Castellani, along with Claire Stetzer, Bethany Buck, Cindy Loh, Melissa Kavonic, Kerry Johnson, Regina Castillo, Oona Patrick, Erica Barmash, Emily Ritter, Lizzy Mason, Courtney Griffin, Anna Bernard, Beth Eller, Brittany Mitchell, Cristina Gilbert, Kay Petronio, Ellen Lindner, Danielle Ceccolini, and Donna Mark. My wonderful family supports my writing on the great days and the tough days. Thanks to Ella, Jake, and Tom, and all the Schirmers and Messners.

I am especially grateful to the people in my life—both in person and online—who ask hard questions and who share ideas that challenge my thinking, the way Nora's experiences over those unsettled June days challenged hers.

If you're interested in thinking more about those big ideas, here

are some great books for
further reading:

For younger
readers:

Baseball Saved Us by Ken Mochizuki, illustrated by Dom Lee
    (Lee & Low Books, 1995)

Crossing Bok Chitto: A Choctaw Tale of Friendship & Freedom
    by Tim Tingle, illustrated by Jeanne Rorex Bridges
    (Cinco Puntos Press, 2006)

Each Kindness by Jacqueline Woodson, illustrated by E. B. Lewis
    (Nancy Paulsen Books, 2012)

*Gordon Parks: How the Photographer Captured Black and White
    America* by Carole Boston Weatherford, illustrated by Jamey
    Christoph
    (Albert Whitman, 2015)

Last Stop on Market Street by Matt de la Peña, illustrated by
    Christian Robinson
    (Penguin, 2015)

The Other Side by Jacqueline Woodson, illustrated by E. B. Lewis
    (Penguin, 2001)

*Separate Is Never Equal: Sylvia Mendez and Her Family's Fight for
    Desegregation*, written and illustrated by Duncan Tonatiuh
    (Abrams, 2014)

Sit-In: How Four Friends Stood Up by Sitting Down by Andrea
  Davis Pinkney, illustrated by Brian Pinkney
  (Little, Brown, 2010)

A Sweet Smell of Roses by Angela Johnson,
  illustrated by Eric Velasquez
  (Simon & Schuster, 2007)

Teammates by Peter Golenbock, illustrated by Paul Bacon
  (HMH Books for Young Readers, 1992)

This Is the Rope: A Story from the Great Migration by Jacqueline
  Woodson, illustrated by James Ransome
  (Nancy Paulsen Books, 2013)

*Voice of Freedom: Fannie Lou Hamer, Spirit of the Civil Rights
  Movement* by Carole Boston Weatherford, illustrated by Ekua
  Holmes
  (Candlewick, 2015)

We Came to America by Faith Ringgold
  (Knopf, 2016)

We March, written and illustrated by Shane W. Evans
  (Square Fish, 2016)

When We Were Alone by David Alexander Robertson, illustrated
  by Julie Flett
  (HighWater Press, 2016)

Ain't Nothing But a Man by Scott Reynolds Nelson and Marc Aronson (National Geographic, 2007)

American Born Chinese by Gene Luen Yang (First Second Books, 2006)

The Blossoming Universe of Violet Diamond by Brenda Woods (Nancy Paulsen Books, 2014)

Brown Girl Dreaming by Jacqueline Woodson (Nancy Paulsen Books, 2014)

8th Grade Superzero by Olugbemisola Rhuday-Perkovich (Scholastic, 2010)

Flying Lessons & Other Stories, edited by Ellen Oh (Crown Books for Young Readers, 2017)

Ghost by Jason Reynolds (Simon & Schuster, 2017)

Ghost Boys by Jewell Parker Rhodes (Little, Brown, 2018)

Inside Out & Back Again by Thanhha Lai (HarperCollins, 2011)

A Long Walk to Water by Linda Sue Park (Clarion Books, 2010)

One Last Word: Wisdom from the Harlem Renaissance by Nikki Grimes (Bloomsbury, 2017)

1621: A New Look at Thanksgiving by Catherine O'Neill Grace (National Geographic Children's Books, 2001)

Unidentified Suburban Object by Mike Jung (Scholastic, 2016)

For upper elementary & middle school readers:

For teen readers:

All *American Boys* by Jason Reynolds and Brendan Kiely
    (Atheneum, 2015)

The Hate U Give by Angie Thomas
    (HarperCollins, 2017)

How It Went Down by Kekla Magoon
    (Henry Holt, 2014)

The March Trilogy by John Lewis, Andrew Aydin, and Nate Powell
    (Top Shelf Productions, 2013–2016)

Monster by Walter Dean Myers
    (Harper Collins, 1999)

Piecing Me Together by Renée Watson
    (Bloomsbury, 2017)

This Side of Home by Renée Watson
    (Bloomsbury, 2015)

A Wish After Midnight by Zetta Elliott
    (Skyscape, 2010)

A Young People's History of the United States by Howard Zinn
    (Triangle Square, 2009)

Kate Messner is passionately curious and writes books that encourage kids to wonder, too. Her titles include award-winning picture books like *Over and Under the Snow*, *Up in the Garden and Down in the Dirt*, and *How to Read a Story*; novels like *Capture the Flag*, *All the Answers*, and *The Seventh Wish*; the Fergus and Zeke easy reader series, and the Ranger in Time historical chapter book series. Kate lives on Lake Champlain with her family and is trying to summit all forty-six Adirondack High Peaks in between book deadlines.

WWW.KATEMESSNER.COM
@KATEMESSNER

Despite herself, she couldn't help a little sad cry. *Brandon! Where are you?*

"Oh no, poor kitty. What's wrong?"

The concerned question came from the human, Ruby, who had entered the courtyard unnoticed while Zuki was playing nurse. She tossed a tasty smelling roll of some strange food to the pit bull, who paused in her first aid duties long enough to swallow it in a single gulp. Ruby, meanwhile, gently shooed away the canine and sat beside Ophelia. She dangled a single large shrimp before her.

"Here you go, little girl. I saved this just for you."

Ophelia's smooth black nose twitched. *I can be sad and full at the same time*, she decided.

While Ruby gently scratched her ears, she made quick work of the tasty crustacean. Once she'd finished, Ruby scooped her up so Ophelia was sitting in her lap.

"Now what happened? Let me see." The human shoved her black spectacles, which had slid down her nose, back into place. Then, gently, she lifted Ophelia's foreleg and examined it.

"Your poor paws, they're all scraped. Come on, let's go inside and I'll fix that."

Clutching Ophelia more securely, Ruby got to her feet and started toward the door. Ophelia considered struggling free, but then changed her mind. She might be leaving on her journey to find Brandon tonight, but no reason that she shouldn't take advantage of the human's help, in the meantime. And so instead she tucked her muzzle into the crook of Ruby's arm and let herself be carried back into the shop. Zuki, still licking her chops over the spring roll that she'd swallowed, followed after.

Ruby brought her all the way back into the main shop and carried her behind the counter, to where its far edge was butted up against the